Voodoo Cruise

Special Thanks
Christine LePorte, Webster, Texas
Your editing skills are exceptional

Copyright © 2018 by Mario Iezzoni

ISBN-13: 978-0-9789187-6-7

1. Adventure—Fiction. 2. Romance—Fiction.

Dedication

To My Beloved Mother

Billie

In Loving Memory
Neil Lamana
Father to My Sweetheart, Mary Ann

Adventure is worthwhile in itself
– Amelia Earhart

Voodoo Cruise

Mario Iezzoni

A Novel

Chapter 1

Alligator Alley ♦ *Fort Lauderdale, Florida*

Distracted by her recent on-air embarrassment that led her to file for a divorce, Gail Stroud failed to notice Alligator Alley's changeover as she drove eastward. The piney mushroom hammocks lining the famed highway had sunk into the treeless, reedy expanse of the Florida Everglades. Gail's thoughts were elsewhere. Should she not wear her wedding ring on the cruise ship? Had her ring finger indentation finally disappeared? Where would the money come from to pay the divorce lawyer? What other surprises lay in wait from her slime-ball husband? Should she lure a debonair Latin man into her inside cabin for a quickie, with the hope he'd unknowingly impregnate her with the child she'd yearned for, for over a decade?

The incident she dwelled upon occurred one month before her well-deserved Caribbean cruise on the *Sapphire Orchid*. Gail, the morning anchor for WKMC Channel 5 Tampa Bay, waited for her cue to go live. Her jealous television producer, Emmitt Stooch, was about to pull another unthinkable, victimizing stunt to drive up ratings. The upcoming news segment was of a police raid of a cockbird gambling ring in an abandoned Ybor City cigar factory. As the camera lit red, the green screen behind her projected a close-up of a well-dressed white man led in handcuffs—it was her husband, Richard. And Gail, who tended not to proof scripts prior to newscasts, started to read. "Tampa City police arrested Richard Stroud, husband of WKMC morning news anchor Gail—" She froze in midsentence. The surprise seized her always perfect diction and steadfast facial control. The on-camera moment had reduced Gail to a yammering, wobbly-eyed series of utters. It was the moment childless Gail came undone, learning of Richard's long-time gambling addiction. That she was flat broke and heavily in debt.

Covered in a splatter of May lovebugs, her silver Tahoe sped eastbound. As she stared straight ahead, entranced, locked in thought, tears filled the edges of her enormous, brown television eyes. This time it was of a 9/11 memory, her big break in the news business. A captivating story of a woman who had lost her trapped husband after learning she was with child. Jumping to his death. Gail had so desperately wanted to replace the loss of life she witnessed that day with a child of her own.

The traffic thickened. Gail wiped away the sadness that flowed. Looking down at the center console for another tissue, she failed to see the swerving vehicles ahead. A Volkswagen Passat had struck an alligator and flung it into the air. The in-flight gator skipped across the roof of a minivan directly in front of Gail and torpedoed snout-first, smashing through her windshield, shattering it—the gator landing in the rear amongst her suitcases. The spiny tail of the alligator thrashed and busted open the rear door, sending her luggage tumbling into oncoming traffic. And as Gail's heart beat wildly, the Tahoe swerved, skidded, and spun on the roadside gravel into the swale, kicking clumps of black muck as it pitched left and lurched to a halt.

White-knuckled, covered in shattered glass, she flipped the door lever, which opened faster than expected. But the seatbelt caught her, which was a good thing, because the still-alive gator was now trapped beneath the running board with its snapping jaws set right at her feet. That's when Gail Stroud let out a bloodcurdling scream.

It was the fifth vehicle that cared to stop; a royal blue Jeep with its cloth top removed. Out leapt a shirtless, bronzed, blond-haired man. But as he trotted through the uncut *bahia*, he halted at seeing the trapped gator nipping for Gail's dangling Jimmy Choos.

"Don't go!" she pleaded, holding her feet perilously above the gator's head. She watched him turn and run away.

"Don't be a coward!" she cried, thinking an insult would stop him in his tracks.

The rugged man gestured to wait. He went and dug in the back of his Jeep, freeing a roll of duct tape, then raced back, the roll between his teeth. Approaching the passenger side, he crawled across the Tahoe hood, then slid off and onto the gator's back, pinning it. Quickly, with one hand, he clamped shut the gator's jaw, unfurling tape, wrapping the gator's snout shut.

It happened fast—Gail suspended within the arms of the muscular rescuer. Carried and set in the sheepskin passenger seat of his Jeep. It was his cologne, mixed with his manly odor, that she first noticed. And when the tingling in her fingers cleared, and the fog that clouded her senses dissipated, she realized her red-polished nails had dug deep into his massive triceps.

"Are you okay?" his firm voice asked, his left hand loosening Gail's death grip.

Her cheeky chestnut look that required no fillers, the honest and captivating expression the television camera loved, blinked. Her eyelashes fluttered. Her enormous brown eyes opened wide and round. Gail nodded, as her mind inventoried her five-foot-three-inch frame. "Nothing's hurt. I'm okay," she heard herself say.

Voodoo Cruise

She sat there for a full minute before she spoke. "What happened?" Gail asked, repositioning among the lumps of wool fibers, her thighs quivering from the trauma.

"You weren't watching where you were going and reduced the Everglade alligator population by at least one. Possibly more, if that young cow hasn't laid her eggs yet."

"What!" Her stomach tumbling. Gail was shocked. She expected sympathy, a comforting phrase, a possible flirt from the rugged man, but not an insult.

Numbed, angered, deceived by her husband, and embarrassed by her television producer, Gail reconsidered. What insensitive thing would this stud guy say next? Why was he as ignorant as other men in her life?

His deep blue eyes studied her, as if he were searching for her soul. Then he broke away, distracted, looking toward the busy stretch of highway. "Are you going to let your luggage litter the highway like that?"

Gail wanted to claw him. "Are you serious? Look at my Tahoe!"

He offered no sympathy.

But her journalistic wit and the acting lessons paid for by her TV station on how to control and project facial expressions afforded some composure. "Can't you be the teeniest bit sympathetic?" Gail asked, again adjusting to the fibrous clumps. "What's with this seat? It's uncomfortable."

"It's wool. And supposed to keep you comfortable."

"It's not," Gail said, crossing then uncrossing her legs.

"Feel free to walk to the cruise ship terminal. It's only another twenty-seven miles."

"What makes you think I'm heading there?"

He paused, as if he were about to lay out an insult, then pointed to the highway. "Judging from the contents of your luggage, it's a pretty good guess," he said, just as he darted off up the grass incline to the edge of the highway.

"Where are you going?" Gail called. Then, watching him as he flagged down a state trooper, "Sorry, I thought you were abandoning me."

A square-jawed state trooper pulled over, got out, and set out flares. He spotted the subdued gator and acknowledged Gail's rescuer, thanking him.

"Morning, ma'am." The Florida state trooper touched the brim of his stiff cap. "You okay?" The intonation in his voice had a strong Tallahassee quality.

"Yes, I think so," she said, her frustration lingering.

"I take it, based on what's on the roadway, you were heading on a cruise."

"Yes, I was."

The handsome man whose vehicle she occupied interrupted. "Am, or was?"

It was a perplexing question. Why would he care?

She must now decide . . .Terminate her desperately needed vacation and quest to sleep with a man other than her soon-to-be-ex-husband, or return to Tampa? She'd booked the inside cabin months in advance on what was rumored to be a fertility cruise, on a ship where, for some unexplained reason, infertile couples conceived at a very high rate. Gail had monitored her ovulation cycles for an entire year to ensure the booking coincided with the peak of her cycle. She was thirty-five, and soon, any latent pregnancy would be deemed high-risk.

"Oh . . . uh . . ." she stuttered. "It's already paid for. I can't get a refund. Besides, it's the only time . . . uh, my cycle . . ." She searched for words. "It's the best time to make a ba. . . I mean, take off work."

"What kind of job controls you like that?" her rescuer inquired, leaning on the window frame over her head, his cologne lingering.

Voodoo Cruise

Gail had to think about his question. *Am I that employment-dependent that I've lost control of my life?* Then the investigative journalist in her took over, and her thoughts diverted to an entirely unrelated issue. *What's he doing wearing cologne? He doesn't come across as someone who would wear gentleman's clothing.*

"I'm a television anchorwoman," she said with pride. "A journalist. Ratings and advertising revenues drop when I'm not on-air."

"Huh—aren't you just a reader?" he said, rather callous.

Again, another comment that boiled her insides, but this time she couldn't fault him. Prior to moving to Tampa, she was an investigative reporter for a Philadelphia television station in one of the toughest viewer markets in the northeast. She'd loved Philadelphia, its demand for journalistic integrity, the grimy, corrupt politics, the brutality of its sports fans, complicated news stories, and impossible work deadlines. But Gail left Philadelphia because she believed the stress was the root cause of her infertility. And as her baby clock ticked, she feared a life without children, choosing the warmer climate and comfortable lifestyle South Tampa offered. She wasn't proud of that fact, especially after receiving a Pulitzer nomination for her 9/11 story, which had set her career on fire. In Tampa, the work was easy—just read the teleprompter. No stress, work on having a baby with Richard.

"Where do you want the vehicle towed?" the trooper asked. "Do you have Triple-A?"

"Oh, no!" Last week she learned she'd had no auto insurance for quite some time. She'd trusted her gambler husband to manage their now-gone finances.

Meekly, she responded, her expression loosening, releasing shame, big eyes pleading. "Officer, I have no insurance coverage."

The trooper shook his head and looked over at the blond-haired man. "You care to help the poor lady?"

Nodding an affirmative, the shirtless man mumbled, "How can you be so irresponsible?"

"I heard that!" Gail said. A twitching snarl came to her face.

He leaned through the passenger side window and reached into the glove box for his wallet. His cologne was subtle and fresh and not right. Yet, Gail wanted to slug him.

Inside, next to the wallet, was a small doll with dreadlocks wrapped in a colorful Caribbean smock. The figurine was the size of two of his hands, its torso made from the fine, hair-like fibers of what appeared to be shredded palm bark. The doll slipped from his fingers as he attempted to remove it from the stuffed glove box. It bumped Gail's knee, landing atop her foot. Gail's quick eyes fell upon what had been hidden beneath the doll: a chain of glittering diamonds. And as his towering shadow moved away, the sunlight struck the stones, shooting a shimmering prism that briefly blinded her.

"What's that?" she asked, blinking several times, the state policeman preoccupied with paperwork.

"A rosary," he said, snatching the brilliant string and shoving it into the deep pocket of his khaki shorts.

He reached down between her ankles and retrieved the handcrafted figurine that'd fallen.

"Here, hold this."

"What's in your pocket?"

"A rosary made of crystals," he answered. "They are special, and none of your business!"

He opened his wallet and handed her a plastic insurance card. "Use my Triple-A service. Deliver your gas guzzler gator-killer to your house."

She glanced up, eyes wide, letting his insult pass this time.

An observant reporter, Gail inspected the name on the card—her penetrating eyes also speaking. "Thank you . . . uh . . . Mr. Applegate."

Voodoo Cruise

"Jason, Jason Applegate," he added, completing his name.

After handing the card to the trooper, who offered to assist with getting her Tahoe towed, Gail realized she had no way to get to the cruise ship. And Mr. Greenpeace, with the back of his sneakers cut out, didn't seem such good company.

"Uh, Officer," Gail asked with a softness in her trained tone, "any way you can take me to the terminal?"

"No, ma'am, can't leave until the gator is euthanized." Then, "Are you heading east?" the trooper called loudly to Jason, who'd run out onto the highway while there was a lull and collected Gail's soiled and shredded belongings. He returned and stuffed the garments into a clear plastic garbage bag he'd retrieved from the back of his Jeep.

"Can you help the young lady out?" the trooper asked a second time.

"I got better things to do," Jason said.

The trooper gave him a hard stare. "I'm asking if you can help her out. She's already in your vehicle."

"What cruise ship are you heading for?" Jason asked, tying a knot in the plastic.

She leaned out the window to check her makeup in the side view mirror, not wanting to look at him directly, as she answered, "The *Sapphire Orchid*."

As the words *Sapphire Orchid* left her lips, Jason froze. The knot on the garbage bag grew tight, the plastic tails stretching. He deliberately waited several seconds before saying anything else.

"The *Orchid*! . . . Where's your husband?"

How does he know about the Orchid? she thought. *He certainly isn't the marrying or cruise ship type. He's rugged, an outdoorsman. Appears to be a free spirit adventurer, a National Geographic type and not a family man at all.* Except for that damn great-smelling cologne that she couldn't shake from her sense of smell.

"You're not with someone?" he said, shoving the bag of gathered clothes beneath some netting so it wouldn't fly out the back of the Jeep.

Gail turned and looked over the back of the seat. Her secured belongings rested partly atop a duffel with an embroidered logo, RJA Foundation, and what looked like a collection of scuba gear with a sticker on the tanks with the same logo.

"Is Jason your middle name?" she asked, digging, thinking the RJA Foundation had something to do with him.

"What gives you that idea?"

"Just a hunch," Gail said, not wanting him to catch on to how observant she was, which was what made her a great reporter.

"You know about the *Sapphire Orchid*?" Gail changed her line of questioning as Jason climbed into the driver's seat.

"More than I care to." His response was sharp. "I'll deliver you only because I'm heading to the port myself."

Releasing the clutch, rolling along the roadside, looking for a break in traffic, Jason mashed the gas pedal. He jerked the wheel and merged onto the busy highway, shifting gears until he caught up with the pace of the eastbound traffic.

Gail studied the contents of his vehicle. The aged Jeep, its worn, unkempt interior and its shirtless driver, tanned with a straight and firm posture. He wore glacier sunglasses that wrapped his eyes, concealing the direction of his sight or a measurement of his mood. A circular dashboard sticker with a blue heron, identifying membership in Friends of the Everglades. A swinging keychain with the logo of the *Rainbow Warrior*, the Greenpeace ship. *He's one of those environmentalists that travel these parts,* she thought. A nature lover who emailed her press releases about the ruination of natural Florida, looking for free TV publicity to raise awareness, but more importantly, to tug the heartstrings of the elderly and sympathetic credit card–carrying college students, pleading for donations to his great, earth-saving cause. It was how he earned a rather lucrative living, Gail was sure.

The Jeep sped along, a buffeting wind tossing Gail's frustrated hair. She wanted to run a brush through but realized she had nothing but the clothes she wore, the purse in her lap, and what Jason collected off the highway. She hoped to meet her close friend Vera, from the fertility clinic's therapy group of which they were both members. Vera had booked the same cruise. Gail could possibly borrow a few things she needed.

"What is this?" Gail asked, lifting the doll-like figurine, fashioned from bound brown bristles, that sat in her lap. She'd recognized its body, made from the fine hair of cabbage palm bark. And only knew this trivia after doing a story about early settlers of Cedar Key and the diverse products formed from the stripping of cabbage palm bark. One such company shredded the bark into fine, baby-soft strands for use in cleaning medical instruments. Other uses included handmade children toys, such as the doll she held.

Jason looked over and chuckled. "It's a voodoo doll."

"A what?"

"Voodoo doll."

"What are you doing with such a thing?" she asked.

"It's a good luck charm."

"Isn't voodoo a bad thing?" Gail questioned.

"Only the black magic. Much of it is good."

"Are you some sort of sorcerer?" Gail said. "A witch doctor?"

Jason laughed as they passed under the toll booth transceiver. "It was a gift."

Gail noticed that his laugh was genuine. It didn't match the cynicism that came with the individual she'd labeled him as.

A fearlessness settling in, she pressed him. "Come on, give me a scoop. On your dangerous journeys into the remote Everglades to count the number of surviving speckled six-toed banana frogs, you discovered an isolated Indian village where voodoo is practiced?"

"Yes, how did you know that, TV reader?" he said sarcastically. "Correct, six toes, like Hemmingway's cats, and no speckles, by the way. And the village would have been of the Taino Indians."

Reader!

"What's your hang-up with what I do for a living? Why do you care what I do?" Gail asked, challenging him. "I'm a journalist, not a reader!" Gail bit her lower lip, a trick she'd learned to express a hint of controlled anger. "Are those diamonds you put in your pocket? Are you a diamond thief?"

"No!" Jason answered firmly. "I told you before, a rosary. I've had them my entire life."

Jason turned his attention to the busy highway and maze of twisting interstate ramps.

Gail observed he'd not shaved in several days—a thickened beard showing a rose hue. He had no body fat. His shirtless frame was nothing but toned muscle. Gail wondered what her children would look like should he impregnate her—handsome towheads, or possibly soft-skinned twin girls, with shimmering bushy-blonde Shirley Temple curls.

A jet passed overhead on approach to Fort Lauderdale airport. To her left, just south of the Fort Lauderdale skyline, several cruise ships loomed—gigantic monoliths, looking almost out of place. Gail was anxious to be rid of Jason's presence. They hadn't hit it off; in fact, were polar opposites. Sleeping with him was totally out of the question.

"We're at the port," Jason said, working the wheel, rounding a sharp off-ramp, exiting the interstate and onto Federal Highway.

"I clearly see that," Gail remarked. She craned her neck to locate the *Sapphire Orchid* with its stunning violet-blue emblem painted across the bow.

"Do you have your passport?" Jason asked as he downshifted and came to a stop, waiting in a line of vehicles at the port entry security gate.

"Yes," she said, relieved she hadn't packed it with her destroyed luggage. "In my purse."

Gail lurched in her seat as the Jeep rolled over raised traffic spikes.

An African-American woman stepped from the booth. "Good to see you, Jason," she said. "Who's the sweet-looking honey seated next to you?" She winked.

"Why do you ask, Charlene? Are you jealous?" Jason said, winking back.

"You know you light up my world, honey pot. I might not let her in if you are cheating on me."

Gail's face grew pale. Was this a joke or something else? How did he know her?

Charlene leaned into Jason's window and reached across with her hand out for Gail's passport. Gail placed it in her hand. The security guard studied it briefly and then handed it to Jason, passing him a giant smile and waving them through. "See you later, my love stud."

"Bye, Charlene, my little pot of gold."

Gail did a double-take as they drove off. "Why didn't she ask for your passport? Are you two an item?"

"If she didn't ask, why should I give it to her?" Jason offered no further explanation.

"You travel quite a bit, don't you," Gail remarked. Seasoned reporters she'd come to know in the northeast market did the same when crossing international borders. Border guards sometimes formed relationships with regular crossers. Often a bribe was involved.

"I'm not going back to show her," Jason said, turning left at the first intersection, following ground-level signs directing to the *Sapphire Orchid*.

Chapter 2

Behind the terminal building, painted in bright Caribbean colors, was the impressive, thirteen-deck *Sapphire Orchid*. Splashed across the bow of the vanilla-cream hull was a rich, violet-blue bouquet of orchids. Gail counted the levels, wishing she'd booked the top deck, a balcony cabin in the Emerald Class with exclusive dining arrangements. Her research had hinted that the higher your cabin, the more likely you'd conceive. But her now defunct Richard sperm bank had booked an inside cabin, halfway up, arguing her theory was nonsense.

Awestruck at the size of the cruise ship, Gail grew impatient as they waited in the long line of vehicles unloading. She recalled the *Miami Herald* article in a recent Sunday Travel Section that described, in literary terms, Emerald Cruise Line's signature luxury liner, the *Sapphire Orchid*:

> . . . *A royal bouquet of tropical sensuality, with sleek nautical lines cutting the sparkly seas so cleanly only the trailing wake confessed that she passed in the moonlit night. At 123,000 tons, the Sapphire has a 1,305-foot ivory hull, brushed in a dazzling, bursting arrangement*

of succulent sapphire orchids that appeared so visually luring you could taste the sugary nectar of each flower merely by sight. Atop the thirteenth deck, twin funnels hung the ship's two-story trademark logo—a brilliant blue orchid, tempting a hovering green-back honeybee; where from the depth of the widening lip of its center petal, a blazing wedding-white ivory, bled ever so thin into the veins of the solid blue of its broad pedals.

But what made the Sapphire Orchid special was its life-giving magic; a truth never advertised, never confessed by the cruise line. That for some reason, infertile couples miraculously conceive. It was the true-type font of the blogosphere, short-wit retweets and the addictive cry of social networks that gossiped the Orchid's secret. Telling of the joyful tears of infertile couples holding pregnancy tests pee'd positive; surmising an itinerary that included the Atabeira Lagoon at the peak of ovulation was somehow the secret. But never did Emerald Cruise Line explain, or admit they had something to do with this miracle, somehow linked to the private Haitian peninsula leased on the southern shore of a pristine, turquoise lagoon.

Embarking couples who traversed the high-up gangway were greeted with a rich aphrodisiac design, one that played on each of the five senses. In the promenade, champagne stairway and narrow cabin corridors, the smell of almonds drifted—said to arouse desire and passion in women. On every menu, and heaped high at every buffet and late into the night at each raw bar, were chilled oysters, thick, limy and juicy— brimming with zinc to raise sperm counts and to activate the testosterone that motivates his libido. High in omega-3 and anti-depressives, her mate became clam-happy and as uncontrollable as a valiant stallion. In bites of entrées there was a hint of chili pepper chock-full of capsaicin, a body-temperature and heart-rate booster that'll get him hot and bothered in a hot flash. And there was, for a premium price, pomegranate juice, a natural liquid Viagra, prominently displayed with top-shelf liquors.

For her, it was honey, a passion kick-starter packed with fast-acting simple sugars—great for instant pep, anytime, anywhere. In giant bowls and mealtime desserts was the presence of dark chocolate, a natural source of serotonin. And in nearly every sellable nook, a chocolate bar. There were sensual fruits; cherries, strawberries, and big bananas oddly positioned vertically. It was an arousal in every way, every food, every color, texture and aroma—designed to lure and please and engage one to mate. And in the middle of the night at random times, an infusion of oxygen came from somewhere. It woke slumbering couples who became oddly aroused. But none of it ever was admitted by the cruise line—no one could explain the unusually high pregnancy rate of desperate infertiles onboard.

And of course, the orchid flower itself—its name derived from the Greek word for testicles—was an aphrodisiac merely by sight.

Anxious to tend to his own matters at the port, Jason squeezed his Jeep between a limo and a tour bus. He pulled too close and ran onto the curb. The jolt lifted Gail from her seat.

Voodoo Cruise

"Tight squeeze," Jason remarked.

Mesmerized by the giant cruise ship, Gail did not react to the sudden jolt.

Jason nudged her elbow; her mind was elsewhere. "What's wrong?"

She did not answer as a tear released from the corner of her eye. "It's a memory, reminding me why I'm here."

"It's a sad memory, I can see," Jason said. He turned off the engine.

Just outside the vehicle, couples lugged tagged suitcases along the broad walkway toward intercepting porters. The female spouses were excited, dressed exceptionally sexy in their slimmest wear.

"There you go," Jason said, as he leapt from his seat and dug out the clear plastic bag with Gail's soiled clothing and came to the passenger side. "The *Sapphire Orchid*, you'll be the only single woman onboard."

Gail snapped her head right, delivering a hard stare. She wanted to lay into him, release her festering men frustration, but thought better. *Soon, he'll be another bitter memory.* And without thanking Jason, she handed him the voodoo doll she'd held the entire time, gathered her purse, and crawled ass-first from a vehicle that'd seen better days. She angrily yanked the plastic bag from his grasp, not saying a word as she turned her back and headed for the building.

Luggage lined a sidewalk tiled in pairs of leaping dolphins, pointing the way to registration. Gail stepped past the jumble of suitcases and joined the thicket of arriving passengers. She followed a couple through the swinging glass doors into the cavernous steel building—a courteous husband allowing Gail to enter ahead, holding the door. Immediately, she grew chilled from the excessive air-conditioning. Heading for the registration counter, she felt as if all eyes followed her, and could guess every woman's thought. *Where's her husband? What's with the garbage bag? Why did they let a single woman on this cruise?*

Embarrassed, and anxious to check in, Gail was desperate to locate her cabin, get clean, meet Vera for dinner, and consume lots of alcohol to rid her memory of the recent months. And when the time was right, get drunk enough to lower her inhibitions, so she could lure a vulnerable, fertile sailor to serve as her free sperm donor.

As she waited alone in the slow-moving line, her introspection continued. How should she deal with the absence of a mate for the next seven days; the likely murmurs, stares, and whispers of eyeballing women her age, dressed sexy and ready to copulate at any moment? She'd scheduled the cruise as recommended by the infertility blog that speculated when onboard conception would likely occur. "Your timing must be right, particularly if you can only afford the less-desirable, lower deck cabins." Gail's cycle would peak in three days; the day after the ship arrived at the Atabeira Lagoon. She must find an unsuspecting male that night, for just one moment of insemination. It had been years since she flirted. *A crew member?* she thought, as the registration line moved along, Gail questioning her motives. This wasn't a singles cruise. In fact, if Emerald Cruise Line knew she was stag, they might not allow her to board.

She was next in line. Getting on onboard was her only hope. At a cost substantially less than a fertility clinic, she had placed all her bets on this trip. It was all Gail could financially spare. The tick of her biological clock, the sheen in her hair, and the pitch in her deeply angled waist would soon fade.

"Welcome to the *Sapphire Orchid*," a pleasant Haitian woman greeted in a British accent. "Can I see your confirmation, my lady?"

Dropping her bag, Gail fumbled through her purse and handed the crumpled boarding pass to the full-figured woman.

As she keyed in the confirmation code, the reservationist's pearly grin flattened. "Mrs. Stroud, there's a problem. Your deposit was processed but the balance never paid."

"What!" Gail said, shocked. "That can't be!"

"Do you have a credit card to pay the ten-thousand-five-hundred-dollar balance?"

Her mind raced. Because of her work schedule, she let her jerk husband handle the reservation. He'd lied. Did not pay in full and must've hidden the balance due notices.

"I don't understand," Gail said. "Why wasn't my reservation cancelled?"

"Inside cabin," the receptionist said. "If no one books on top of you, the reservation isn't cancelled. It's held open with the hope you'll find the money."

As excited passengers behind her waited, Gail nervously dug through her purse and produced a credit card.

As she swiped the plastic, the Haitian's grand smile flattened once again. "I'm sorry, my lady. Can you go and sit on that bench?" She pointed to the long wall straight back. "I will contact an account manager to see if there is something we can do."

"Isn't the card good?" Gail asked.

The woman shook her head side-to-side and pointed toward a wall bench. "No, my lady, I must keep this card."

Embarrassed, lugging a plastic bag like a homeless person, Gail trudged past the turning heads and sat on the uncomfortable, multicolored plastic seat as directed. Off in the corner a TV screen displayed CNN Headline News. It had been her lifelong goal to make it as a primetime reporter for a station as prestigious as CNN, but it took a great news story to get noticed by the big networks. It happened to her once already, but her career trajectory had stalled when she left Philadelphia for Tampa, a less challenging market. And she'd not wised up as to how bad her financial situation had become. Her work, leaving at 3 a.m. to prepare for the 6 o'clock news, left little time to pay attention to household details. In the evenings, demanding neighbors wanting to network with Gail, a prominent Tampa personality, failed to respect her downtime. So-called friends visited the moment she arrived home from the station, commenting on the morning news, her makeup, selections of outfits, and even the presentation of her breasts; too much cleavage, no cleavage, wide cleavage, bra type, cup shape. Her typical night, when she had a chance, was an early dinner, a Pinot Noir, then to bed, while Richard watched sports or was at the Derby Lane dog track playing poker.

As the line dwindled and the early afternoon passed, Gail wondered where Vera was. A true friend, Vera was not enamored with Gail's television notoriety, often waiting patiently whenever they shopped at International Mall as admirers asked for autographs and Gail-selfies. But Gail didn't care for Vera's husband, Ian. He showed too much attention to the other desperate women in their infertility support group. Vera had offered Gail to ride with them from Tampa to Port Everglades, but Gail refused, making a work-related excuse, because the real reason was Ian and his purposeful, undressing gaze. It was obvious what was on his mind, and she felt sorry for Vera because she too had locked onto a husband as creepy as Richard, unwilling to abandon him because of her ticking baby clock. Vera had booked the Emerald Class, far away from the lower deck cabin Richard had selected.

While she waited for the account manager, her thoughts drifted. That was the role of the account manager; work out a payment rather than let the cabin go empty. How to pursue her backup plan of sleeping with someone on the cruise? And why couldn't she shake the thought of Jason, clenching his thick triceps as he carried her to his Jeep, a rich, yet subtle cologne of a man who lacked the intellectual sophistication to wear it. It was out of character and odd. And the rosary, the blinding brilliance, were they really crystals?

As the afternoon passed, the registration lines dwindled. The headline news had cycled through and was repeating. Gail kept distracted, analyzing word choices of the CNN newscasters, scrutinizing the reporters' facial expressions, measuring the word count of each sentence, intonation, syllable emphasis, grading each reporter, until suddenly, a blood orange Breaking News banner flashed across the screen. "Fire in a cruise ship engine room strands 3,000 passengers in the Gulf of Mexico." The screen switched to live video from a helicopter hovering over the passengers, waving white towels as smoke billowed. But as fast as the news broke, the terminal's TV screen went black.

"What happened?" Gail searched to see if there were other monitors. Near the restrooms, another screen went dark.

How odd, she thought. *Someone's monitoring the content. Are we being watched?*

Another half hour passed, and the monitors never went back on. Only the very late and overly worried arrivals dribbled in to register. Bouncing her knee, Gail grew nervous. Did they forget her? Was the ship going to leave without her?

Feeling the weight of the world, she buried her head in her hands. Her plan had come to a screeching halt. And now, she had no way back to Tampa. How to return without a credit card or cash? A fear that she'd have to panhandle, beg to return home. The countless stories she reported on, of how Tampa and St. Petersburg wanted to stop panhandling, raced through her head. Lonely and growing sadder, she watched as a tear dropped and splashed onto a concrete floor brilliantly lit from overhead fluorescents. She fumbled through her purse for a tissue, but suddenly, the concrete grew dark, the presence of an arriving shadow. *Someone's looking at me,* she thought. Her eyes leaking, she kept her head buried. But there was the scent of his cologne. *Oh no, it can't be!*

"Take my good luck charm," the voice said. Jason slipped the voodoo doll she'd held earlier between her locked forearms into her lap.

She didn't dare look up. The roughly made doll sat within the crease of her closed thighs, a folded twenty-dollar bill held fast by a tie-dyed handkerchief-size scarf wrapped around its torso.

"What!" Gail blurted, eyes red, head upright, shocked, emotionally shaken. She bolted to her feet and stood defiantly inches from Jason's chest. Infuriated, she angrily scolded. "I don't want your money. How dare you ridicule me in this way, you horrible person!"

Flipping back her thick hair, she slammed the doll into his chest, cursing him, releasing the doll. It dropped to the cold concrete.

Using his sandal, Jason nudged the doll her way, near the bag of clothing, and walked off, saying, "Don't be so mindlessly antiseptic, it would do you some good to be superstitious. The money is the blessing of the doll, to bring you financial peace, not for you to spend."

Gail's head spun wildly. How did he know she had a financial problem? What was he doing here! What business did he have at the port? The flirtatious security gate guard knew Jason and didn't ask him for his passport. Gail couldn't gather her head around the situation.

Jason had walked away, not up the escalator with boarding passengers, but toward a guarded exit that opened to the loading dock, where forklifts whizzed about.

Suddenly, a voice called from across the wide-open space. "Jason . . . Jason Applegate."

Gail watched Jason stop midway through a doorway held open by a security guard. A dark-complected man in a sailor's uniform crossed the open space and greeted him. They hugged, kissed cheek to cheek, then talked for several minutes. Gail noticed the officer turn his head and look over. Then he lifted his cell phone and talked into it.

Moments later, both disappeared through the door to the loading dock.

Reaching for the doll on the floor, Gail considered kicking it across the lacquered surface. Instead, not wanting to draw attention, she set it in her lap. *Something's not quite right with this ship,* she thought. *There's a comfort with Jason, ranging from port security to the ship's staff. There's a story here, a connection . . .* Then, for some reason, her sadness dissipated, replaced by an energy she hadn't felt since leaving Philadelphia to become a Tampa anchorwoman. It came upon her like a rush of adrenaline. "I must board this ship!" The mysterious man that she despised; her creep of a husband not paying the balance due for the cruise, bankrupting her, all that had happened, she was not going to allow herself be beaten down anymore. Gail Stroud, the once tough, award-winning South Philly investigative reporter, was hot on the trail of a major story.

"Mrs. Stroud," a feminine voice called.

"Yes," Gail answered, searching for where the voice came from. A female sailor approached, hair neatly braided, running under her pinned white cap, her uniform a sharp white, pressed and clean. "I'm the ship's account manager. Sorry for the delay, the *Orchid*'s turnaround is always extremely time-limited and challenging. Anyway," she continued, "we checked your employment and discovered you're a newscaster."

"Yes, the morning news anchor," Gail said. "WKMC Channel 5, Tampa Bay."

"Where's your husband?"

Fearful the sailor would not let her on the ship without a spouse, Gail told her unfortunate story as concisely as a reporter, all the time worrying and wondering about Jason, and her journalistic need to get onboard.

"I am sorry for your situation, Mrs. Stroud. I have it within my authority to extend you credit for the cruise and to purchase proper attire in our onboard shops," the account manager said. "Emerald Cruise Line would hope your TV station would be most grateful with reciprocity for our generosity."

The well-dressed, smart-looking sailor smiled.

Gail knew what was happening. The cruise line was trading for good publicity—the type of advertising that dollars could never buy. It happened often. And she, as the TV personality, the talent, was the gatekeeper of such incredible goodwill, judiciously doled to a captive audience, paying in spades money the cruise line was willing to forget to use her viewer-trusted notoriety. And when a disaster occurred, such as the cruise ship now stranded in the Gulf of Mexico, video of desperate passengers pleading for help, smoke billowing, Gail would go easy on the cruise line.

Tactfully, Gail asked, "How about an upgrade to the Emerald Class?"

The strictly dressed manager nodded. "Of course, nothing but the best." Then she called for a porter to gather Gail's plastic bag.

"Come with me." She escorted Gail up the escalator and across the gangway.

"Welcome aboard," a Russian-accented female voice greeted as she entered the second level of the promenade. The leggy Russian crew member invited her to take a glass of pink champagne.

"Thank you," Gail said, lifting the flute off the tray. The champagne quickly disappeared.

"What do I smell? Is it chocolate?" Gail asked. But the Russian didn't answer. She simply smiled.

Conspicuously, Gail set the glass on a nearby gold granite tabletop, returned to the Russian, and helped herself to another.

She glanced at the packet of information the account manager handed her. *It's for real, Emerald Class! I can be with Vera,* she thought, finishing her drink in one lift. She passed a bank of richly designed elevators and took a seat. Gail sat there for a moment taking it all in. What an incredible ship, the colors, the quality. She was onboard! . . . *What's that smell? Almonds? . . . Hmm.*

Gail had a craving for some odd reason. Not far from where she sat, across the richly designed carpet and bank of golden elevators, was a cupcake bar tucked in a corner. Leaving her comfortable armchair, passing late-thirty-something couples as they milled about the lobby, Gail approached the counter. Beneath was an incredible collection of dark chocolates, cupcakes, and mounds of fudge. "What do you have for a person who's had an exceptionally bad day?"

Dressed in a chocolate-colored apron, the woman wore a name badge that said she was from Switzerland. She smiled and pointed to a tray of freshly made fudge. "Dark chocolate fudge," she said in broken English.

"I'd love a quarter-pound." Gail handed the woman her room key card, which doubled as her onboard credit card.

"Emerald Class," the Swiss clerk observed. "I have a special chocolate for your husband, if you'd like." She smiled and raised her eyebrows in a manner that insinuated his lovemaking would be better.

Gail was at a loss of words, not wanting to reveal she was stag. "Give me a half-pound. But why is his different from mine?"

"It's the recipe with a spice that will make him feel like a virile mountain goat," she whispered with a knowing expression as she packaged the fudge. "Stop back in two days and you can have my special blend of honey fudge."

With the boxed fudge, Gail left for the elevator, where she could see everyone who passed behind her in the mirror-like wall cover. She was the only person alone. Pushing the Up button, she fumbled with the strings on the fudge box. Other couples gathered and waited for the doors to open, each male with a firm arm wrapped around his mate. As the long elevator wait continued, Gail could see in each of the women's faces, questioning why she stood alone, unaccompanied, spouseless.

After a very uncomfortable ride up six decks, Gail exited and turned left, entering a narrow hallway that led to her cabin, Room 1113. Her starboard suite was on the highest deck. Swiping the keycard, she entered. The steward had delivered her tattered belongings, removed them from the plastic bag, folded them, and laid them on the bed. In her purse was the voodoo doll Jason had set in her lap. She removed it and set it on the desk, below the mirror. She wasn't quite sure what to do with it. Did it really bring her good luck—a twenty tucked beneath the colorful, tie-dyed handkerchief wrap?

She unknotted the fudge and bit into a square. "Mmmm . . . Did she say honey fudge?" she said, taking the box with her, squeezing past the queen-size bed to look out the sliding glass door that opened to the balcony. She lifted the curved handle and yanked open the thick, plate glass door. "Oomph." A rush of warm air came. Eleven stories below, loaded forklifts rumbled and sputtered across the dock and up a ramp, vanishing into the *Sapphire Orchid*'s hull. There were several security guards milling about. Gail sat in a chair, savoring the taste of chocolate, tossing another square into her mouth.

She watched the scramble below. Then, *he* appeared, Jason, from somewhere inside the hull. He came trotting out onto the dock, stopping to talk to a forklift driver. Moments later he jogged toward the terminal building and talked to a security guard. They seemed to be waiting for something. Two more pieces of fudge and five minutes passed when a solid white van pulled to an open gate at the corner of the building where Jason and the guard stood. Her eyes grew wide as the gate unlocked and the van rolled inside. Jason started toward the van. He looked back toward the ship and waved. Moments later, from somewhere below, a line of young, dark-skinned children appeared and marched in step to the van, climbing inside it.

Leaving her chair, leaning against the rail to get a better look, Gail squinted and watched Jason dig into the pockets of his khakis. He had changed into something presentable. *But the facial hair's got to go,* she thought.

Jason handed over a wad of cash to an adult who got into the passenger side. *What's he up to? He can't be trafficking children in broad daylight? A security guard is watching. Is everyone at the port on the take?*

Suddenly, Jason's attention turned to an arriving tractor trailer. It came through the same gate and backed near the hull, where the children just left. A forklift removed several pallets covered with dark green netting. Jason lifted the netting. His head disappeared beneath for several seconds. Moments later, he gestured the forklift driver to follow him as he disappeared into the hull of the *Orchid*.

Pressing her stomach against the balcony rail, Gail watched to see if Jason was going to exit the ship or stay onboard. Several minutes passed. There was no Jason. She pulled her chair close to the edge and waited. And as the *Sapphire Orchid* prepared to depart, longshoremen tended to their final tasks. But there was one person who had not moved since the vanload of children left. He'd been leaning against a light pole in the parking lot, on the other side of the fence. She recalled he had ducked behind a parked car when Jason passed, reappearing shortly after.

Gail strained her eyes. He was a short, thin man. He wore a green cap with black hair poking from the edges. And as the ship readied to cast its thick lines and sealed the large door that opened the hull, the observer disappeared.

Who is he? Gail wondered. He seemed keenly interested in Jason. Was he tailing him? Something was not quite right.

She returned to the coolness of her stateroom, feeling a buzz from the sugary fudge. *What to do next?* Gail thought. *I'll head for the top deck and watch the departure from there.*

At exactly 4 p.m. a steady, deep-throated bellow of the *Sapphire Orchid*'s horn announced its Port Everglades departure. Slowly, a rush of gray chalk-water shoved and boiled against the starboard seawall. The massive curvature of the Dutch-welded steel side slipped from its nine-hour refresh. A pair of tugboats sat ready as the gigantic vessel eased into the short channel. Gail left her cabin and headed for the top deck.

As she climbed the multicolored, carpeted staircase with polished oak rails, a relaxation came upon her. A sudden freedom from her job and creep husband back in Tampa. Jaded by the on-air antics of her station manager, Emmitt Stooch, in his relentless effort to embarrass her as often as possible, she'd grown bitter toward men. The drama of her life had gone on too long; she'd lost the capacity to relax. Perhaps that was why she couldn't conceive a child, she thought, searching for an answer as she had a thousand times before. She didn't want to live her life alone, empty, absent the chaos and love of child rearing. Absent someone to love her unconditionally.

Emerging from the top deck stairwell, Gail hooked the tip of her sandal on the lip of the last riser. She stumbled, but quickly gripped the rail to stabilize her footing. She stood straight and made her way outside. A healthy sea breeze tightened her summer dress, nearly knocking her over as she tried to walk. *Where are my sea legs?* she thought, feeling the forward surge of the ship as it headed along the channel toward the break in the sea barrier.

Crossing a patch of the deep-green imitation turf, Gail leaned against the outer rail that angled inward and watched as the *Sapphire Orchid* traversed the narrow channel and split the basalt barriers heading into the open Atlantic for the warm waters of the Gulf Stream. And at the point where the vessel cleared the channel and broke for the open sea, Gail saw him, the man in the green cap, standing on the jetty, watching the ship. She strained her eyes to see if a vehicle was close by. In a parking lot, off by itself was a red pickup, a small one, old and beaten. Again, her reporter's instinct required her to log the sighting in her memory.

Voodoo Cruise

"Excuse me," Gail heard a voice say. She felt a bump on her elbow. It was a woman's foot, suspended in her mate's arms, whisking her off the top deck, no doubt heading to their cabin for some hanky-panky. All around were couples, holding hands, shoulders nudging, lips pecking—lovers. How did she end up in such a situation? How could she have been so naïve, wasting so much of her biological clock on Richard?

But Gail knew why, her denial, her reasoning, it was a desperation that started in New York City on 9/11. A memory that today had caused her not to pay close attention to the swerving traffic on Alligator Alley. Had she'd been more alert, she would have missed the alligator like the cars in front. But her fate would not have led to her encounter with Jason. He'd be just another deckhand, moving about, unnoticed. And there'd be no story to investigate.

Chapter 3

The *Sapphire Orchid* cut cleanly through the ocean swell. Beneath the stern, an endless spiral flush pulverized the Atlantic white, then blended as a boil into an aerated green, and finally the rich blue of the Gulf Stream. From the top deck, a firm easterly sea breeze tossed Gail's hair across her face. Brushing it back, she thought back to the incident on Alligator Alley, guessing the expression on her ex-husband's face when the tow truck dropped off their SUV in Richards's apartment complex parking lot. *It's his problem, and the delinquent lease payments, that's on him also.*

As gathered seagulls darted within the *Orchid*'s invisible slipstream, her thoughts shifted to her rescue from the jaws of the alligator. Why did Jason stop to help? It was a selfless act. What was Jason's story—children in a perfect line, walking from inside the cargo hold; dealings with the *Sapphire Orchid*? Again, she couldn't imagine the cruise line an accomplice for trafficking children. But she trusted her reporter's instinct; she'd come across a great story on what was a very unusual cruise ship.

Fifteen years ago, another great story happened that catapulted her career. Gail, a recent journalism graduate, had accepted a street reporter position at a Philadelphia TV station. Raised in a middle-class, stable household, Gail was aware her career choice wasn't what her parents wanted. Her father, though not college educated, was a successful suburban custom home-builder; her mother, a homemaker and full-time elementary school teacher. Both expected Gail to marry, provide them with three grandchildren, and teach at the local grade school, as did her mother until retirement. Family was important.

Majoring in English, Gail attended West Chester University in Pennsylvania and pursued a teaching degree until her junior year. It was while taking a journalism course, and with the inspiration of a worldly English professor, that she discovered herself—a passion to capture the raw and complicated inner-city lives people often lived. It intrigued her, because her childhood had been so protected, a want for nothing. The best way to give back for her great life was to expose the ill will inside downtrodden, urban communities. Philadelphia, and across the Delaware River in Camden, was the perfect setting, fertile ground for the start of a journalistic career.

She'd been working at WFIX 29 for three months and grew hungry for her own stories. They gave her softball stuff, short blurbs on renovation of historic buildings, the gentrification of blighted neighborhoods, city council meetings when there wasn't much on the agenda. Until finally, a topic came where she had some background, thanks to her father. Her station manager asked her to do a story on construction building code changes that would foster inner-city redevelopment. The manager, who'd interviewed Gail for her position, was aware Gail had some construction knowledge. So, he sent her to New York City to interview a Philadelphia City Planner who happened to be speaking about Form-Based Codes at a conference in the World Trade Center. The date, September 11, 2001.

The budget-minded TV station had sent her alone in a company car with a camera and tripod. Already familiar with New York, Gail planned to be at the World Trade Center by 9:00 a.m. She exited the Holland Tunnel at 8:20, but couldn't find a parking spot close to the building. Circling the congested streets, she found a space several blocks away in Battery Park. At 8:44, she hoisted the bulky camera to her shoulder and was making her way when American Airlines Flight 11 crashed into the North Tower. The impact knocked Gail on her ass—camera still set on her shoulder. She sat in shock as debris rained. *What happened?* she thought. What next? . . . Race to the World Trade Center, or film from where she parked?

Returning to the car, she retrieved the tripod and stationed it on the wide sidewalk that bordered Battery Park. Gail recorded the horror of the 9/11 attack, including the United Airlines Flight 175 crash into the South Tower. The camera rolled as people rushed in confusion and panic. But it was the woman who came down Broadway and crossed the intersection to the sanctity of Battery Park that became her story. Smartly dressed, barefoot, carrying designer heels, her hair singed and small lacerations on her cheeks and forearms, the woman crossed the chaotic intersection and collapsed on the park bench next to Gail.

In her right hand, she clutched an envelope. Frantically, she dug in her purse for her cell phone. She was crying, talking to herself, stunned. "Oh my God! Oh my God! Oh my God! I got to call Chris. Oh my God!" she said, out of breath, swiping her cell phone.

Close enough to record audio, Gail swung the camera in her direction.

Her name was Dawn. She was coming from an early doctor's appointment that morning and had just entered Tower Two when the plane struck. She worked at an insurance company on the 103rd floor with her husband. She'd been trying to get pregnant for nine years. This morning, she'd gotten good news and wanted to share it with her husband, where it was most important to them, where they'd met at their jobs in the World Trade Center with supportive coworkers.

Gail zoomed in on Dawn's stressed face. But it was the cell phone call that was most disturbing.

"Chris, Chris, thank God I got hold of you. Are you all right?" Dawn said, her hands covered in gray, caked powder.

Gail couldn't make out what he was saying on the other end. Only her expression conveyed her serious concern.

"Chris, get out of there!"

Another pause . . . behind the camera, Gail closed in on her expression and filmed the woman's tearful sadness at the realization her husband was about to die.

"Can you get to a window so I can see you?"

There was a pause.

Holding the cell phone to her ear, Dawn stood on the park bench trying to make out where she might see him. She waved her arm while holding the cell phone. "I'm in Battery Park standing on a park bench. Do you see me, Chris?"

Gail panned to the top of Tower Two. She zoomed in on waving arms from blown out windows; smoke billowing, obstructing her shot briefly. Then she captured the horror, as one by one people jumped, audio picking up the sound of bodies crashing onto the street canopy.

"No, no, don't jump, Chris," Dawn screamed into the cell phone. "You are going to be a father. I'm pregnant. I'm pregnant," she screamed. "Honey, wave your arms . . . I see you, I love you. You are going to be a dad."

And ironically, as Gail zoomed in on people trapped above where the jet had crashed, and thick black smoked billowed, she focused on a man waving his arms, blowing a kiss with both hands. Then, as the black smoke enveloped him, he disappeared.

"No, Chris!"

Gail kept her camera locked on the window, hoping the smoke would clear—the mother-to-be standing on the park bench screaming, sobbing—Chris no longer on her cell phone. But the figure that fell from within the smoke was Chris. He'd jumped to his death.

It must've been from either her family values or the sheer shock, as Gail went over and comforted the woman—Dawn crying, explaining they so desperately wanted children and tried for so long. In a flash, her joy had changed as she told Gail her story. A love story, soul mates, and a tragic ending as the Towers collapsed—the new mother completely crushed by her horror.

The news footage captured of this new mother about to be widowed, holding her womb, had garnered Gail several awards. Which got Gail plenty of airtime, an opportunity to refine her on-camera skills and build her brand, a break that put her in front of the camera on a regular basis. It helped that her look was pleasing to viewers.

She was dating Richard at the time of the 9/11 event. They'd met at a Philadelphia Main Line nightclub two years ago. It was her 9/11 experience that compelled her to press Richard to marry. He did. Gail wanted children right away, replacing the lost lives she witnessed. But it never happened, and she reasoned it was her own post-traumatic stress that prevented her from conceiving. The fertility doctors, after many tests, indicated that though Richard's sperm motility was low, she could conceive and should keep at it.

But when many years passed, she reasoned it was the stress of her job. And though she anchored Friday and Saturday evenings, well on her way to weekday work, she didn't want to waste the notoriety gained from her 9/11 story. Gail applied and got the morning anchor position in Tampa, thinking the warmer climate in a less challenging viewer market would afford her the opportunity to have a child.

On the upper observation deck, the Fort Lauderdale skyline faded as the *Sapphire Orchid* sailed east. Gail felt a tap on her elbow. The nudge broke her train of thought. "Champagne?" A waiter offered a drink. But she refused. All around, celebrating the beginning of the cruise, were happy couples. A few feet away, a late-thirties husband lifted his slim, platinum mate into his arms and carried her off, across the artificial lawn, past a raw bar toward the elevators. Gail could feel Jason's arms cradle her in the same way—her nails digging deep into his biceps; forearms thick with rose hair, and his cologne-infused perspiration. An arousal came, then a fear, a broken sweat. She was alone with no male partner, certainly the only single woman onboard. *I should go to my cabin and hide until dinner,* she thought, fanning herself, a fleeting thought, wondering if it was a hot flash.

When she was ready to leave, the latch that opened the thick glass door to exit the observation deck did not give. "Why are these damn doors so heavy?" She shoved her hip into it. There was a sucking sound, the result of the difference in air pressures. The super coolness from inside arrived as she entered the stairwell. Goose bumps jumped to her bare shoulders.

Just inside was a single elevator. Next to it a carpeted staircase. Deciding it was quicker, Gail took the stairs. Making her way, she noticed on each landing, a watercolor of paired animals; oddly with backs turned, peering across an exotic tropical landscape. Moments later, she arrived at her cabin, inserted her keycard, and entered the tight quarters, then dove to her bed. It'd been an exhausting day, a predawn journey from her Tampa troubles, and a long-needed vacation.

But her relaxation was short-lived. Gail lay there, restless, staring at the blank ceiling, and considered how she had missed Richard's gambling ways. How he had hidden his vice for such a long time. Was it that she worked too much; focused upon her success, distracted by her producer, Emmitt, a good journalist in his own right, but a jealous nemesis who worked to embarrass her at every turn? Or was it that she'd convinced herself it'd take too long to find another mate? All the good men were married, she thought. She'd fallen into a mediocre marriage and feared the early onset of menopause, not wanting to delay having children any longer, not leaving Richard.

Rolling onto her right side to face the balcony, Gail pulled into a fetal position, peacefully staring out at the passing nothingness of the Atlantic. The *Orchid* had turned and headed south. The setting sun had dipped behind thunderheads, rumbling cumulous clouds drenching the distant Miami skyline. But over the ocean, the sky was blue and clear. Gail wanted to put her life on pause, recapture the piece of herself she'd lost—a fearlessness she once had working city streets—a confidence that eluded her in comfortable South Tampa.

Her thoughts drifted, something she often did to clear her memory of the horrible murders she read on the teleprompter. Of a baking Tampa baby left alone, strapped in a car seat in the hot summer sun. Of a python swallowing a newborn because careless parents didn't possess the education to know better. How, as a mother, she wouldn't dare to be so reckless should she be so fortunate to have children.

If she were to conceive, Gail wished it a daughter. And the moment she was born, a lullaby would play throughout the hospital announcing a new life on this earth—something good, replacing the death she witnessed on 9/11. She'd name her Dawn, a new beginning, after the woman she sorrowfully captured on video as her husband leapt to his death. And each year, on her daughter's birthday, they'd take selfies— many of them. And when she was old and shriveled, her daughter would be her best friend, caring for her. Gail had reported on sad stories about nursing home abuse; lonely and abandoned spinsters. And with the probability of outliving Richard, the lack of a child, or family when she needed it most, she feared loneliness terribly.

The fresh air from the open balcony door had turned warm and moist—the *Sapphire Orchid*, surging in rhythm with the tide, had entered the Gulf Stream. Gail closed her eyes. The fact that she'd sit at dinner alone tonight on what was jokingly known as the Love Boat was disheartening. She must find a way to deal with it all, or decide not go to dinner, eat in her cabin. But first, she must find something to wear should she sit with Vera at dinner.

Sitting up, she reached and opened her cruise packet and found a violet, onboard credit card with the logo of the *Sapphire Orchid. What better way to rid my blues?* she thought. *What a great-looking card. Let's take this for a test drive.*

Walking the promenade, window shopping, Gail felt her spirits lift. Her credit seemed to have no upper limit. There was no problem with the nearly thousand dollars in overpriced dresses, beachwear, handbag, and imitation jewelry she purchased. A one-piece bathing suit fit so well, she didn't want to take it off; fashioned from a Spanx fabric that made her mid-thirties, slightly thickening figure look better than what it was—narrowing her waist by reallocating subtle gatherings atop her hips and winching up her buttocks. When she presented the colorful cruise credit card, staff became incredibly kind. Yet, the shop she avoided was an imitation version of Victoria's Secret. Later, perhaps, she thought, not abandoning the notion of bedding one of the many handsome, polite, olive-skinned, uniformed crewmembers that walked about. There'd certainly appeared to be plenty of available candidates.

Returning to her cabin with an armload of purchases, Gail had no desire to locate her friend Vera just yet. This was her time, she needed space. She opened a chilled bottle of Pinot Noir, a gift supposedly from the captain. How did they know this was her favorite wine?

Lifting an inverted wine glass buried in a readied ice bucket, she uncorked the bottle and filled the entire glass, spilling as it overflowed. The outside of the glass wet from the chill, Gail went into the tiny bathroom and sat in a small space to apply her makeup. *I'm not used to putting on my own face*, she thought. At the station, it was someone else's job to make her look pretty. She felt a bit absentminded on how to apply makeup. When it came to the limited combination of jewelry to adorn her dinner dress, she felt inferior—accustomed to better selection, the property of the TV station. *How to do my hair?* Her two male stylists bickered endlessly about her onscreen hairstyle. Gail feared she couldn't dress to the level of television beauty others made her out to be these days. Her appearance at dinner would be plain and somewhat flat. But a healthy dose of alcohol would reduce the self-consciousness . . . She poured another glass, mindful not to go near her balcony or the ship's railings on her way to dinner.

Feeling a buzz after emptying the entire bottle, she finished dressing—one last look in the mirror, a dash of perfume and thick lipstick, and a brush through her hair. She made her way from the cabin and along the richly carpeted hallway with more framed watercolors of paired wildlife. "What's with these paintings? Am I on Noah's Ark?"

Arriving at the shimmer and glitz of the atrium, where the library stood three stories aft of the elevator, she waited. Seeing her reflection in a thoughtfully placed, decorative etched mirror, Gail adjusted her hair, making sure an appropriate amount of split fell on each side of her bare shoulders. She tested if the bounce in her curls was enough.

Waiting for the elevator, looking downward through the sparkling glass atrium, she gauged the first floor of the library would be on level seven.

A text message came from Vera. She was running late.

Gail decided not to wait at the dining room bar—a woman without a spouse. Instead, she chose to head down to the library. "Might as well find a good book to read for the stag woman at the table tonight."

The Pinot had numbed her nervousness and worry of a spouseless dinner. Two couples, conveying the body language of affection and sharply dressed in evening attire, joined her at the elevator. The golden doors parted. They entered, the men politely allowing the women. Quickly, the all-glass elevator dropped three floors. And as Gail exited, she saw *him*, Jason, in the library. The elevator doors closed too fast for her to slip away—trapped. Jason sat in an empty lounge chair, a laptop on his knees, his legs extended onto a coffee table. He was making notes, maneuvering the cursor. Dressed much neater this time, in pleated taupe dress pants and a Tommy Bahama shirt. He'd also shaved.

Gail pushed the elevator buttons—both the Up and Down. She jabbed the lit circles, anxious for Jason not to notice. She tried to remain out of his line of sight, standing behind the decorative glass wall. The elevator was not coming. Everyone was heading for dinner, and this wasn't a favored floor.

Peeking through the tinted glass, she took to observing Jason—his hair freshly washed and unknotted this time. The thickness of his blond hair had a healthy wave. She remembered his teeth, perfect, white, no Starbucks stain. His shoes were stylish, European, made of soft, quality leather. The fabric of his clothing was rich and relaxed, not stiff, as with poor quality fabric. It was hard to believe this was the same shirtless male she'd labeled a Greenpeacer—the pious type that grew scraggy beards, wore muddy cutout sneakers, nylon shorts, never a shirt, and emboldened in conversation.

The elevator couldn't come fast enough. *Why won't it stop at this level?*

But as she waited, she thought of her sudden fear and lack of composure. *He doesn't own this space. I want a paperback to read! It's been years since I've read a book.* She took a deep breath, stiffened, and walked confidently toward Jason, excusing herself as she made her way boldly to the stacked shelves of used and donated paperbacks.

"Excuse me," she said.

Jason didn't look up; he seemed consumed.

Passing, Gail looked back. "I said excuse me!"

Slowly, he turned, smiled, and said rather politely, "Do you need help reaching a book?"

What to say next? "No thanks," she said, forcing a feigned smile, waiting for some provocative statement to depart his lips.

But none came, as Jason had gone back to work.

Huh! Does he even recognize me? She was confused, the alcohol she drank prior to leaving her cabin making her temporarily a bit braver. Then she heard him say without turning to her. "I see the money spirits solved your boarding problem. You must've hung onto my good luck charm."

Gail didn't know what to say or how to respond.

Slowly, he swiveled and looked squarely at her. "You look good for the few hours that you've been onboard. Your tension is dissipating."

Gail remained speechless; his conversation was different, unprovocative. He was handsome in every way. Beneath her dinner dress she could feel her body temperature rise. *Oh please, not another hot flash.*

Gail finally thought of something. "Aren't you the person that drove me here? I didn't recognize you."

"Of course," Jason said. "How could you forget?" He laughed and turned back to focus on this computer work.

Perplexed, Gail wondered how someone could be so suddenly entirely different. *It's got to be a ruse.*

"I have to ask," Gail said, standing next to a stack of books, interrupting, wanting answers to the many questions regarding what he was doing on this ship, his relationship with port security. The kids and the large, delivered pallet he inspected.

"You can't ask," Jason answered.

"What was I about to ask you?" Gail said, feeling a word dance coming.

"You can't ask," he repeated. "You know what kind of ship this is. I know why you were coming here. However, I don't know why you did not return home, since you've no mate."

Voodoo Cruise

"It's complicated," Gail said.

"It's complicated for me, too," Jason said. "That's why I won't tell you. Let's not know either's personal business."

He slapped closed his laptop, rose to his feet, paused for a moment as he towered over her, then walked off.

It was the pause that got the best of her intoxication. He stood with a confidence, a politeness, and the virile presence of a professional that sent a chill through her. Gail was flush and warm and frozen in her stance, the alcohol working the last of its digestion. Jason came across a different person this time. A much more complex man than the rugged egomaniac in the Jeep. Not the environmentalist free-spirit, hair loose in the wind kinda guy she'd labeled him.

Chapter 4

V era, great to see a friend," Gail said, wearing a strapless, light-red dinner dress as she arrived at the richly designed Emerald Class dining room bar, located at the entrance to the main seating area.

Sitting on a leather barstool in a short, tight-fitting, black dinner dress was Vera. Standing next to her was Ian, cheeks rosy, missing a tie, sporting a gold neck chain, black chest hair rising to his Adam's apple. He'd obviously already had several cocktails. Gail paused as the expected annoying glare lunged for the formation of her chest. And Vera, as she often did, slid between and hugged Gail to block Ian's visual assault.

"What happened? I didn't hear from you when you arrived at the port," Vera said. "I need details."

Gail told of the accident on the toll road, the damaged Tahoe, the alligator at her feet, and the encounter with Jason. How she'd seriously considered returning home but after some contemplation, opted to continue her vacation regardless.

"It's great you showed the courage," Vera said, supportive, still wedged between Gail and Ian as he maneuvered to improve his scan of Gail. "Let's go and enjoy dinner."

Voodoo Cruise

Vera took Gail's hand and led her to the dining room.

"Good evening," the maître d' said in a cordial, yet thick accent. "I'm Mauricio, welcome to the Emerald Class dining experience. Your names, please?"

"Ian and Vera Haas." Vera turned to look at Gail for a moment with a concern that conveyed if she'd include Richard's name.

"Gail Stroud," Gail responded. "My husband is not with me." She didn't care to elaborate.

He scanned the list, confirming the last name.

"Seating for four? . . . Uh, excuse me, Ms. Stroud, my apologies."

And there it is, Gail thought. The assumption. Correcting the maître d' would have drawn undue attention. Fortunately, Mauricio understood her dilemma. But still, the other women in the dining room would notice and question the absence of her spouse—a wasted seat.

"This way, please."

Ivory tablecloths with multicolored embroidery of paired sea life in each draped corner adorned every table setting. Vases prominently displayed bouquets of large violet-blue orchids. The wall coverings were a pastel aquatic decor with paired dolphins leaping into an endless oceanic horizon. A waterfall behind the maître d's podium trickled over etched glass of the *Sapphire Orchid*'s trademark logo. Across, at the farthest side of the dining room, floor-to-ceiling plate glass brought the blueness of the passing seascape literally into the dining area. Tables set in twos and fours filled the entire dining room.

Escorted, the threesome passed seated couples. Mauricio invited Ian and Vera to sit closest to the tall window. Gail stopped at the seat next to Vera. As Mauricio pulled the seat aside to allow her to sit, a nearby spouse dared to display an oddity to her expression, curious as to why the lone woman was seated without her mate.

Noticing the snide look, Gail cringed. *Soon everyone will see no one is sitting across from me.*

Their waiter promptly came and stood at the corner of the four-seater. A female sommelier appeared. The waiter introduced himself as Estevan. His name tag indicated his homeland was Hungary. "Is your husband running late tonight?" Estevan queried in broken, Hungarian-accented English.

Gail wasn't expecting the question. "Uh, no!" she heard herself say, thinking how she could finish the reply. "My husband isn't coming."

"She's stag tonight," chided Ian, his loud, drunken voice heard by nearby occupied tables.

"Got any single men on this ship?" Ian announced.

Gail wanted to leap overboard.

"Put a lid on it, Ian," Vera said, barely tolerant of her drunk husband's behavior.

Without hesitation, the waiter placed the cloth napkin in Gail's lap and spoke French to the sommelier. The sommelier nodded, then meticulously uncorked a wine bottle. "On the house," Estevan replied.

It was clear to Gail that Estevan understood, as the trained professional he was, and immediately diverted. However, Gail couldn't help notice the head turns of the well-dressed women in nearby seats— their eyes drifting in her direction, heads cocked to listen—a flick of hair as an excuse to check the lone lady and vacant seat across from her. Gail caught many sneaking peeks, pretending to look out at the vast ocean, craning, wondering why this woman had no mate in a class of dining that guaranteed conception of a child; a wasted life.

Gail knew from the online reviews that the Emerald Class experience yielded the best pregnancy results. The seat without a mate made her a standout—perhaps part of a threesome; a surrogate could be the justification. Or, what did she do to drive her spouse away? Was it an argument? Why was this woman allowed to sit for dinner without a counterpart? Somehow, Gail felt her presence cheapened the reputation of this exclusive and costly eating venue.

Voodoo Cruise

For Gail, dinner couldn't finish fast enough. Amber-skinned young men serving as busboys hurried about, clearing tables for the next course, politely filling water glasses. But what struck her as odd was the busboy staff seemed of another race that she couldn't quite place. It was easy to assume they might be Filipino. But what puzzled her most, they appeared young, perhaps barely eighteen, and eerily similar to the young boys she saw marching to the van on the terminal dock, where Jason stood just before they departed.

"Excuse me," Gail said to the busboy to get his attention as he finished filling her water.

The young man, looking to be in his late teens, politely smiled.

"What country are you from?"

The young boy stood there and didn't say anything. He smiled, then turned to look for Estevan.

"It's likely he doesn't speak English," Vera said.

"You know, you're right, but look at his smile, it's constant. He seems such a pleasant boy, I wonder where he's from."

Estevan, always attentive to the comings and goings of his support staff, had taken note of Gail's questioning and came to the table.

"Can I help you, madam?"

"This young man, and his smile. I was wondering what country he is from."

"He's Chuukese," Estevan said. "There's several onboard our ship. They are from the poorest region in Micronesia. All are from orphanages where once they turn eighteen they must leave."

Estevan nodded for the busboy to go.

"Every time he approaches one of the tables, he gives the biggest, most beautiful smile. I wish I had that type of temperament," Gail said.

"It part of their culture," Estevan replied. "The Chuukese are known as the Smiling People. Living on remote islands as they do, they've never incorporated the desire to think about tomorrow. It's very much about today. They simply have not learned to worry about the future. Being alive is the greatest gift to celebrate each day."

"How profound, don't we all wish that," Gail said. "Thank you, Estevan, for educating me."

"You are welcome, Mrs. Stroud."

Gail looked out at the ocean and imagined where Micronesia was. The Atlantic had settled quite a bit. The softening sun was about to set, allowing for a darkening shade of blue in the clear sky, except for a small cloud that had formed. Gail, not wanting to look back across the busy dining room, contemplated the endless ocean horizon and compared it to the emptiness in her life, and the empty seat directly across from her. Outside, a wind had kicked up beneath the lone cloud in an odd way. A fetch suddenly formed and blew in the direction of the ship. And as dessert arrived, the cloud darkened. It thickened and grew skyward.

How odd, Gail thought. *So sudden!*

"Vera look . . . over there!" Gail pointed toward the port bow at about ten o'clock. "Looks like a waterspout is forming."

Heads turned; even the busboys paused. They all watched the ocean surface turn into a whirlpool the size of a backyard swimming pool. A tiny tornado rose from the center. And as the density increased as water droplets sucked into the funnel, the waterspout lifted and connected with the cloud. Quickly, all attention directed off the port side—a twister, its diameter growing.

The captain's Greek voice bellowed. "Attention! Attention! We have a natural anomaly taking shape off the port bow. All passengers and crew are to remove from all open decks. Don't be alarmed, guests, it just a waterspout that's tracking alongside the ship."

Several guests came to the window and snapped photos using their cell phones. Ian took a selfie.

"It's moving with the speed of the ship, like it wants to follow us," Gail said to Vera. "It's turning green."

The miniature tornado drifted closer, now barely forty feet away. "What's that? There's something inside the spout. Looks like green blobs."

Then suddenly, whatever filled the spinning funnel released and flung blobs toward the ship.

Smack!

Gail lurched in her seat. There were dozens of thumps as the blobs struck the glass. Some burst and splattered what looked like blood across the window. There were screams and the sudden shuffling and toppling of chairs. Disturbed, many couples ran from the dining room.

"Frogs," Ian called, observing one that did not burst and stuck to the glass. "Look at the tiny suction cups on its feet." He took another selfie.

As every window was covered, a grotesque red slime ran the length. Grossed out, couples left in the middle of their meal. The Haitian kitchen staff came from the galley and gathered in the farthest corner. The maître d' scolded them in their native language, "Back to work." But the Haitians called back and pointed. "Voodoo, voodoo, black magic."

Again, the captain's voice asked for calm, warning passengers and crew members not to go onto the open decks until they were clean. His diction was clear, confident, and matter-of-fact, like this happened regularly, as he explained it wasn't unusual for fish or smaller sea life to be drawn into a waterspout. However, Gail found it odd that they were frogs with batlike wings; that they were too far out to sea for such a reptile. The calls of voodoo and black magic she also found strange.

With dinner now ruined, Mauricio asked everyone to leave before the mechanical cleaner started to wash away the frogs. "Please depart the dining room." he asked, indicating they may not want to see what happened to the frogs that got squished by the wipers. "We will gladly accommodate you in the downstairs main dining."

Gail noticed there was no apology from the captain or management staff. Either they were frightened too, or something else. There wasn't the presence of panic amongst them, just the same trained matter-of-factness the captain displayed.

Leaving, Gail didn't want to spend any more time near eyeballing Ian. She decided to skip dessert on the promenade and spend the evening in her cabin, not wanting to be around for the first night romance that came with the enticement of being onboard the *Sapphire Orchid*. But first, she wanted to pass the library. And as expected, she found Jason in the same chair, busily typing. She'd considered approaching to ask if he'd heard about the waterspout and the unusual frog episode, but decided not to. Still, she wanted to find a good book to read and went to the shelves.

"Jason, Jason!" she heard, as she froze at the far end of the library. Someone had called his name.

The sailor she'd seen greeting Jason while she waited in the terminal raced in from behind two swinging service doors, dragging a plastic bag along the carpet. Out of breath, he sat across from Jason. They conversed. The sailor opened the bag for him to look. Gail, wanting to overhear, took a distant seat with the back facing them. She'd selected a book within reach, pretending to read the inside jacket.

Jason opened the plastic bag and looked inside. "La Hotte glanded frog. A message from the mambo," she heard him say, as he inspected the contents of the bag.

Then she heard him say something else, his voice carrying in her direction. "Do you mind?"

Jason stood to face Gail.

She felt his presence. *He's not so naïve. He knows I'm snooping.*

"Why don't you come and sit with us?" he said sarcastically.

Voodoo Cruise

Calmly, Gail went to the bookshelf and returned the paperback. "Looks like I have some research to do," she said. "La Hotte what mambo?"

But before Jason could respond, she jetted away. It was time to do some reporter research.

Gail had a clue—La Hotte glanded frog. Why was the sailor in such a frenzy? And how did Jason recognize the frog so easily? Was he an expert? Mambo, what was a mambo? There was a reason Jason was onboard, a relationship that involved Emerald Cruise Line. *What's with this voodoo stuff?* she thought.

Leaving the library, Gail passed a row of interior windows down the hallway. On the other side of the library in a separate room were rows of computers. *An Internet cafe, I can log online,* Gail thought, entering the empty room.

Swiping her cruise pass card at one of the many unoccupied workstations, Gail accessed the Internet. Her name appeared on the screen and a video ran an advertisement for lingerie sold on the promenade deck. *Not funny,* she thought, not liking the idea that whenever she swiped the card an algorithm gathered and tracked her every move. "I wonder if it knows I'm husbandless. Perhaps it will deliver me a sperm donor," she said cynically, vividly reminded of the purpose of this ship and her mission to conceive.

Gail typed the species name into the search bar. Images appeared. She considered snapshots of the frog and read the Wikipedia narrative. The frog was indigenous to Haiti and considered to be extinct for nearly thirty years. It was rediscovered in a pond at the edge of a fishing village in the Atabeira Lagoon.

La Hotte Glanded Frog (E. glandulifer). This frog is called Old Blue Eyes: its most distinctive feature is its striking blue sapphire-colored eyes – a highly unusual trait among amphibians.

As she read, she found something else unusual. In Haitian voodoo, frogs are a sign of fertility.

What's the connection? Was it some sort of threat directed at the *Sapphire Orchid*—the bloodied windows a warning? Gail entered the word "mambo wiki" into the search bar.

Mambo is the term for a female High Priest in the Voodoo religion in Haiti. Mambos are the highest form of female clergy in the religion, whose responsibility it is to preserve the rituals and songs and maintain the relationship between the spirits and the community as a whole. They are entrusted with leading the service of all of the spirits of their lineage.

Gail contemplated what she'd read. Voodoo was somehow involved. Interesting, she thought, recalling the voodoo doll Jason gave her. There was a connection, but what was it? It puzzled her.

"Lots to sleep on," she said, logging off and leaving.

Tired, on mental overload, Gail headed to her cabin. The bed had been turned down. A bowl of fresh fruit prepared. Slipping off her dinner dress, she let it drop to the floor. Stepping out of the sleek gathering, she went and tugged open the sliding glass balcony door to let the soothing sound of the nighttime ocean inside. Her head spun with the confusion. She collapsed to the bed and slept soundly.

Chapter 5

Gail did not recall waking at all during the night, a rarity. At the foot of her bed, on the dark brown desk below the black flat-screen television, sat the voodoo doll Jason gave her. Propped against the low mirror, the doll was in a sitting position. "Did my cabin attendant position it that way?" She contemplated the twenty secured to the scarf tied to the waist of the bristle-formed figurine. Did it bring her the good fortune that allowed her to go on the cruise? A skeptic, she was not convinced; voodoo, mambo, a waterspout of sucked-up frogs, and the black magic fear portrayed by kitchen staff—should she believe in such things?

She felt a tingle in her head. "I need coffee before my caffeine headache arrives."

After slipping from the fresh sheets into her slippers, Gail tossed on a solid-colored summer outfit, again purchased with her limitless onboard credit. She departed the cabin for the breakfast buffet on the same deck.

The early morning buffet wasn't at all busy, as expected. Of the few early-rising passengers, all were paired with their mate. They looked tired. *Probably working overtime trying to make babies,* Gail thought, as she admired the layout of food, craving fresh strawberries for some odd reason.

Loading her plate with a selection of fresh fruit and cereal, she avoided the empty main-seating and went outside to the rear deck, a more private space. Seeking a quiet corner shielded from the buffeting wind, she found a wicker chair set with thick seat cushions and a coffee table. She sipped her coffee and mixed in the fruit with her cereal. Below and off the stern was a steady gush, whipped into a white flush that trailed the *Orchid*. There was the noticeable hum of the electric motors and the smell of smoke drawn from the stack into the wind eddy created by the displacement caused by the ship speeding along at nearly thirty knots.

There was a story here, a great one. She sensed it.

It'd been some time since she'd worked as an investigative reporter. The hard work and odd hours weren't part of her life anymore—comfortable Tampa was. Lattes and fruit smoothies on an outside porch, beneath palm trees in the dead of winter in Hyde Park Café, was her life now. She considered if perhaps she should work on what she needed to do. Find a crew member horny enough for a quickie. In another day, she'd be at the peak of her ovulation. A child would make everything right in her life again.

"Hello," a voice called as Gail contemplated her thoughts. An older woman greeted her and settled into an adjacent chair. "I like it back here," the woman said. "There is a healthy wind to keep the air fresh."

She looked to be in her mid-fifties, with jet-black hair and olive skin. Her build was thick and sturdy. Her voice clearly indicated she was Mediterranean.

"Relaxing, isn't it?" the woman said, gathering her thick hair, knotting it into a kinked ponytail to keep the wind from messing with it.

"Yes, and needed!" Gail answered, suddenly realizing this was the first woman she'd seen without a counterpart.

Voodoo Cruise

"You're older," Gail said. "Why are you here?"

The woman laughed. "You think I'm one of the passengers?" A warm, engaging smile came. "My husband is the ship's doctor. The *Sapphire Orchid* is our home."

Someone who may enlighten me, Gail thought, *perhaps with information on Jason and his connection.*

"What did you think of that episode with the frogs, yesterday?" Gail asked, biting into a strawberry, looking down to swirl her spoon, toying with the blueberries that turned the skim milk in her cereal purple.

The women's softened face grew into a more serious expression. "Yes, that can be annoying," she responded, repositioning to fully face Gail.

"Wait," Gail said. "Does this happen often?"

"Not very, but there are occurrences."

"What!" *An admission such oddities do occur on this ship?*

"Are there other occurrences beside frog tornados?" Gail inquired.

"What do you mean?"

"Natural anomalies, like the captain announced," Gail said. "I heard Haitians believe a curse has been put on the ship. Do you believe it?" Gail hadn't heard that; she made it up, fishing for information.

"Yes, of course, what else could explain it?" The woman laughed.

Was this woman toying with her? Gail wondered, taken by her affirmation.

"You live onboard the most mysterious cruise ship in the world, where no one admits to or even discusses the unusually high conception rate. It's got quite a reputation. And you can't deny the fact, couples conceive in a way that can't be scientifically explained."

"You've done your homework," the woman said, extending her hand. "My name is Marie, Marie Battar."

"Marie, I'm Gail Stroud."

"Yes, Gail, odd things happen, and there's lots else you don't know."

"Like what?"

Marie paused for a moment and pondered. "Like the goodwill that surrounds this ship and Emerald Cruise Line's generosity to Caribbean children."

"Goodwill?"

"Isn't helping infertile couples a form of goodwill, allowing new life to enter the world?"

"It certainly is, and couples pay generously purely based on nothing else but the results discussed on infertility blogs," Gail said. "How does it happen here, yet nowhere else in the world?"

"That's a secret," Marie said, chuckling.

"Secret! You mean you know?"

"What do you think? My husband is the ship's doctor. He's a kind and giving man at that. We don't keep anything from each other, not even that."

Astounded, Gail realized she had lucked out, finding an information source who might cooperate. What a story this would make if she could reveal the *Sapphire Orchid*'s deepest secret. She'd be world famous, land a high-paying news anchor job in a bigger city. Solve her debt problem and begin a new life. Only if she had proof of whatever it was this ship did to make babies.

Gail pushed further. "Do you mind telling what your husband has shared with you?"

"Yes, I do mind."

Gail's expression fell flat.

"Aren't you here to have a baby?" Marie asked, sitting back in her chair, crossing her legs.

"Yes, but my husband didn't come."

"Oh! I'm sorry to hear that. But why?"

Voodoo Cruise

"I'm not sorry at all!" Gail responded, which led her to share with Marie her sad, desperate story, revealing her personal circumstances; even that she'd try to lure one of the crew into the sack.

"Oh, that's easy, I can arrange that for you," Marie said.

"A crew member?" Gail blushed.

"Yes! I live aboard and know the entire staff. I know who's vulnerable, a casino dealer, perhaps a bit macho and horny, and of good breeding stock. But you need to wait until we depart Atabeira."

Gail grew nervous. She fanned herself. This woman would arrange for her to have sex with another man—the first "other guy" since Richard. This was highly unusual for a woman she just met.

There was a paired silence. Reality had arrived for Gail. Sleeping with an unknown man was a big step; not even in her college days did she have a one-nighter. Her thoughts deepened. A child would bring stability to her life. Her life was a mess. But was she about to mess it up more? Gail had to think. Should she take this woman up on her offer? What if she conceived? How to explain the absence of a father to her child?

"I see you have doubts," Marie said, restarting the conversation. "You Americans are too uptight when it comes to your sexuality."

Gail remained silent, contemplating, considering; she was becoming emotional for some unexplained reason. *A mood swing? Menopause? What's with me?*

"I'll tell you what," Marie said. "Why don't you come to the Atabeira village tomorrow? It may be best that you see what people don't know about the goodwill this ship provides. Like I mentioned, for children of the Caribbean."

Gail turned away, her eyes filled with tears. She sniffled. "Go with you?"

"Trust me," Marie said. "You deserve some good in your life. Tomorrow—you won't regret it. Then, in the evening, we will go to the casino to check out a nice man to give you the child you desire." Marie chuckled. "I know you are sad. But—you must excuse me—lighten up, Gail. Take life less seriously . . . Go for it. The dealer is handsome and smart, of good breeding quality and gentle."

Marie's chuckle surprised Gail. Perhaps she was right and Gail should behave a bit more liberally. She so desperately wanted a child.

The door next to them swung open. Again, the sucking sound of the air temperature differential. A rush of super-cool air. A uniformed sailor came through the double-doors that opened to the buffet. It was the man she'd seen with Jason. He came to Marie, knelt, and kissed her on the cheek.

"Hello, my love," he said, greeting Marie affectionately with exceptional warmth in his eyes.

Marie allowed the man to lift her hand and fold it within his. She turned toward Gail and introduced her.

"Meet my new friend," she said to her husband.

The man smiled. "I'm Lou." His accent was as thick as Marie's

"I know you," he then said, recognizing Gail. "You are the young lady Jason asked me to let on the ship."

"You know him?" Gail asked, head spinning. Too much happening entirely too fast . . . *Asked to let me on the ship?*

"Jason . . . asked you to let me on the ship?"

"But of course," he answered. "Said you had a rather challenging circumstance and desperately needed a change of venue, some luck, and a cure to whatever frustrates you."

Gail wanted to pepper him with questions about Jason.

"You mean he had something to do with the cruise line letting me aboard?"

Lou nodded. "He offered to pay for everything, but the captain felt there was a greater value in good publicity for the *Sapphire Orchid*."

"What?" There were two sides to Gail's thoughts. Jason was wealthy enough to cover her expenses, and the captain vetoed his generosity because they wanted something from her—great press. Was something about to happen?

"I'd like to talk to the captain," Gail said.

Marie interrupted. "When we get back from Atabeira, I can arrange. But I must warn you about the captain."

"Warn me?"

"He's Greek and you are alone. He has mistresses onboard, if you know what I mean. Like you, he wants to sire a male child. He's not a gentle man."

Again, Gail's head spun. Odd—was that the reason he captained this vessel, so he too, could sire offspring?

"How are your husband and Jason connected?" Gail asked, deflecting the notion the *Orchid*'s captain might want some action with her.

"Good friends. My Louis and Jason go back many years—to their Peace Corps days."

Peace Corps—Jason! *It figures,* she thought, a curiosity stirring. A man she had difficulty with, offering to pay her way. To care for her financially! The only other man in her life who cared was her father. Why suddenly Jason? Though he initially refused to take her to the port when the state trooper asked, he still did. Maybe he didn't want her to witness what he was up to. Was he truly a nice guy, different from the horrible men in her life?

"I saw you both in the library and overheard you talking about the frogs," Gail said to Lou.

"Yes," Lou said. "Jason is a consultant for the cruise line."

"Consultant!"

"He's a marine biologist and quite an expert when it comes to sea life, such as the frogs that were sucked up inside a waterspout. He's spent much of his life on the ocean, much of it in the Pacific where we met."

"I'd certainly like to know how he'll explain a frog twister. It makes no sense," Gail said.

"You'll have to ask him when you see him," Lou said.

"What purpose as a consultant does he have on this ship?" Gail asked, using a rapid-fire sentence, hoping to trick him into an honest answer without thinking.

Lou didn't bite. He turned his attention to his wife, kissing her again, saying he had to go and prepare for tomorrow, then left. But not before saying it was a pleasure to meet Gail, offering she enjoy the rest of her itinerary.

"He didn't answer my question," Gail said.

"I know," Marie responded. "He doesn't know you that well, even though you apparently have something to do with Jason, his good friend."

"Jason and I didn't hit it off," Gail confessed. "We seem to be oil and water, unfortunately."

"It's not you," Marie said. "Jason is a rather intense and focused individual, and cares lots about different things. He's very bright, and will often challenge you in conversation. If you couldn't converse, it's not you. I assure you, his mind is always working on something related to his life mission. And sometimes it gets in the way of simple, casual conversation. That's why I think he's still alone. I wish he'd take someone into his life. It's time he has a family."

Marie glanced at a wall clock that hung over a laundry cart of pool towels. "Oh, I'd forgotten. I have a meeting with the ship's nurses."

"Nurses?"

"Yes!"

And as Marie stood, she looked down at Gail and contemplated for a few seconds. "Please join us tomorrow. Come to the fishing village on the far side of the Atabeira Lagoon, where the *Orchid* will anchor."

Gail thought for a moment. "Okay, I'll do that," she said, sensing an opportunity to delve deeper into the mystery of the *Sapphire Orchid*. The village might have a direct connection.

"When we arrive in the lagoon in the morning, instead of going to the private beach with all the couples, come with me and my husband to the Atabeira village. We deliver medical supplies and care for children. It's a charity effort on behalf of the cruise line. Besides, if you go to the beach everyone will stare at you, all alone with no mate. I'm sure it doesn't make you feel good about yourself."

"I won't feel comfortable walking the private beach alone. A part of me regrets coming on this trip," Gail confessed.

Marie smiled. "Few women desire a life alone."

A tear came to Gail's eye. She was relieved at having found a friend. A single female passenger onboard was more difficult than she'd imagined. It wasn't a vacation anymore. Also, getting off the ship and closer to the clues that might yield answers was what she needed to keep distracted, to occupy her mind for the next six days. With her bruised self-esteem, the investigative reporter lurked deep inside. It certainly stirred up an emotion.

"Wear something to cover your entire body. Bring a broad-brim hat," Marie said, as she departed, holding the door open to the buffet area. "Oh, I'm not sure if you are current on your reading about how the *Sapphire Orchid* will get to the lagoon tomorrow. I highly suggest you get up at dawn and watch as the ship navigates the Navidad Narrows. It's quite an experience, like when large ships traverse the locks of the Panama Canal with only inches to spare on each side."

"I'll be up," Gail answered as the door closed behind Marie.

Gail was excited. Would Marie reveal more information? What if Jason warned Marie not to disclose any of the ship's darkest secrets? Would Marie clam up? Not to publicly reveal a story was an ethical issue for Gail. The public had a right to know what was unique about this cruise ship as it headed south toward Haiti.

Chapter 6

Having finished breakfast, Gail returned to her cabin and put on the just bought swimsuit she loved. Strolling the *Orchid*'s starboard outer deck on her way toward the solarium, Gail felt compelled to pause. There was no land in sight. Thunderheads had formed across the vast expanse of the seascape and seemed to go nowhere as curtains of gray drained beneath the stationary clouds. The ocean chop was subtle. The big ship, with pectoral stabilizers spread like a soaring humpback whale, held the top-heavy deck stacks stable. Leaning over the rail, Gail could make out the *Orchid*'s underwater fins and wondered what would happen if they struck a reef or hidden outcrop. What if they broke off? Would the ship fill like the *Titanic* and slowly sink?

With the vastness, there seemed an eerie vulnerability. What if the Caribbean swallowed them whole—would anyone notice?

The solarium pool was the only peaceful place Gail could go to limit her exposure to the constant shipboard canoodling. The cruise ship director had scheduled activities that assumed every onboard passenger was a couple. The theater featured a comical version of the Newlywed Game. Always a good laugh at the expense of unwitting couples. The pool bar band played upbeat love songs, another reminder of the absence of true love in her life. To avoid it all, Gail tucked herself in a far corner on a rather substantial, soft, reclining solarium pool lounge. A few feet away was a bubbling hot tub. Soft jazz played. She closed her eyes and fell asleep.

It was the cold splash from the spray as someone dove into the pool that woke her so suddenly. Her mind danced in the sudden release from what must've been a rather deep sleep. So deep that she'd forgotten where she was. Swimming laps was a man moving at an incredible pace. With each flip and underwater turn, he jetted a distance beneath and resurfaced, charging for the next wall. Gail immediately knew from the thickness of his biceps and deep tropical tan and slender body that it was Jason. Who else could it be? she thought. Crew members were not allowed here; the wall plaque at the entry said so.

Gail buried herself beneath several towels, covering her head just in case Jason walked past.

Waiting for the moment he would stop swimming and perhaps stroll by, she contemplated if their conversation would be adversarial this time. What trick questions could she ask about the secrets of the *Orchid*? Why did he offer to pay for her passage?

Jason's swim continued for what seemed forever. Back and forth, hard charging breast strokes. It amazed her the degree of shape he was in. It explained, when she saw him shirtless on Alligator Alley for the first time, how he got like that. And she couldn't help to think that if by some dumb luck, it would be him she'd sleep with to conceive her children, if they'd get along forever.

Twenty minutes had lapsed when the splashing stopped.

"Where'd he go?" Gail asked, flipping up the edge of the towel that had concealed her face. From where she lay, Gail could not see into the pool, only the edge of the deck and the ripple of the surface. *Did he have a heart attack and drown? Should I go and save him?* Gail came from beneath the bundle of towels and stepped to the edge of the pool. There beneath the surface was Jason, gliding like a dolphin the entire length, flipping at the wall, not breaking the surface, swimming in the opposite direction. *How can he hold his breath so long without passing out?* And as Gail turned to hide once more, Jason lifted his head out of the water.

Gail struggled with her towels to hide, then gave up.

"We meet again." Jason called over to her.

No words came from her mouth as Jason swam to the edge and hung his elbows on the tile. "Did you learn anything about frogs and mambos?"

"Oh, uh . . ." Her mind raced. What to say?

"Yes, in fact I did," she said, standing and walking the short distance to where he hung on the tile.

Wearing a rather nice and comfortable swimsuit, Gail searched his eyes to see, as men would do, if he was measuring the desirability of her physical features. For men could never resist checking out a woman's physical qualities and Jason was no different.

Jason flipped back into the water, onto his back like an otter. She could see his eyes scan every inch, measuring her. He clamped his hands together as a child would do in the pool to playfully shoot a stream of water that jetted toward Gail, striking her in her midsection.

The water was colder than Gail imagined. It tingled.

"It's the Haitian frog of fertility," she said, pretending to ignore the childish behavior—or was it a flirtation?—and that her front was dripping wet. "The mambo is, for the lack of a better term, the keeper of the voodoo. One who summons the spirits."

"You've done your homework," Jason replied. He rolled to his stomach and swam half a pool length. Came to the edge, pressed his hands to the pool deck, and lifted his entire frame from the lap pool.

It was when he stood and reached for the towel to dry himself that Gail came undone. She fainted to the floor, and once again found herself suspended in his arms and carried to her recliner. Jason lowered her onto the soft cushion.

"Are you okay?" he asked. "Do you need a doctor?"

Lying there, with Jason leaning over to comfort her, Gail struggled to say the word, "No. I was a little light-headed when I stood." It was the only excuse as to why she fainted. It was Jason who made her faint, a burning desire that overcame her to want of him. He was in incredible shape, standing there in his tiny bathing suit and not another stitch of clothing. It was overwhelming to the point where she'd lost consciousness.

"You're likely dehydrated," Jason said. He went to where a waterfall trickled over a wall of hand-assembled river stone at the long end of the pool. On a low table to the right was an ice bucket filled with water bottles.

Jason returned with one, unscrewed the cap, and offered it to Gail.

Drinking the entire bottle in four chugs, Gail felt much better.

"Who are you?" she asked. "Why this ship? Why me? Why did you offer to pay my way?" she asked, subconsciously crunching the plastic bottle.

"I'm Jason Applegate. A marine biologist. And blame it on the spirits of the voodoo that we meet like this. I offered to pay your way because I felt sorry for you. I'm not the creep you think I am."

Gail smiled. It was the first time they'd conversed in a manner that wasn't antagonistic.

"Nice, clear, and concise answers," she said, wanting to push more. "Do you care to add to anything else?"

"Not really, but if you must know, I'm here to monitor the quality of the natural fringe reefs that support the village at the back of the lagoon near Emerald's private beach. And to report to the captain, the village elders, and the Haitian port authorities. There's been a considerable amount of destruction to the reef from the ship's turbidity."

"Is that what all the writing is about in the library?" Gail asked, repositioning, draping a towel across her exposed legs.

"Yes. My thoughts on the matter."

"Tell me what fertility frogs and summoning of the spirits have to do with why couples on this ship are likely to conceive."

"I won't tell you."

"Why not?"

"You seem like an educated person. Do I need to reason it out for you?"

Gail was taken aback just a bit. Much of her job required deductive reasoning and innate intuition.

"You've got me there, Mr. Applegate. But help me out anyway, to make sure I understand."

"There's only one captain in the world who can navigate a ship this large into the lagoon. And apparently, rumor has it that it's the visit to the lagoon that has something to do with the birth rate on this ship. I'm sure you've read the same stuff I have that convinces people there is something special going on in the lagoon. Now think about it, Mrs. . . . What is your last name?"

"Stroud, it's Gail Stroud."

"Gail. The reef is severely damaged, as is much of Haiti. You telling the world does no one any good. Whatever perspective you decide to convey will send people here in the tens of thousands and upset the delicate balance that is currently in serious jeopardy."

There was silence. Gail could tell the intensity of Jason, that if she said one more thing, the dialogue would break down and become adversarial. He'd given her plenty. She needed to end the encounter.

"Thank you, Mr. Applegate. Your point is well taken. I appreciate your candor." Gail stood from where she sat and went over to the hot tub, an indication that the conversation should end.

Jason, a bit more intense, dove back into the pool and swam several more laps.

Concerned as to why she may have fainted, Gail returned to her cabin and had lunch delivered. Maybe Jason was right, she was dehydrated. It may be stress related; she'd had lots on her plate for a considerable time.

Vera called her room. They talked a bit, Gail saying she wanted some me time. Vera, the true friend, allowed her the space. Gail mentioned Marie and the offer to tour the village, indicating it was better than hanging out on the private beach with her and Ian. Vera understood and agreed the change of pace might do some good.

When evening came, Gail spent the night alone, much of it on her cabin balcony, quietly contemplating, annoyed by the watchful look of the voodoo doll on her desk, not sure what to do with it. She considered tossing the creepy thing overboard, but feared the black magic. Though skeptic, and though Jason had something to do getting her onboard, there was just enough of a superstition. The sheer thought of falling overboard scared her—sliced in half by an underwater stabilizer, or perhaps chopped to bits by the propeller, or bobbing alone in shark-infested waters, bleeding, the floating voodoo doll tossed overboard, drifting alongside, reminding of her naivety.

The air fresh and relaxing, Gail fell asleep on the balcony, but somehow in the middle of the night made it to bed, leaving the glass door wide open.

Rising before daybreak and craving a shot of hot caffeine, Gail ordered room service. Showering, she wrapped herself in a thick bathrobe with its signature *Sapphire Orchid* logo, the embroidered hovering bee a metallic green. Coffee arrived with a knock of a dark-skinned steward. Gail thanked the sleepy woman and returned to her balcony recliner and waited for daybreak to arrive. If she were at the TV station right now, she'd likely be in front of the camera, reading the all-too-routine edited sequence of the morning newscast. Her two stylists pampering, applying makeup, fussing with her hair, pinning her dress in forbidden, non-camera body-shot locations, tightening her top, making sure her figure was clean, robust, and neat—lipstick, bold and glossed, long eyelashes, a thin line of mascara, and neat eyebrows. The right set of high heels to force her natural stance at a sexy separation, showing off the length of each leg should the camera lens drift in that direction. There was once a time when she didn't need to wear Spanx, but now it was a necessity. They all did it these days, no matter how Twiggy-thin the female reporter.

The mechanics of the morning broadcast was habit and too easy for Gail these days. Seamless, never nervous, yet she was unable to conceive. The red light on the camera would brighten and Gail would straighten in her stool, illuminate her bleached teeth, and say. "Good morning, this is Gail Stroud and . . . *blah, blah, blah, blah, blah.*" It all had become a blur.

The wind stirred with the arriving sun. The stacked decks of the *Sapphire Orchid* cast its morning shadow to the starboard side. On the western horizon, the island of Haiti had appeared, lifting from the Caribbean, its terrain mountainous.

An hour passed. The *Orchid* turned, its shortening shadow swallowed by the maneuver. In the months planning her trip, Gail had read about the narrow passageway leading to their first port of call, the Atabeira Lagoon. The nautical charts called the deep water route a nearly impossible channel to navigate, the Navidad Narrows, famous because Columbus's *Santa Maria* ran aground in the shoals after spending Christmas Eve in Atabeira. It was a tight passageway, but well worth the result. The lagoon was one of the most beautiful enclaves in the entire Caribbean.

Mario Iezzoni

The water had changed to a super-blue clearness. Where the morning sun penetrated enough to reflect off the ocean floor, patches of light blue appeared. Gail thought how she'd describe the underwater seascape in as few words as possible, as a TV anchor would do. Was the seafloor jagged? How close to the ship's hull? How many galleons of early explorers sank to the bottom? What would happen if a ship the size of the *Sapphire Orchid* sliced open like the *Costa Concordia*? How much bedlam? Would she survive?

The small, random islands surrounding Haiti grew larger and more numerous. The big ship slowed as it seemed to track along an invisible guide wire—the starboard side shallowing, volcanic outcrops breaking the surface, a darkness in the channel, where the below, the abyss, the basalt bottom passed far beneath. A wake had formed near the bow, a sign they'd entered the Narrows. The wake pushed out to each side like a pair of open scissors. At each edge of the channel, the energy collided, crested, washed over, and briefly exposed the jagged black stone and attached coral. Fish flipped and flopped, the delicate ecosystem in brief chaos, a backfill flush; then again, a series of lessening crests until the reef that contained the passageway was back in recovery mode.

At two miles from the mouth of the Atabeira Lagoon, two jagged volcanic spires rose from the deep blue glare. The twin structures were nearly as tall as the ship. *How will we fit?* Gail wondered, as the vessel neared. She'd read the *Sapphire Orchid*'s captain, Nickoli Lavaki, came from generations of famous captains with impeccable seafaring records, never a mishap in a century and a quarter.

Scooting to the edge of her lounge chair, Gail pulled close to the railing. She stood and leaned over. Up and down the stacking of decks, early-rising passengers watched in awe as the bow centered the spires and gracefully threaded the unique formation. She felt she could reach and touch the black rock where cormorants dried their feathers on its jagged ledges. Then her memory of 9/11 came and the roar of the each of the twin towers, collapsing. Quickly, she dropped back onto the edge of her seat. Her heart raced. A panic attack came. *What would happen if the spires collapsed?* She recalled years back, when she had the chance to anchor the weekend news in Philadelphia. An earthquake struck Haiti. She had to quickly bone up on her geology, learning two tectonic plates slid past each other at this exact spot. A reverse fault, it's what created the narrow pathway to the lagoon.

A pod of dolphins arrived and raced alongside, as if to celebrate the *Orchid*'s successful navigation of the Narrows once again. The mouth of the lagoon was in clear view. Just inside the south side, a lengthy pier jutted out, partially blocking a quarter of the lagoon entry. A coral reef that attached to the shoreline ran the entire concave section of the miniature bay, across the back where the village of Atabeira was tucked away. The reef ended at the base of steep ridge that formed the north side of the lagoon.

The ship's handbook described the shelf-like reef as a fringe reef, because it grew attached to the volcanic base rock of the mainland. Rich in sea life, the reef supported the economy of coastal villages for centuries. And without the life-sustaining reef, Atabeira would not exist. The handbook added that when Christopher Columbus's *Santa Maria* ran aground, he ordered his beloved Spanish galleon dismantled, leaving the crew behind, Columbus promising to return. And when he did, Columbus found his crew killed by the Taino Indians—the village nearly wiped out by smallpox. The village had another major setback a century ago, when a massive mudslide came through the center, wiping out its schoolhouse, killing nearly every school-age child. The handbook added that Emerald Cruise Line was sensitive to the peacefulness of the Atabeira inhabitants and that passengers were forbidden to visit the tiny fishing village.

"I feel sorry for the village," Gail said to herself. "How was it able to rebuild its population?"

And in that fleeting thought, the answer arrived. *They conceived!*

"But how?" she asked herself as the mountainous terrain that trapped the cove gathered in the *Sapphire Orchid*, the entire lagoon surrounding the oversized ship, the ever-present hum of the *Orchid*'s power plant suddenly absent. The vessel drifted toward the pier that attached to a stretch of elevated land that formed the south-side arm, a peninsula of sorts—Emerald Cruise Line's private beach. There was a shudder, the balcony floor vibrating as a rush of milky seawater shot from the bow thrusters. The big ship rotated to align with the concrete pier. The sunlight shifted. The shoreline adjusted. The *Orchid*'s eerie shadow resized as the towering vessel drew parallel to the concrete pilings. Another flush of chalk and another shudder as the giant cruise ship delicately kissed the massive, black rubber buttons that cushioned the glossy white hull. The *Sapphire Orchid*'s thousand-mile journey had concluded.

With the *Orchid*'s bow pointing toward Emerald's private beach, Gail watched the big ship's preparations from high above. Far below, uniformed deckhands appeared and secured thick mooring ropes with large plastic cones to block waiting rats, likely hiding on a crossbeam beneath the concrete deck somewhere. A hundred yards up the shoreline, inflatable floating play structures wobbled in the disturbed waters, their carnival colors clearly out of place. Tour guides and concession operators prepared jet skis, parasails, and party catamarans.

Near where the ocean waves broke on the opposite side of the private beach, cabanas laced in white curtains offered ample shade. And at the farthest reach into the Caribbean, a concrete bunker anchored eight zipline cables, hung like a clothesline above the entire expanse of the peninsula, the coiled steel rope running uphill and disappearing into the deep green leafy jungle. Beneath, waves broke on an actual beach, formed from the crushing tracks of bulldozers and not the decade-long wash of the Caribbean.

Finishing the last of her coffee, Gail set the empty cup on the small table just behind her and returned to the balcony railing to take in the beauty of the seascape. The broad starboard side faced the Atabeira village, three quarters of a mile away. But her eyes quickly diverted. Directly below, at the watermark, a murk erupted, the bow thrusters once again shoving water. The lashed tethers grew taut as another flush shot beneath the pier, this time forming a wave on the other side, as if an underwater jet engine went to full throttle. The disturbance lasted for nearly a full minute.

What's that all about? Gail wondered, the reasoning for the sudden disturbance not making sense. Was this standard operating procedure?

Gail watched as a giant waterborne cloud formed and surrounded the pier, as if a colony of albino octopi had released lime-colored ink. *Extreme turbidity,* she thought, the balcony railing pressing into her stomach. *Is this intentional? My gosh, what a mess!*

The crystal clear lagoon became gray as the massive cloud rose from the seafloor and spread like a creeping fog. Beneath the barnacle-encrusted pillars, the ink invaded like a rolling storm cloud, growing, fanning out, spreading toward the village, filling in the openness. Gail watched in amazement as rolling milk-filled waves crested and washed onto the distant fringe reef—sediment from the seafloor, rinsing, suffocating the coral, one wave after another.

In the village, tiny boats tossed and tugged at their leashes, dirty hulls whitening with each toss. A tether lashed to a water taxi snapped, and villagers ran the length of the undulating dock, complaining in an unfamiliar language, panic in their voices, pointing at the ship as the small, colorful watercraft headed for the shallow coral.

Gail imagined how she'd describe it in a newscast, how the villagers felt about this intrusion into their way of life. The obnoxious arrival of aliens, just like Columbus. The bulldozing and westernizing of its southern peninsula. The construction of modern structures on a sand spit, making way for noisy and unwelcome explorers. The death of their fishery, invaded by Caucasians once again, this time a different pox, a doom soon to come no doubt.

There was a knock on her cabin door.

"Oh, I forgot. It's Marie!" Gail said, snapping from her thought and the plight of the village.

"Give me a minute while I toss on something," she called out.

Moments later Gail opened the cabin door and greeted Marie.

"Thought you changed your mind," Marie said, entering with a pleasant smile, wearing a skirt that touched her sandals. "It's time to head for dry land."

Halfway down the tight corridor, they entered a doorway labeled Crew Only.

"Follow me," Marie said, holding one of the inward swinging doors open.

This is the area passengers never see, Gail thought. The walls were glossy white and damaged on the lower half from service carts. There was a sparseness, not the rich and impressive design on the passenger side of the double doors. Gail followed Marie down endless flights of steel stairs that were steeper than passenger stairwells. Minutes later and a bit winded, Gail arrived in the cavernous cargo area, three decks in height. Much of the ship's supplies sat on shrink-wrapped pallets. The place she'd seen Jason enter when in Port Everglades.

As they walked mid-ship amongst the stacked rows of labeled supplies toward the stern, a warm breeze mixed with the dry coolness came. The dim light grew brighter until it became day-bright as they exited an aisle. A giant loading door the size of the back of a tractor trailer had lowered.

"This is our staging area," Marie said.

Voodoo Cruise

Still catching her breath from the trek through the hollow framework of the ship, and the arrival of the thickening humidity, Gail asked, "Marie, can we take a break for just a minute?"

"Sure, we must wait for the rest of our boarding party anyway."

Squinting, adjusting to the sudden brightness, Gail heard the chatter of women's voices. From amidst the alley of pallets, seven women she'd never seen arrived. She turned to Marie, the expression in her eyes asking, "What's up?"

"Volunteer nurses," Marie explained. "They are here to examine and care for the Atabeira children. Consider it our payment for use of this beautiful and peaceful place for such a short period of time."

"How come I didn't see any onboard?" Gail asked.

"You're a Floridian, have you ever been underground at Disney's Magic Kingdom?" Marie replied.

"No, but I understand it's built on a giant stage."

"Exactly, you are now beneath the stage; no longer part of the show. So are these nurses. Though guests, we treat them as staff."

"Guests?" Gail sensed something was not quite right.

The thick door with rounded corners had fully retracted and stretched out over the water. From what Gail gathered, they were on the opposite side of the pier, facing the open Caribbean and the maze of tiny islands that hid the narrow passage that led to the lagoon. And as the temporary dock prepared, a water taxi from the village rounded the stern and headed their way.

Gail heard a familiar voice call Marie's name. It was her husband. "Hello, my love, I see you have brought a guest this time. This is a first."

"Yes, my love," she answered. "She's a friend and deserves special treatment."

Gail noted that although Marie and Lou communicated orally, there was a second language spoken as they stared into each other's eyes. A close couple, much more said—a collusion of thoughts.

A Zodiac attached to a lift rolled to the doorway and lowered to the water using a portable crane.

"What's she doing here?" a firm voice called from where the Zodiac came. It was Jason.

Marie stepped forward as Jason appeared from the dimness into the daylight. He was with sailors who pushed a pallet forward—the pallet she'd seen Jason inspecting in Port Everglades.

Jason pushed a cart loaded with scuba gear and several silver waterproof cases toward them.

Marie touched Jason's shoulder warmly, like a mother, smiling, charming him, stopping him. "Jason, she is a friend of mine. I've invited her to see all the good we do for the village."

"You do know she's a television reporter?"

"Yes, but I don't care how she makes a living. Besides, isn't that what we want, someone to tell the world what good we do?"

"You know how I feel about humanitarian efforts. The only importance is the people we care for. Are you taking her to the temple?"

"Yes!"

Gail thought to herself, *Temple!*

Jason approached, stopping a few feet away. He smiled. "Due to the kindness of Marie, your life is about to change."

He then pushed his loaded cart to the large doorway.

Once again, Gail found herself without words. Why the white-toothed smile and the intense look?

My life is about to change? What does he mean? Gail was becoming undone, as was always the case when Jason was around—a flashback, suspended in his arms, setting her down in the seat of his Jeep. In the solarium, emerging from the water, lean, muscular, an athlete. Her mind spinning, fainting, Jason catching her.

Voodoo Cruise

She watched him load his gear into the waiting Zodiac. With a yank of the cord on the outboard, it started. Jason revved the engine and sped away, alone.

"Is Lou coming with us?" Gail asked, turning her attention to their own preparations to depart.

"Yes, but he will be heading over with the supplies. I'll meet him at the schoolhouse where we'll care for the children," Marie said as it became their turn to depart.

"Temple? What did Jason mean?" Gail asked.

"There's a Haitian ceremony we take part in once the children are cared for and the supplies distributed. It's a form of thank you from the villagers. It's quite an experience if you've never seen such a ritual, better than the entertainment you'll experience if you went ashore to the private beach. Besides, it might bring good fortune, perhaps even tonight at the roulette table, his name is Fabrizio. If you approve, I will arrange a way you can invite him to your cabin."

Marie's last sentence was unexpected. Should she say anything like, "I'm afraid to have sex with a man I don't even know"? The consideration made her incredibly uncomfortable, even though she'd worked it out in her mind that she could get through it if she drank enough wine. Maybe she'd be more comfortable if she solicited the sperm donor by picking someone up on her own.

"Trust me," Marie said. "Take a chance. Keep an open mind. Fabrizio is a handsome man, the best-looking man you've ever made love to."

It suddenly dawned on Gail she was now part of her own story. Her college journalism professor had warned not to become emotionally involved with your subject matter—the individuals you need to draw information from—it's easy to fall into that trap, he warned the class.

Marie came across as a rather forceful person. She was hard to say no to.

But having sex tonight . . . Was Marie pimping her out?

"What's with the scuba tanks?" Gail asked, deciding not to dig deeper about the temple event; she'd learn soon enough.

"Jason monitors the condition of the fringe reef. Whatever damage occurs, the cruise line must make up for it somehow. That pallet of relief supplies is part of the payment for the damage to the reef."

"So that explains why he's here."

Marie smiled. "Price of doing business in paradise."

"So, Jason is a contractor of some sort for the cruise line?" Gail knew the answer, but she wanted to see if Marie would offer more information.

"Don't you know anything about him?" Marie said.

"No, like I said, our conversation is vinegar, as you can see when we just talked."

"He's actually a mediator between the Haitian government, Emerald Cruise Line, and the village."

"How did he land that job?"

"His adoptive mother. She lives in Atabeira."

"Huh? I'm even more confused," Gail said.

"Tell you what," Marie said, wanting to hurry the nurses aboard the arriving water taxi. "Why don't you join Lou, Jason, and I for dinner tonight. I will have Lou and Jason share with you how they ended up here on the *Sapphire Orchid*. Also, I think it would be good for Jason to have a beautiful woman at the table and you not alone. He's not the rough guy you think he is."

"Wait a minute. I thought you were setting me up with Fabrizio from the casino to come to my cabin tonight."

"I am, but after dinner we go to the casino to check Fabrizio out," Marie said. "It's unlikely Jason would accommodate me, he's not the type. But he certainly is good-looking and would bring you some beautiful children.

"Besides," Marie continued, "Jason meets with the captain after our meal. No telling how long that will last, or what mood Jason will be in after he meets with Captain Lavaki. Jason can be a bit of a workaholic and will likely retire to his suite."

"Suite?" Gail noted.

"Yes, Gail, Jason's given nicer quarters than ours."

"Meet with the captain for what?" Gail hoped Marie wouldn't think about the question too long.

"Like, ah . . ." Marie paused, thinking about the question. "Like the frogs," Marie continued. "Do you honestly feel that some sort of natural phenomenon like that can actually occur?"

"No, I've never heard of such an unusual event in all my days of reporting the news." Gail could see Marie was stalling, contemplating her response, as when someone is dealing with a reporter and not wanting to be forthcoming. Gail believed Marie had a different perspective than Jason, one that was more forthright. In her effort to speak honestly, Gail believed Marie found herself in a difficult position.

"As you can see, the Atabeirans aren't fond of what we've done to their beautiful and self-sustaining place on this great earth. Jason's role is to work out an arrangement—keep peace."

"Why is that his problem to solve?"

"I'm having a difficult time finding a way of explaining in a way that would make sense to you, Gail, without ruining my friendship with Jason."

"That's honest and refreshing," Gail said.

"I think what you are alluding to, Gail, there's a link to this village and the frog twister?"

"Obviously," Gail replied. "What I know is such frogs as found in the twister are in Haitian culture a form of spiritual fertility. And now you are telling me about a ceremony that will take place in the village later."

"True," Marie said. "And if the people of this little village have such powers to send a message like that, it doesn't hurt Emerald Cruise Line to employ someone like Jason to keep the peace, to protect the cruise line's investment on the peninsula and possibly their billion-dollar ship."

"Billion-dollar ship! Is it in danger?" Gail asked, shocked, a lead to a much bigger story.

Marie deliberately walked away, toward the waiting nurses. She instructed them to fill each of their packs with medical supplies, including a healthy portion of candy for the village children.

Gail's mind whirled. There was much to think about. Did this little fishing village have the capacity to compromise the safety of the *Orchid*'s passengers? Hard to believe, but Emerald certainly was not taking any chances. It also explained why Jason had a suite and not a tiny cabin.

Lou came over and kissed Marie goodbye. "See you ashore, my love." He left in the tender loaded with supplies.

"We're next, Gail," Marie said, inviting her to move through the large cargo opening and down the ramp onto the floating dock. A colorfully decorated water taxi eased up to the ship.

"You first, step in," Marie said.

A dark-skinned, shirtless Atabeiran captain with missing teeth stood at the steering wheel. His rump leaned on a narrow 2x4. There was no seat for him. A young boy was there to help everyone board. The floor wasn't flat, just wooden ribs and a narrow board that crossed to keep feet dry. A six-inch plank ran the curvature of the inside gunwale and served as perimeter seating. Like the captain, passengers mostly stood with their sandals on the board that spanned the ribs, and leaned against the hip-high gunwale seating. The water taxi, with its bright-blue hull and sharp canary-yellow posts to support a flat corrugated metal roof, rocked. An undersized, fifty-horsepower outboard with a hose hooked to a grease-covered gas tank sputtered.

The vessel listed heavily as Gail reached for the young boy's hand. His legs split wide as he straddled the gap between gunwale and the dock. She braced her other hand against a yellow post to make her way onboard. "Thank you," Gail said to the young deckhand as she stepped onto a board, water sloshing beneath. She leaned against the angled plank that served as a seat and sat somewhat sidesaddle. The taxi continued to rock as the nurses boarded, backpacks slung from their shoulders, each finding an uncomfortable spot to position for the short trip ashore.

The sun was high and in the east, the murk of the lagoon had settled. But the clearing seawater still held a bit of a lasting haze. There was a puff of exhaust and a whirl of the outboard as the captain shoved the throttle forward. The young Haitian boy leapt aboard. The tiny, top-heavy craft went into a healthy lean. It looped around the *Orchid*'s giant stern and headed toward the village of Atabeira.

Chapter 7

Fishing Village of Atabeira, Haiti

There was no sea breeze. A rolling, glass-like wake followed the loaded water taxi. "I appreciate your advice on what to wear, Marie," Gail said, leaning in a quasi-sitting position, speaking louder to compensate for the sound of the straining outboard.

"There is a practicality to Caribbean garb, much of it cotton to keep cool. And bright colors to celebrate life." Marie smiled, her face in the shadow of the flat canopy that shaded the tiny watercraft.

"This visit will be something special for you," Marie added, also speaking louder.

"I get that," Gail said. Her mind was on the collective of nurses. Why didn't she see them aboard? Why the secrecy with the humanitarian mission?

As the shoreline drew close, Gail noticed a rather nice, single-story home with a substantial porch several hundred feet up on a ridgeline. The ridge ran down from the highest peak behind the village and disappeared into the sea at a step angle. Jason's Zodiac headed past the house on the hillside. The Zodiac slowed. Jason waved to a woman on the porch overhang.

Voodoo Cruise

What a beautiful view from there. But the structure seems out of place, though, with the third-world shacks scattered about the village. And what's with Jason waving to the woman on the porch?

"That's Ruth, Jason's mother," Marie said, guessing Gail's thoughts. "You should go and meet her."

"Where's she from?" Gail inquired.

"The States, just like you," Marie answered. "Go, talk to her while we attend to the children. She'll be good company and is a fascinating lady. You may learn a bit more about Jason, given you ask so many questions. But when you hear a bell, followed with drumbeats, come to the temple. You'll find it near the central square. I want you to be a part of the ceremony."

"Part of the ceremony. . . I thought I'd only observe?"

"Not if you want to be a mother."

"Mother—how are you going to manage that . . . with magic?"

"But of course," Marie said, laughing. "Aren't you religious?"

"Uh . . . to a degree. When I have children, I guess I'll attend a church." Gail's parents were devout Catholics. Anytime she went back to Pennsylvania, her parents expected her and Richard to attend Sunday Mass with them.

"You do know voodoo is as much a religion. In fact, to Haitians, it's engrained in their Catholicism."

"How's that?" Gail asked, the water taxi cutting across the lagoon, halfway there.

"You have saints you pray to all the time."

"Yes, Catholics do!"

"Voodoo is the same. Certain spirits have special powers."

"For example?" Gail led her along.

"Erzulie Fréda is the Haitian spirit of love."

"Er . . . zullu who?" Gail stumbled with the pronunciation.

"Fréda," Marie said. "Call her by her last name. It's easier. Aren't spirits essentially the same as your Catholic angels and the unique powers they have as Catholics often pray to?" Marie observed.

"Yes, true," Gail answered. "I pray to Saint Anthony any time I lose my car keys."

"Voodoo, though the name sounds odd, is tied to a similar form of religious belief. The temple is a church. So, when you hear the pounding of drums, head to the chapel, it's time for Mass, or in our case, a ceremony."

A hundred yards out, the tiny watercraft slowed. A narrow, floating walkway running approximately forty feet crossed the sharp coral and connected to a poorly maintained seawall. Villagers gathered.

"Where did Jason go?" Gail asked.

"On the other side of that ridge. There's another, smaller lagoon, an inlet of sorts." Marie pointed to where Ruth's home perched. "He's counting fish, taking samples, and monitoring the health of the coral. Because of the presence of the cruise ship and the turbidity, this lagoon is fished out. The reef on the other side is relatively healthy but is showing signs of stress."

"I can see why," Gail said. "Did you notice what happened after the ship was tethered? A blast came from the cruise ship and stirred up the water something awful. Why did that happen?"

"I don't know," Marie said, "I'm not the captain. Perhaps you can ask him when we return.

"You don't know much about who Jason is, do you?" Marie asked, changing the topic, the taxi altering its course, listing.

"No, he's not forthcoming."

"He's spent much of his life on the ocean. His expertise is with the ecology of volcanic islands. His work has been mainly in the Pacific, mostly Micronesia."

"But why here, with the cruise line?"

Voodoo Cruise

"Jason has a special relationship with this village. You'll find out when you meet Ruth." Marie pointed to the house again.

"Huh! I'm confused," Gail said, focusing on the onshore activity, the villagers gathering.

"Not for long," Marie answered. "I'm sure by the time we depart Atabeira you'll have a greater understanding and appreciation for the humanitarian mission of the *Sapphire Orchid*."

The tiny craft cut its engine. The taxi drifted over a section of jagged coral and smacked the aged dock, absent any cushioning.

"Oooh!" Gail caught herself from slipping off her seat.

Turning and looking back at the giant cruise ship, Marie pointed at the *Orchid*. "See the villagers' perspective. For centuries Atabeira was a peaceful place. Now look, with that obnoxious steel vessel and hordes of foreign invaders polluting their waters, killing their fish. There's nothing to gain. We are poison."

"So why doesn't the village evict them from the cove?"

"Complicated," Marie said. "Look up. The government turned the rainforest surrounding the village, including the fringe reef, into a national park to protect it. The government then leased Emerald Cruise Line the south-side peninsula for forty years. Atabeira has no say in the matter."

Gail could see how out of place the massive vessel was, with its ornate painted *Sapphire Orchid* emblem across the bow.

"I get it," she said. "They're pissed and don't want this ship here."

"At eighty dollars a head to Port-au-Prince, it's unlikely that will happen. Jason's job is one of mediator, keeping the peace."

"Isn't eighty a bit steep?"

"Haiti is a poor country. The mountain that surrounds the Atabeira inlet has one of the few untouched tropical rainforests in the entire country. Emerald Cruise Line pays for the protection and exclusivity."

"When I was in the library, I saw Lou race to Jason to identify the type of frog that came out of the twister. Another word was mentioned. Jason said it was a message. My interpretation was it was some sort of warning," Gail said, wanting to know more than what'd she learned on the Internet.

"What word?" Marie asked.

"Mambo?"

"The mambo is the village high priestess. Think of it as the female version of one of your Catholic priests, or a bishop. From her all voodoo originates. You'll see when we get to the temple."

Gail shrugged her shoulders. She wasn't superstitious, more of a realist, but wanted to get down to the issue of a warning.

Marie shrugged her shoulders. To Gail, it seemed Marie didn't care to elaborate.

"Look how many children there are waiting for us," Gail said, moving on. "What's the demographic of the village?"

Marie paused, then answered.

"It's why the nurses are here; to care for the too-many children. The average family has seven children. Atabeiran women are an exceptionally fertile group."

Lots of children, something extraordinary, Gail thought. *What a story this will make if I discover the reason.*

Two young Haitian lads, with more watching, snatched hemp ropes tossed by the captain's deckhand. The boys skillfully secured the taxi to wooden poles hollowed into a section of coral.

Across the lagoon, the *Sapphire Orchid*'s passengers disembarked. Reggae music played, the pleasant rhythm carrying across the water. The first of the disembarking passengers had already reached the private beach.

"What an incredible contrast," Gail said, waiting her turn to climb from the water taxi. She stood silent, the towering cruise ship clearly a disturbing presence. The ant trail of couples disembarking, then marching along the pier.

Gail was last to step off the tiny watercraft. Careful, looking down at the plank decking, she walked the wobbling wooded dock, avoiding the missing boards. She stepped onto the seawall. Children had emerged from shanty homes and headed their way. The small contingent of nurses greeted the arriving children, handed out candy. Forming a small parade, the children took the nurses' hands and escorted them to a thatched roof structure located in the central park.

"Marie, if you don't mind, I'm going to explore on my own," Gail said, wanting to separate from the group, to investigate without interference, discover what the warning may be about.

"It's a tiny place," Marie remarked, as Gail walked away, returning to the waterfront. "There aren't any roads out of here. It won't be hard to locate us you if you get lost."

"See you in a bit," Gail said. "When I hear drums, right?"

Marie gave her the thumbs-up. Each departed in a different direction.

Gail guessed Atabeira was about four blocks deep, its ability to get any larger severely limited by the mountainous terrain that encapsulated the village. Above the rooftops and Brazilian palms, starting at about two hundred feet, a series of terraces were cut into the hillside and lined with hedges at the lip. The ledges appeared to serve the purpose of preventing the mountainside from washing into the village during periods of heavy tropical rains.

Returning to the waterfront, Gail made her way along the water's edge. Jason had waved to the house on the ridge from his Zodiac. His mother might be a good place to start.

The dirt street, topped with crushed shells, paralleled the seawall. It quickly narrowed and became a walking path. Like she often did on the dark streets of South Philly, Gail looked for clues, often along a back alley and the people that lived there. However, there was no one around and likely would not speak English. She continued and came to a wooden bridge and a stream nourished by the rainforest high up the mountainside—its source from a perpetual cloud that formed on the windward side of the ridge—the rapidly rising, ocean-borne, moisture-laden air colliding with the abruptly rising landmass, condensing as it cooled, drizzling for an eternity at the peak.

Downstream of the bridge, the creek had cut a channel into the fringe reef. A school of pan-size fish jetted within the swirl of freshwater mixing with the salty sea. Two unattended fishing poles leaned against a nearby palm. Several mango trees stood on the upstream side of the bridge. Beneath the tree closest to the bridge was a bench cut from a stump. A spot that offered good shade.

It seemed the village adults were elsewhere, selling handcrafted items in an open-air market regulated by the government to ship passengers, Gail guessed, as a compromise perhaps, the western dollars corrupting the corruptible, to serve the same purpose as Jason, to keep the peace while the obnoxious ship invades for a few hours each week, polluting their homeland.

Besides greeting the woman on the hillside, she wanted to see what Jason was up to on the other side of this ridge. She walked along the waterside path, but a short distance away, the trail ended on a spit of sand that separated the thick jungle from the shoreline. "I guess this is the end," Gail said, returning to the bridge. She paused in the shade of the mangos, taking a seat on the homemade bench.

Where next? she thought, looking around. Her only choice was to climb the hillside somehow, along a trampled path that followed the stream. It appeared the trail skirted the outer the edge of many shacks on what appeared to be the poorer section of Atabeira. "Let's see where this takes me," Gail said, refreshed.

Voodoo Cruise

At about fifty feet into the thicket of brush, the trail turned muddy and rose steeply. With each step, she lifted above the palms and village rooftops. The expanse and beauty of the Atabeira Lagoon came into view. The view of the *Sapphire Orchid* was ominous. The path crossed the creek. On the other side, several well-worn trails from below converged. Gail crossed and continued uphill, switchbacking twice, the final turn ending at a set of steps and a nearly vertical rise.

"The first terrace and steps." she said to herself. "Quite a bit of work has been put into the stonework." Gail admired the mildewed stones wedged into the hillside dirt. And as she made her way, rising higher, a breeze arrived, bringing with it a sudden sweet smell. "Honeysuckle?"

She waved her arms as several bees arrived and circled. "Shoo, shoo . . . is there a beehive somewhere? What's that sweet smell?"

Reaching the top step, still waving her arms to redirect the bees, she came to a plateau big enough to build a small house. There was a shed set back near the hillside and another set of stone steps that led to the next terrace. Gentle wisps of gray smoke drifted from a crooked pipe poking through the rippled tin roof. The shed, made entirely of the same corrugated sheets as the village roofs, had seen better days. On the narrow side of the rectangular structure, where it faced the tumbling creek, was an opening. A loose stack of firewood sat at the entry.

"I wonder what's cooking. That's where the sweet smell is coming from."

Gail approached. "Hello . . . Hello, is anyone around?"

Must be a hive nearby, she thought, the sound of buzzing bees growing louder.

"Beehives!" Gail said, looking through the shed out the other side.

Set behind the hedges planted at the lip of the terrace were wooden beehives set at precise intervals, each perched on stone blocks. A cloud swarmed above each.

"Looks like some sort of honey farm."

Gail stepped back from the doorway and looked uphill. There were many more terraces. "This is no small-scale operation. None of it can be seen from the ship."

She was slightly higher than the smokestack on the *Sapphire Orchid*. Passengers on the private beach looked like rabbits. Jet skis left traces of white as they raced in the dull blueness of the lagoon, not venturing toward the village, restricted by marker buoys.

"There's certainly a connection." Gail looked at the smokestack on *Sapphire Orchid*; its radiant blue flower and hovering honeybee logo. But suddenly, her jaw dropped. "It's the same green bee as the ones buzzing around me!" The hives had a purpose that clearly led to the ship.

"What's cooking in the building?" Gail entered the shed. In the far corner, where the flue poked through the slant of the roof, sat a blackened kettle, charred from the red-hot embers beneath. Suspended over the top of the kettle about eighteen inches was a cylindrical hood that gathered and channeled the rising steam. The edge of the cylindrical hood rolled inward to form a trough that gathered the resin that formed as the steam condensed inside the pyramid-shaped hood. The trough tilted in a way to direct the resin into a flue that dripped into an open barrel.

The aroma coming from the kettle was sweet.

Gail ventured further inside the shed, inspecting the kettle, its unusual design, the gathering of residue. She stuck her finger into the gutter and tasted the sappy substance, licking her finger clean. It was exceptionally sweet. She did it a second time. "Mmmmm . . . Shit, I shouldn't have done that," she cursed, realizing she may have made a mistake.

Immediately, she became flushed. Her heart rate increased. A tingling sensation came. "Why did I do that? I thought it was honey."

Voodoo Cruise

The sweet taste lingered on her tongue. It felt like she was having a rather intense sugar rush. "My gosh! This stuff is potent! What do they do with it? Whatever the secret is of the *Sapphire Orchid*, it has to do with this kettle and those terraces."

As Gail moved within the flat light, she bumped into a shelf on the long wall. There was a clank and a rattle as several bottles toppled over each other like bowling pins, rolling off the shelf, dropping to the dirt floor. Each bottle had a different design, one decorated with sequins, another strung with tiny beads, a jug with a cork plug and decorated in tiny seashells, bits of crab claw and red and white sequins to form three hearts around the body of the jug.

Bending over, she lifted and shook the jug. It was empty.

She'd broken out into a sweat. "What's happening to me! I'm having an allergic reaction. I must get out of here."

Stepping outside, Gail took several deep breaths. More bees raced past as a good feeling overcame her. She felt rejuvenated, like she'd snorted chocolate and cocaine at the same time. Whatever was in the shed made her feel great. "Am I high? How can that be? Then she recognized the terrace hedges—again, from working the beat and the research she'd done as a reporter on the drug trade. The hedges were coca bushes.

She went back inside. Below the large window was a pile of coca leaves. "They are mixing this with the bee honey. The villagers are in the drug trade and slipping it to the ship, mixing it with the food so customers can feel good, frisky, enlightened. But there's got to be more to this . . . coca and honey? If it was that easy, someone would have made a fertility pill and passed the FDA already, or distributed it through the black market."

The sweetness that lingered seemed to drip down the back of her throat. Her craving continued to build. She wanted more honey, but had enough self-control not to. She could feel her body changing, a tenderness coming, and an urge to make love.

"Oh my! . . . My hormones! I've got to get control."

She shook her head, trying to clear her mind as a desire to have sex overwhelmed her. She took several deep breaths. "Get control of yourself, Gail. Get control," she said as her heart raced, her body craving a need to mate.

"Maybe if I jog in place, I'll burn off this high." Gail started to do jumping jacks.

But as soon as she began, she heard voices. "Someone is coming up the steps!"

Where to hide? She looked for a safe place. Her only option was to dart off across the tumbling creek, toward a thicket of trees hung with vines.

Running, worried, trying to clear her head from the effects of the sweet resin, Gail covered the short distance quickly, stumbling as she crossed. *Splash!* She tucked in behind a giant breadfruit tree just as a head lifted from the staircase to the terrace. A round-headed Haitian lady with a stout older white-haired woman emerged. Gail's heart throbbed. She heard bottles rattling in a sack they carried as the two topped the last rise and went into the shed. No doubt tending to the simmering kettle, gathering the honey for distribution to the ship, she thought, hidden in the shadow of the suspended vines.

But before she could turn and dart further into the rainforest, the stout white-haired woman emerged, looking in Gail's direction.

Gail froze in her tracks. The lady spotted her.

Gail's eyes grew big and round. What next? What to say as she came in her direction and spoke?

"You are the curious type, aren't you?" she said.

Gail stepped into the sunlight. She had no choice but to engage.

"Uh, uh, I guess you could say that. I came from the ship."

"But of course," the woman said. "I can see you've discovered our little honey farm."

"Yes, stumbled across it by accident," Gail responded.

"I'm Marion," she said. "You may want to leave before the mambo discovers you've knocked over her bottles. She's not too fond of foreign visitors to her farm. And would likely put a curse on you."

Gail wanted to ask questions. For one, she spoke English, and must know what this was all about. But caught snooping, it was best if she headed off in another direction.

"I was trying to locate the house I saw on the hillside, that's how I stumbled across all this."

Like Marie, Marion's demeanor was such that she was not at all concerned that Gail stumbled across what was obviously a concealed operation. "If you continue in the direction you were heading, down the windward side of the ridge, you'll come across a path that will take you to Ruth's home."

"Ruth? You know Ruth?"

"Of course, this is a small place. But shhhh." Marion put her fingers to her lips. "You best get going, before the mambo sees you."

Gail heeded Marion's advice and left, fearful the so-called mambo priestess might not be as accommodating. She passed beneath the breadfruit tree and disappeared over a ridge that dropped steeply into the Atabeira rainforest. All around was a gathering rising mist, condensing where the warm breeze pushed up the mountainside and quickly cooled. The windward hillside was a thick jungle, a canopy of immense greenery and penetrating thick fog. Broadleaves dripped onto others as the dew teared its way to the soggy ground. Ancient vines with thick stems spiraled moss-covered tree trunks. Standing on softened earth, the sunlight completely blocked, Gail tried to gauge where she was and how to get to the trail without getting lost. The *Sapphire Orchid* was no longer in view.

This was much steeper than where she came from. Squatting, sitting on her butt, she slid downhill, feet out front, controlling her steep descent. Her dress quickly became caked with mud and decaying leaves. "Ouch!" Her ankle twisted on a root as the slick surface gave way. Gail slid nearly out of control for nearly twenty feet, unable to stop.

Thump! She landed on the path.

"Ouch! Crap!" she said, testing her ankle, standing, applying weight until she felt confident she could walk.

"Now where?"

She followed the path. As she descended, the air cleared and the Caribbean and the area Jason sped off to came into view. *It's the second lagoon,* she thought. *It's much smaller.* But as she thought of Jason, another thought had come quickly; his arms around her, carrying her off, and again, that damn cologne. She couldn't control herself. An urge arrived. For some reason, she felt an attraction. "Get that out of your mind. He's not your type."

Gail seemed to have little control over her thoughts. Whatever was inside the shack, or in the small of amount of resin she tasted, it had affected her. Her ovulation cycle was about to peak. She was wondering if that had anything to do with her attraction to Jason. Perhaps a psychosis driven by a determination to conceive, and the very different environment that she found herself. Maybe it was all psychological and stress-driven, and nothing to do with the honey?

"Hello," a voice called, shocking Gail. It was an American voice. A woman had come along the path.

Gail wanted to race away, but there was nowhere to hide.

"Uh, hello," Gail replied, surprised, unsure if she should still turn and run. But why should she? She'd done nothing wrong.

Voodoo Cruise

The woman, dressed similar to Gail minus the mud, was thin and much older.

"Are you lost?"

"No, just exploring the rainforest," Gail said, the distance between them closing.

"It's beautiful here, reminds me of my travels when I was working," the thin woman said. "It's why I live here."

"You are an American?" Gail asked.

"Yes," she replied.

"What are you doing here?"

The lady laughed and redirected Gail's questions. "What are you doing here covered in mud?"

"I came from the cruise ship."

"Are you lost?" the lady said.

"Yes, I am," Gail confessed. "Kinda wandered off. And as you can see, got myself into a pickle."

"You're the curious type, aren't you?" The woman smiled. "My name is Ruth. I've lived on this island for quite some time."

"I'm Gail. I came over with the nurses to the village."

"That's nice, you must've met Marie."

"Yes!"

"You must be infertile."

"Infertile!" Gail was dumbstruck. What a statement to make! "I'm without a child, yes," Gail said, feeling a bit of sadness, a reminder why she was on this journey.

"My home is down this path, not far," Ruth said. "Do you care to join me? It's rare that I get to speak to an American mainlander. Nice to have some company. I think I can help you with a new outfit." Ruth looked down at Gail's mud-caked clothes.

"That would be a big help!" Gail said, running her hands around the waistline of her dress, then down and along the round of her butt to measure the extent of the wetness.

Gail was still curious as to why this woman, so out of place, lived here. She also realized she was Jason's adoptive mother.

The brisk pace that Ruth led seemed to dissipate Gail's allergic reaction to the honey. Her craving went away.

"What a beautiful setting," Gail said as they arrived at the base of the house Gail had seen from the water taxi. Its foundation was made of coral, cut from the reef and hauled up; the stone blocks the same as the village seawall. The stairs were identical to the terrace steps, set in seven-inch lifts, leading to a single-floor, open-air residence. At the top of the stairs was a substantial wraparound porch that mostly overhung the steep mountainside.

"This is home," Ruth said, briskly climbing the staircase.

Birds chirped from somewhere within the surrounding forest. There was a low, noticeable hum that came from the forest fog above them. Gail noticed how winded she was chasing after Ruth trying to keep up. Florida was mostly flat; she wasn't accustomed to the steep terrain.

As she stepped onto the porch an incredible view appeared. The entire Caribbean lay beneath her. "We must be five hundred feet up," Gail said, taking in the beauty of the scenery.

"Give or take a few feet," Ruth said, crossing to the long side that spanned the drop-off. "Ice tea?"

"Yes, and thank you, I could use the caffeine."

"I have a dress you can wear. We're about the same size."

There was a rectangular wicker table at mid-porch with a collection of conch shells and three wicker chairs. A healthy breeze traveled in from the corner of the porch.

Surrounded by jungle, it seemed the perfect place. The air temperature was perfect.

Voodoo Cruise

"I can see why you live here. This view is incredible. The air is fresh," Gail observed.

"Seventy-six degrees all day, every day," Ruth said, returning with their tea and a sleeveless maxi-dress slung over her forearm. "Here, put this on. If you need privacy go behind that partial wall." Ruth pointed inside, near the open area of her living room.

Anxious to be rid of the unclean feeling, she changed, then used the bathroom to remove the mud that covered her in spots.

"You clean up well," Ruth said, ice cubes clanking, directing Gail to the far corner of the porch.

"You have refrigeration?"

"Yes, from a solar generator on the ridge, invented by a Peace Corps friend."

Interesting, Gail thought. Marie had said her husband, Lou, and Jason were Peace Corps volunteers.

"I want to show you why this place is unique," Ruth said. "The small cove below faces directly into the trade wind in a manner that gently gathers and funnels the ever-constant breeze up the hillside. As you can feel, the rising air passes directly through my house. As the air lifts, it condenses rather rapidly, creating the clouds you see over our heads. It's good for growth in the forest that surrounds us."

Gail went to the banister where Ruth's porch reached out, overlooking the second, smaller lagoon. Far below, the water was clear, much clearer than where the *Sapphire Orchid* anchored. The fringe reef was wider, healthier-looking, and filled in nearly the entire cove.

She saw Jason's boat anchored just off the edge of the reef. But Gail couldn't make out if Jason was onboard.

"There's a boat down there," she said.

"Yes, I can see," Ruth said. "Get comfortable, have a seat." They made their way to the wicker chairs.

"This has to be the coolest home I've ever been in," Gail said.

"Thank you!"

"I must ask, Ruth, why here?"

"I'm originally from Washington, DC. I'm a retired lawyer. And like most of us government lifers, commuting in DC traffic for thirty years, we dream of peaceful places where we can live after a lifetime of administering bureaucracy, and the hot DC summers and crowds of tourists."

"What about the *Sapphire Orchid*? Don't you find it out of place that your peace has been disturbed by the presence of the ship?"

"Yes, it's quite annoying. But it has a purpose for women like me and you that can't have children."

Gail's eyes widened. *How does she know so much?*

She pressed further. "I must ask, how much can you tell me about all this? You're a lawyer, no doubt well-read. It would be nice to know what's with the *Sapphire Orchid* and this village. There's an obvious connection."

Ruth sipped her iced tea. Except for the clink of cubes, she stalled, her eyes not fixed on anything. She was contemplating all that she knew.

"You know what?" Ruth said, finally speaking. She leaned to her side and set the tea on the wicker table. "I'll show you; come with me back into the rainforest."

Standing, they headed to the far side porch, opposite from where they'd entered. Another set of stone steps led up and into the steep hillside, a switchback into the thickening overhead mist. At each turn were pie-shaped stones with thick green moss filling in the gaps. Gail followed Ruth as more ledge trails branched off into the canopy of trees in different directions, a network of sorts, following the natural arc of the mountainside. *Something is going on here,* Gail thought as several bees flew past. An obvious hum grew louder as they progressed higher and deeper into the grayness.

"What's up with the bees?" Gail asked.

Voodoo Cruise

"That's what I'm about to show you," Ruth responded.

"These trails appear to have stood the test of time," Gail noticed.

"It's one of the few places in Haiti not been destroyed by deforestation yet," Ruth replied. "It's the only virgin forest left in the county."

As they headed uphill, the ever-present fog thickened. Gail guessed they were about one hundred feet above Ruth's home when the path topped out. It leveled to a semicircular plateau of sorts, just like the shed on the other side of ridge. The substantial section of the ledge cut rather significantly into the hillside. Growing dead center was an ancient, sprawling banyan tree. The flat light and heavy fog made it difficult to see the entire tree. It was massive and likely hundreds of years old.

"Why can't I see the trunk of the banyan?" Gail asked.

There was a powerful scent and a collective buzz, like an invisible swarm lived somewhere within.

Ruth circled to her right, looking for something. "Ooh! I walked right into it."

"Is that a curtain?" Gail asked as she came close to the outer edge of the banyan and the long horizontal reach of the limbs.

"Yes," Ruth said, looking for an opening. "The flap is here somewhere."

A bee flew between Gail and Ruth and pierced perfectly through a tiny hole in the netting.

"Ah, there it is." Ruth separated an overlap in the net and said, "Follow me."

The scent, like blended honeysuckle and violets, grew much stronger. Gail followed Marie behind the curtain.

"My God!" Gail said, as a limitless number of root-drops dangled like a Napa vineyard.

Ruth remained quiet.

"Gosh," Gail said, looking at the uncountable number of vines that dropped from above, each loaded with stunning, spidery blue and white sapphire orchids. "There are tens of thousands of orchids here!"

Ruth smiled. "Yes, all through the hillside is a hidden forest full of orchids. These trees have been here for hundreds of years. The climate is perfect."

"Ooh, a bee!" Gail swatted her arms, the bee nearly caught in her hair.

"Don't worry," Ruth said. "They are more interested in the nectar."

"I don't get it, though. What is this about? Clearly, with the netting, it's a big secret. Help me with this, Ruth!"

"It has to do with the Haitian government and the village wanting to protect the rainforest. Like I said, it's the last virgin forest in the country. Haiti is only one percent forested. Without protection, this mountainside would get clear-cut, and the remaining hardwoods turned into charcoal. The dirt would wash into the Caribbean, killing the fragile ecosystem that supports Atabeira. The village elders allow the cruise ship only because the government aggressively protects this mountainside from deforestation. And as you can see, the Atabeirans have a rather good reason to preserve this forest."

"Tell me more," Gail demanded, her hair straight from the humidity.

"Follow me." Ruth directed her to come further within the suspended vines, where a string of orchids, hundreds of them, hosted an entire root-drop.

"These are bucket orchids," Ruth said. "The more technical name is tropical epiphytic orchid. The flower is co-evolution, meaning they've evolved with the orchid bees you see buzzing about. The orchid and the bee depend on each other for survival."

Huh! thought Gail, confused.

"The flower secretes a fluid into the lip-like bucket of the orchid. Male orchid bees are attracted by the strong scent and use it in their courtship. The bees land, fall into the bucket, and can't get out at first because the lip is lined with smooth downward hairs."

"How do they get out?" Gail asked.

"There are knobs the bee must grip to climb out. The knobs lead through a spout that constricts and temporarily holds the bee in place. At that same moment, a packet of pollen is delivered and glued to the thorax of the bee. The flower traps the bee there until the glue dries, then releases, allowing it to fly off."

"Incredible," Gail said. "It's the reason I enjoy being journalist. You learn the most incredible things researching interesting stories to cover."

"Come close to the orchid and watch," Ruth said as the pair stood shoulder to shoulder at eye level to the suspended flower. A green-back bee arrived in seconds and tumbled into the bucket.

"I get it. A Darwin thing."

"Kind of like that," Marie said, nodding. "Watch closely, see what the orchid does as the bee climbs out."

Imprisoned in the snout of the flower, the bee waited patiently as the pedal delivered the pollen packet, gently holding it in place. Minutes later, the flower's throat opened and the bee took flight.

"Ruth, I must confess, I was up on the hillside and saw the shack and the hives."

Ruth once again had to contemplate her response. As lawyer, she had some degree of ethics and compulsion to be truthful. And for whatever reason, people tended to trust Gail. It was the way she came across in her calm, welcoming demeanor and camera-loving expression. The way she posed questions, a "help me out" needy expression, "let the world know" observant manner.

"You've learned quite a bit since you've been on this island," Ruth said. "Likely you'll find the underlying reason anyway. The village of Atabeira, for centuries, relied upon the bountiful waters of the Caribbean. As you can see, the community is pretty much cut off from civilization, except for traveling by sea. The Taino Indians that lived here were healthy for centuries. But two major events nearly wiped out the population of Atabeira."

"Let me guess," Gail said. "Explorers of the Caribbean and the landslide."

"Yes, how do you know that?" Ruth asked.

"Except for the landslide, it was taught in just about every fifth-grade history class."

"When Atabeira was nearly wiped out by smallpox, the Taino villagers began working on a way to repopulate. Early on, the elders, over many generations, found a way. Normal society might not agree with what I'm about to say; however, you must realize this was a less sophisticated culture at the time, much of it purely animalistic—a will to survive."

Gail spoke. "So, it's the orchid, the rainforest, and coca."

"Yes, it is. But the secret is within the genetic mutualism of the orchid. You see, orchids use sexual trickery, deception, to lure pollinators. They use it in a way to assure a genetic diversity by selecting the bees it wants to carry its pollen. The sugars and chemicals in the nectar, when concentrated enough, has the same effect, but only on women. When ingested, it elevates a woman's testosterone levels.

"Testosterone? I thought it would be estrogen!"

"No, there's often plenty of estrogen at the peak of our ovulation; however, testosterone is secreted in surges around the time of ovulation, as Mother Nature's way to increase our interest in sex."

"But much of what you say is basic biology. Why is this so different?" Gail asked.

"This village has been working on this for many centuries. The concentrated honey increases the male's sperm motility through a combination of chemically altered female vaginal secretions. Also, the female egg is highly receptive, energized in a manner that makes conception likely for those that have struggle with such issues. Often there are twins born. But the honey delivers with such an intensity of sexual desire, woman lose complete control; their mating instincts become red hot."

"Hmm, that explains why the blogs recommend you make sure your ovulation cycle matches with the anchorage in this port. I'm dumbfounded," Gail said, staring at the incredible abundance of beautiful blue and white orchids.

"It looks like the root-drops are trimmed so not touch the ground," Gail noted.

"Yes, when your cruise ship is not invading the Atabeiran homeland, most villagers are up in the rainforest tending to these banyans. They trim the drops so they don't attach to the ground, unless they want it to support the limb as it grows outward."

"Isn't it dangerous to be giving this . . . ah, let's say for a lack of a better word, potion, to the young girls that the village wants to breed?" Gail asked.

"I was about to get to it . . . Atabeiran girls are taught, or should I say scripted, from a young age to follow the instructions of the mambo or risk the consequences of her magic. They know no different. In the village, only the mambo administers the potion. Because the wrong amount can be dangerous."

"Dangerous, how's that? Has anyone been hurt?"

"Yes, there is a story when there wasn't a suitable male to mate with, a desperate young girl, under the influence of the potion, jumped into the lagoon to swim across the Caribbean. She was never seen again."

"Ruth, I've got to ask. It's obvious Emerald Cruise Line gets their hands on the honey, isn't it?"

"Unfortunately, yes, it's evolved to be part of the deal," Ruth replied.

"Isn't there some danger to female passengers?"

"There could be, but from what Marie told me, it's administered in very small doses for a period of days. There's not that much to go around anyway with the number of couples onboard these days, so it's delivered rather judiciously."

"How does the captain feel about this?"

"I don't know," Ruth said, being the lawyer. "You should ask him. But I must say, the captain is quite a stud, and tends to hoard the honey for the five girlfriends he keeps aboard. I've heard it's because he's not sired a son yet."

"Disgusting!" Gail said, her feet wet from standing in the soft soil.

"He's Greek, what can I say."

"Ruth, what about the older lady I saw with . . . uh, what do you call her, the mambo? She looks Caucasian. Why is she here?"

"You mean Marion. She was a nun once upon a time."

"What's she got to do with any of this?"

Ruth laughed. "She is in hiding. She exiled in Haiti."

"Exiled?"

"Marion got into a considerable amount of trouble in the United States. She was a pro-life activist. Would picket abortion clinics and was under investigation for fire-bombing a clinic. Marion heard of the miracles of the *Sapphire Orchid*, jumped bail, and took up with the mambo. For Marion, it is a fulfilling and noble cause to bring life to this earth."

"Interesting," Gail replied. "I feel sorry for the young girls that must have babies."

"Once a young village girl becomes a woman, usually at age fourteen, she's sent to another village either by boat or over the mountain at her right time. She's escorted by the mambo, and Marion, to assure she remains safe. The mambo keeps sole possession of the honey and places just one drop into a rum drink, typically at sunset. The alcohol helps with the absorption and calms the fear in the young woman. It takes about thirty minutes for the aphrodisiac to take effect . . .Then, wham, to put it mildly, she loses complete control—her mating desire extremely strong. She craves male sperm and will pursue the first age-appropriate male she can find until she mates, behaving like a cat in serious heat."

"Let me guess, the reason she goes to a different village is for diversity of the gene pool."

"Correct."

"What is the likelihood the girl won't conceive?"

"Very unlikely, though it does happen. It's only the infertile male where they won't conceive. And somehow, she can sense it, like the orchid's natural selection of which bee it allows to land. She will move on until she copulates prior to sunrise, which is when the powerful aphrodisiac wears off."

"How brutal," Gail said.

"I know, but it's biology, survival of the species. Nearly every girl has no recall of what happened to make them pregnant. The potion is that genetically evolved, it wipes away the memory of the act.

"Let's head back," Ruth continued, walking to the net, opening it to escort Gail out from beneath the giant fig. "We must go, or you'll miss the ceremony. I'm sure Marie invited you."

Gail considered what she just learned. But to crave sexual intercourse to such an extreme degree! She couldn't get her head around it. Her ex-husband wasn't good in the sack at all. In fact, much of it was quick and self-serving, roll over and not even a kiss goodnight. But Marie offered to deliver her a suitor tonight, Fabrizio. The timing was right. Was Marie going to slip her some honey? And if Ruth was correct, she wouldn't remember doing the deed, which could be good and bad, not to know how good the sex was.

The downhill trail took only half the time to return to Ruth's home. Stepping onto the porch, Gail heard a familiar voice call from below the porch. "Hello, Mother!"

There was the rapid thump of footsteps, and Jason appeared. He had no shirt on, as when he rescued her from the alligator.

"Jason," Ruth said, excited, racing to greet him and giving him a bear hug.

Gail's eyes grew big. "Oh no, not him again!"

Ruth turned to introduce Jason.

"No need," Jason said. "We've already met."

"Jason, we meet once again," Gail said, remaining at the edge of the porch, her head swimming.

"I gather Ruth gave you more meat for your story."

"Come, let's all have a seat," Ruth said.

"To be honest, Jason, she told me everything," Gail said, setting her hand at the edge of the chair to lower herself without losing eye contact with him.

Jason turned to his mother.

Ruth nodded, confirming she gave away the secret of Atabeira.

Then Jason said something completely in character as far as Gail was concerned. "I'm hoping you don't reveal any of this to the public. It's much more complex than you know. You should know it will destroy this village and its rainforest should the secret get out. What has brought life back to Atabeira for centuries will only serve to assure its permanent destruction if not managed appropriately."

"I'm aware," Gail answered, but didn't care to elaborate, distracted. He had only a pair of swim trunks on. How could he remain so physically fit? He was in terrific shape—six-pack abs.

The secret she just learned put her in a rather uncomfortable role as a reporter. Currently, there was a considerable amount of good happening. Every infertile couple and corporate interest would beat a path to the village, and would undoubtedly destroy it, should Gail spread the word.

"All I hope is when you gather all your facts, you will not feel compelled to tell anyone."

"Jason, I have even more questions. Like, why this lagoon? What is your role with the cruise ship? How did Ruth become your mom?"

"It's complicated," Jason said. "Like I told you in the library. Ruth is not my biological mother," he added, confirming what she already heard from Marie.

Ruth interrupted to explain some more. "As a Washington, DC, lawyer, I worked for the Peace Corps. The position allowed me to travel quite a bit, which was a passion of mine at the time. When Jason was a child, I found him on an atoll in the Pacific at one of the Peace Corps's most remote assignments. Here was a white male child living on an island with native Chuukese and clearly out of place. Having no children of my own, I adopted him. And when he was old enough, after I'd spent a fortune on his education, Jason went back to where he felt was home and is now quite an expert on coral reefs."

Gail had been studying Jason the entire time. She could see no physical similarities except for they were both Caucasian. He was getting impatient. There was clearly something else bothering him. What was it? Gail wondered. Something was not quite right. She could sense his tension.

"I must head back to Atabeira," Jason said, fidgeting.

"When will I see you again?" Ruth asked.

He turned and looked at Gail. He wasn't comfortable revealing his travels. "You know where I'm going next, to attend to a few matters, then heading home for a few months, but first back to Washington. I'll call you."

"Are you returning to the ship?" Gail asked.

Jason, standing in only his swim trunks, looked down at Gail in her seat, her legs crossed. "I'm getting off in Tortola."

Gail grew flustered. His look was overwhelming. She'd never encountered a man with such confidence and clear self-direction. But there was now an underlying concern written in his expression.

Jason gave his mother a kiss and then trotted off, bounced down the porch steps, and headed down the mountainside.

Ruth left her chair and stood at the edge of her porch. Gail joined her. "This view is incredible," Gail said.

Below, they watched Jason exit the jungle, dive into the water, and swim several hundred yards to his anchored Zodiac. He climbed into the watercraft. Then he waved, started the motor, and sped off. All Gail could think about was, who was this handsome person? And the incredible, physically fit body he had? She wanted to make love to him and would if the opportunity presented it.

Chapter 8

It's time to go," Ruth said as Jason's Zodiac head out of sight. "Soon we'll hear the call of the drums."

Gail had a great story but had not gotten completely to the bottom of the thread that tied Jason, the *Sapphire Orchid*, and Atabeira. What made it more confusing was Jason's link to everyone she'd met so far. She knew a bit more about his life, his role as a mediator of some sort, maybe a government employee, but beyond that, she could not piece it together.

Gail tried to get Jason out of her head, but for some reason fixated on how fit Jason was. *A swimmer's physique.* Certainly, he'd be a great genetic candidate for her child. But there were too many blanks to fill in. And perhaps, in the presence of his mother, he was much more subdued. Raised on an island and of a different culture, he was more in his element here than in a Jeep on a busy American interstate.

"Let's head down to the village," Ruth said.

Not far from Ruth's home, the downhill trail widened. It left the shade of the rainforest and quickly became a sundried dirt alleyway. They entered the back corner of the tiny community. The heat of the day had absorbed into the hard-packed ground. Three blocks further, they came to the central park. Rising above the rooftops and towering Brazilian palms was the invader, just as Columbus, the ominous *Sapphire Orchid*, a reminder to every villager its poison.

At the far corner of the park was a hexagonal building. "They call it the Temple of Hounfour," Ruth told her.

"Again, another odd name, a word I don't know the root of," Gail said.

"It's just another name for voodoo temple," Ruth replied. "Much of the meaning is rooted in African culture. I'm much better with Latin translations."

The nurses had gathered outside the temple and were about to enter the temple. Marie was waiting.

"I see you met Ruth," Marie said, smiling. "And of course, you know she's Jason's mother."

"We had a nice chat about bees," Gail said.

Marie smiled. "There's much more. Let's go inside."

The six-sided temple had a low-sloping roof with narrowing, pie-shaped roof sections that tapered at the peak. A wooden pole, its shape also hexagonal, poked through and continued skyward another fifteen feet.

"What an odd-looking structure. Looks more like a wooden carnival tent," Gail observed, thinking a cross would be more appropriate to symbolize a church.

They followed the nurses inside.

Gail, using her quick wit, asked Ruth where Jason was heading. And Ruth, with her honesty, told her he went to speak with the village elders, then on to meet with the captain. "It's the reason he is here."

"What about?" Gail hoped for an unexpected answer.

"I'm sure you can reason why, or ask him later when you board the ship, what he discussed with the elders."

Voodoo Cruise

For Gail, Ruth's response didn't add much. Just that it confirmed what she already knew, his role as a mediator.

Inside, the floor was mostly dirt except for the center, where a decorative ceramic pad encircled the hexagon pole painted a rich blue. The ceramic pad looked like some sort of ceremonial altar. Opposite their entry, at that far side, was a smaller entry with an ornate hardwood chair just to the right. It reminded Gail of her Catholic church days and where the priest sat just after holy communion.

"Gail, we are to stand at the edge of the concrete with the nurses," Marie said.

"No, I prefer to stand against the back wall."

"I understand if you are nervous," Marie said, moving forward with the nurses.

"I'll keep you company," Ruth said. "And interpret what's happening."

"What's going to happen?" Gail asked as they made their way to stand near the exterior wall. "Is there an animal sacrifice?"

"No, no," Ruth laughed. "It's the reward for the nurses, for helping care for the children. A ritual that takes place every time the *Sapphire Orchid* is in port."

More villagers arrived, filling the temple, standing shoulder to shoulder, crowding Gail and Ruth. Gail tried to blend in, but the color of her skin made her a standout.

From the smaller, opposite entry, barefoot men with drums came, making a clumsy ruckus, all beating their instruments. Lacking any organization or formal dress, the band came to the concrete pad and circled the center, at times nearly colliding with each other. They danced, spun, and beat their well-worn instruments heavily decorated with painted figures, strung with seashells, bits of coral, skeleton fish heads, and dangling beads. Still, there was no logic or rhythm, like a bunch of fumbling third-graders making noise.

But when the back door reopened, the drums abruptly stopped. The band left the center of the temple and gathered off to the side. There was a silence.

"The mambo is about to enter," Ruth whispered.

"Mambo?"

"Yes, she's to conduct the ceremony. Invite the spirit to enter her body."

Gail looked at Ruth, perplexed. "Spirits? Surely you don't believe in such things."

"Judge for yourself."

A proud, full-figured, charcoal-black woman appeared through the rear doorway, barely clearing the width of the frame. Her dress was solid white and handcrafted with embroidered red hearts ringing the bottom of her skirt. Her hair, in tight braids, was strung with white beads, with fire-red coral at the end of each length. Her entry was deliberate. The drumbeat started, but in rhythm this time. Several in the audience began to chant. Behind the mambo came Marion, carrying an assortment of bottles and jugs tied together with twine and draped over each shoulder. Marion was dressed like the mambo, except for the embroidery at the bottom of her skirt.

Gail recognized the mambo. She'd seen her at the shed.

Marion stepped to the side and waited behind the altar. She unslung the bottles, taking a seat in the hardwood chair.

The mambo started to dance, circling, deliberately avoiding the altar.

"What's she doing?" Gail asked.

"Summoning the spirit of Fréda?" Ruth answered.

"Fréda?"

"Yes, the spirit of love and fertility."

The drumbeat intensified and grew into a strong rhythm. The chant from the witnesses who had gathered grew louder and fell in line with the dance of the mambo and the beating of the drums.

Voodoo Cruise

Though she couldn't understand the words or the harmony, it appeared the mambo, with raised arms, was calling the spirit from the heavens.

The beat of the drums increased, intensifying, deepening.

"This better get going or we'll miss the ship," Gail said, growing inpatient.

"Shhhh . . . watch, the possession is about to happen," Ruth whispered.

The mambo danced past them, twirling in the dirt and then onto the ceramic for the first time. Tightening her circle, shuffling her bare feet, spinning, closing the circle, finally freezing in position. A shiver overcame the mambo. The drums abruptly went silent, but the chant of the villagers continued.

The mambo opened her palms and placed them against the center pole. She raised her eyes to the heavens. She shuddered with an incredible shake—the rolls of body fat vibrating, her hair braids dancing. And as her expression had clearly changed, the chanting immediately ceased. There was an eerie silence.

Facing the onlookers, the priestess's plump expression had changed, her huge pearly-white grin turned into a blank stare. There was a presence about her, a possession of her soul, and gasps from the audience.

"Fréda has entered her body," Ruth said.

"I take it you've seen this before," Gail said, matter-of-fact.

Ruth nodded. "Many times."

The drums struck a slow, subdued rhythm. The mambo, possessed, now Fréda, summoned Marion with the bottles and jugs. The short, white-haired woman came from behind the altar to the edge of the tile. And one at a time, the mambo pointed to a nurse and rolled her finger to come—eyes fixated, pupils constricted, another person within. More dancing, but only on the altar, the beat of only a singular drum, then sudden silence with one last hard thump. Again, dead silence. Fréda chanted and directed the nurse to kneel.

"She is blessing the potion and delivering its power," Ruth said. "Each nurse will be rewarded for helping their children today."

But Gail had already figured there was more to this. Several must be a plant by the ship. If this potion, or supposed honey, was what it was supposed to be, then this was how it made its way back to the *Orchid*.

One through seven, each nurse received the blessing.

"They forgot me," chided Gail, although she was relieved she wasn't part of this bizarre ritual, having no reason to be.

"You think so?" Ruth asked. "Any childbearing woman in this temple is fair game, particularly with the last blessing."

"I've brought no value to this village," Gail said, puzzled, yet suddenly suspicious. *What are Marie and Gail up to? Jason helped me get onboard with no money. Marie invited me to the village. And Ruth revealed Atabeira's deep secret. Is that why I'm here? Do they believe in this stuff? Can I really get pregnant?*

Fréda pointed and summoned Marie. She knelt and Fréda delivered a decorated bottle. Marie stood and hugged Fréda in a way that, even though there was a spirit inside her, was as if they knew each other.

Gail grew more concerned. Marie wasn't of childbearing years.

"I need to go." Gail said, suspicious she was about to be included in this bizarre ritual, somehow.

"Just one more," Ruth said, "a special blessing."

There was one jug left, with white lace around the neck, the body designed in hearts and decorated with shimmering sequins and beds, identical to the design on the hem of Fréda's skirt. The drums started. Fréda chanted and danced while working the drawstring on an iguana-skin pouch attached to her hip. She opened the soft pouch by separating the drawstring and lifted a voodoo doll much like the one Jason had forced Gail to take. Raised it into the air, touching it to the blue pole, summoning a possession.

"What's she doing?" Gail asked Ruth, her anxiety reaching its limit.

"It's the assignment of twins."

"Twins?"

"Yes, it doesn't happen all the time, but Fréda feels for the last blessing someone in the temple is prone to bearing more than one child."

"That's a crazy notion," Gail said, releasing a cynical chuckle. "And how do you know that?" The reporter, sensing something was not right, cornered Ruth.

Ruth smiled, the lawyer inside recognizing Gail's intuitive question. "There's one jug left. See, there are three sequin hearts painted on the side, one large heart and two smaller ones."

Gail squinted, trying to make out the hearts on the jug Marion held. Ruth was right.

"Yes, and you know this, how?"

"It represents the beating hearts of the mother and her unborn children."

Rolling her index finger, Fréda summoned Marion to bring the jug, then gestured her with her eyes to reach into the pouch.

Removing whatever was inside, Marion stretched out her clenched fist.

"What's inside her hand?" Gail whispered.

Ruth didn't have time to answer. Marion unrolled her fingers, revealing a pair of pearls, one black, the other white.

There was a gasp in the audience, then laughter and cheerful chatter in foreign language.

"What's happening?" Gail asked.

"It's the final gift," Ruth said. "One that guarantees conception. But it's a bit odd this time and explains the laughter. Marion has pulled two different color pearls."

"What do the pearls mean?" Gail asked.

"They represent the babies; the white pearl is a girl, the black a boy. Some lucky woman will conceive twins of different genders. The male twin in the village has the right to become a village elder; typically recognized as the dominant male. The female twin . . . well, think of her as the princess."

"Twins!" Gail chuckled. "Like all this is for real. I'd like see that happen. Huh!" But deep inside she was nervous. The unexplained reason as to how so many infertile couples conceived on the *Orchid*. Her own belief that she too would conceive had she still been with Richard. It must be true, which conflicted her.

From the same pouch, Fréda lifted a light pink scarf and flung it, unraveling it, waving it about in ceremonial dance. Fréda lifted the doll and pointed it to the peak of the sectional ceiling. The doll shook as if it had received the spirit. Fréda's big white eyes panned the audience and measured the entire room. She stepped off the ceramic. Danced in the dirt a bit differently, with less intensity, melancholy, the doll possessed, scarf and pearls within her hand. She passed the doll over the heads of the young village girls in the temple. But Fréda felt nothing. Again, she danced, this time touching each childbearing woman just below their stomach.

"What's she doing?"

Ruth answered. "The spirit in the doll will tell which womb is likely to conceive twins within the next twenty-four hours."

Gail let out a nervous chuckle.

Standing against the wall, Gail, Marie, and Ruth watched as Fréda circled again, touching each of the girls, holding the doll for several seconds. Fréda's face would go sad and move on. Gail looked over at the young girl next to her. She was barely fourteen. *Poor child, I hope she doesn't conceive twins, she's too small and too young.*

But as Fréda was about to approach, she paused as the doll shook in her hands. Her eyes became full and rolled directly toward Gail, the doll quivering, Fréda trying to hold it back. But she seemed overpowered. The doll wanted to jump from her grip. Fréda's arms extended and touched Gail's womb. The audience cheered.

"Seems you are the lucky one, Gail," Ruth said, as Gail looked down at Fréda holding the figure pressed to her stomach.

Gail wanted to step back, but the wall prevented it. Fréda smiled and lifted the doll to show everyone. She rotated her hand to lay it flat and used her other hand to insert the two pearls into the fine fibers that made the torso, just above the hipbone, where the womb would be.

Fréda summoned the last remaining bottle. She widened the mouth of the pouch and slipped the jug inside. Untied the pouch from her waist, reached around Gail, and secured it in a manner that the pouch hung from her hip.

Frightened, Gail allowed Fréda. The mambo knotted the pink scarf around the doll where she'd inserted the pearls and placed it in Gail's hands, folding Gail's fingers around the figurine dressed as the mambo, decorated in little hearts. Fréda gathered Gail's hands within hers, blessing her, praying.

Nervous, extremely uncomfortable, Gail wanted to pull away—Fréda had invaded her personal space—but she thought better of it. All eyes were watching—Gail, an island guest, was forced to maintain her composure.

As the drums beat, the entire temple erupted in a chant. And as Fréda's grip tightened, Gail suddenly dropped to her knees, pulled to the dirt by the possessed, big black woman drenched in sweat. Gail fell on top of Fréda, who'd lost consciousness. Fréda's arm flopped to her side, as the spirit left her body. Instantly, the chanting and pounding of the drums ceased.

"This can't happen!" Gail said, holding the doll, rolling off the unconscious woman's round body and coming to her knees, inches away.

With the help of Ruth and Marie, Gail rose to her feet and backed away; the pouch secured to her waist, voodoo doll in her hands. But she couldn't move as the women in the temple surrounded her, touching her stomach, speaking in a language she didn't know.

Holding the gift, she wanted to shoo them away, but felt it impolite. And as the mambo regained consciousness and was helped to her feet, everyone filed out of the temple. The horn on the *Sapphire Orchid* was blaring, summoning passengers.

"It's time to go and conceive your twins," Ruth said with a rather hearty laugh. "Don't you dare toss that doll away, or the black magic will come," she warned. "You may not believe in all this, but it's not in your best interest to chance it."

Gail was distraught. "Am I to conceive twins within the next twenty-four hours? Well, that'll be easy to disprove. Just keep my legs closed. Huh!"

Villagers followed the nurses back to the waiting water taxi. "Here, use this," Ruth said as they walked to the waterfront. She handed Gail a sack made of hemp, like what Fréda had as a pouch that held the jug around Gail's waist. "It won't draw as much attention when you get onboard."

"Why don't you take the doll?" Gail suggested. "Let it stay here."

"No, no, you mustn't. It will bring you and me both the black magic. No one on this island will dare take it. And don't you dare leave it here in the village. You do not want that pox upon you."

Annoyed, Gail shook her head. "I gotta be dreaming," she said, as they stepped onto the plank boards of the dock, making their way to the moored taxi.

Voodoo Cruise

Ruth stopped midway. She took hold of Gail's hands and held them in hers. "We are all far from perfect, including Jason. We've all learned far more by our travels to unfamiliar places, and are better people because of the people we meet in our life journey. I hope for you, Gail, your visit takes you in a direction that enriches your life considerably."

"It has, Ruth," Gail said. "Thank you for your honesty and those kind words."

Marie had gone aboard the tiny watercraft. Gail, the last in line, allowed the young deckhand to assist her into the crowded boat.

"Congratulations," Marie said as Gail joined her on the uncomfortable seat. "You are lucky. Your wish will be granted with not just one child, but two."

"I don't think so," Gail said. "To conceive within twenty-four hours, preposterous. Watch me prove you wrong. Want to place a wager?"

Marie laughed. "Don't you want a handsome surrogate tonight? You don't know of the power of voodoo. The spirit is in your doll. It's your destiny. It can't be undone."

Gail wanted to laugh out loud, but felt compelled not to, worried she had no choice in the matter.

The pilot revved the outboard, turned the wheel, and left the dock.

"All I have to do is keep my legs closed. Besides, not much good has gone on in my life. I don't believe I'd be so lucky as to have a child in my life."

"You Americans are so nervous about promiscuity. Bringing a life into the world is a blessing. Tonight, we'll go to the casino, where your man will be waiting, and I'll give you instructions."

"Marie, what are you doing with your gift from Fréda? Why you?" Gail asked, seeking to change the conversation.

"It's for my husband and me. We are such great lovers. Fréda's gift for helping the children, as you know. I won't conceive, but our lovemaking keeps us close."

"What?"

Marie's face grew serious. "I must warn you, Gail. Don't try the potion Fréda's given you without me to assist for the first time. Only a certain amount is necessary. It will take over your body and bring you great pleasure and a desire to conceive. Tonight, I will help you take some, when the time is right, before your lover arrives at your cabin. And if you don't conceive, you can use it repeatedly until God grants your wish."

Gail reached down and lifted the small sacks around her waist, allowing the jug and the doll to rest on her thighs. Motoring toward the *Sapphire Orchid*, she pondered the entire experience.

Chapter 9

A second horn blast startled everyone in the taxi. The deafening sound was longer this time, followed by two shorter ones, a final reminder it was time to board. From the middle of the Atabeira lagoon, the *Sapphire Orchid* looked like Noah's Ark, as sunburned couples lined the pier in pairs, boiled lobsters entering near the stern.

Gail shook her head. "What a television shot this would make, with a reference to Noah's Ark and a memorable line just before a commercial break."

She laughed silently to herself, yet she worried about what took place at the temple.

At the afternoon's thickest humidity, the heat of the day had increased considerably. Gail was thirsty. In her head, she replayed the day's events; the shack with the simmering honey pot and the many terraces of beehives. Her allergic reaction to the licked resin and heightened inclination to mate. Most disturbing was the moment Fréda, in a rather intimidating manner, selected her—the voodoo doll quivering and the prediction of twins of different genders. She couldn't get it out of her swimming head that she would have a lover. Sometime soon, she was to conceive. Who would it be? Sex with someone onboard! She still wasn't sure her idea of luring a willing crew member, a casino dealer as Marie suggested, was what she wanted. Would Marie have something to do with it, provided the mambo's blessing was real and predicable?

"Marie," Gail said as her thoughts fell upon Ruth and Jason. "Your husband knows Jason well. What's with Ruth and him?"

"Let's get onboard first, out of this heat, and I'll tell you."

The taxi came alongside the *Orchid*'s solid white hull. Sharply dressed sailors waiting to assist helped them to the platform, Gail supporting the sacks that held the doll and jug of honey.

"What's the story?" Gail asked as she walked an aluminum ramp with a rope rail into the cavernous hull.

Entering, Maria pulled Gail aside. "Ah, a welcome coolness. Let's go over by the forklift and talk before we head upstairs."

They separated from the nurses.

"Jason, what an odd story," Marie said, leading Gail into the cool shadow near a forklift. "Have a seat," Marie said. Gail placed her hand on a pallet suspended on the protruding forks and lifted to take a seat, her feet dangling.

"How do you mean?" Gail asked as she adjusted her rump to the uncomfortable slats of the pallet.

"Lou told me about Jason's childhood," Marie said, taking a seat behind the forklift steering wheel. "Ruth found Jason in one of the most remote places on earth, in Micronesia, in the state of Chuuk."

"Micronesia, isn't that in the Pacific?"

"Yes."

"Ruth indicated she worked for the Peace Corps," Gail noted. Then she said, "This isn't going to work." Gail slid off the pallet and leaned against it, rubbing her butt.

"Exactly," Marie answered. "Ruth was the director of volunteer placement. She often traveled to inspect volunteer living conditions, making sure volunteers were safe and treated well."

Voodoo Cruise

"On one of her trips to a field office, Ruth learned of the discovery of a young white boy living on a remote outer island atoll named Lekinioch. The atoll had the distinction as the Peace Corps's most remote assignment. And to find this child was quite a chore. Ruth had to fly from Weno, a Peace Corps base of operations, then to a World War Two Japanese landing strip two hundred miles south, near the equator. Then hire a boat to cross thirty miles of open ocean to reach Lekinioch."

"That's some journey," Gail said. "Sounds dangerous."

"Ruth didn't know much about this white child that thrived amidst an indigenous Polynesian population. He spoke no English, only Chuukese. When she spoke to the Peace Corps volunteer assigned to Lekinioch, Ruth learned Jason, as a child, had been dropped off by a Japanese tuna trawler. The trawler found him alone on a disabled catamaran. His parents weren't aboard. From what Ruth gathered, based upon the weather conditions and the dates they found him, his parents were likely swept overboard during a tropical storm. The Chuukese cared for Jason because they were that way with children. A village elder by the name of Mau had taken him in. It didn't matter who you were born to, the island lifestyle was one of subsistence; everyone shared and depended upon each other. Jason had assimilated. It wasn't until Ruth arrived that the Lekinioch residents decided to do something."

Gail was enthralled. It explained why Jason was single-minded and clearly different from the men in her world.

Marie continued.

"But it's the story that Ruth got out of Jason, as he grew into an educated young adult, that was most intriguing. A story that took years to release, passed on to Jason by Mau, his so-called Chuuk grandfather. You see, for centuries the Polynesians have used storytelling to teach and pass along their navigation knowledge to the next generation. Mau was such a navigator. It's the story that's embedded within Jason that's intriguing. He tells of an island atoll that was perfect in every way; lobsters were plentiful, breadfruit trees big and thick, coconut meat exceptionally sweet, a taro field so plentiful, the fish they caught with flesh as sweet as butter. Apparently, the Lekinioch inhabitants were displaced descendants of this perfect place. An atoll that sank, and the only reason the inhabitants survived was because of the . . ." Marie paused. "Let me see if I can say this correctly. *Chopot mi Auchea* as they would say."

"Choo . . . pot mi auchie?" Though correct pronunciation of a name was a required skill for Gail's profession, she fumbled with the expression. "What does it mean?"

"In Chuukese, it means woman of great importance, or Great Lady."

"Who would that be?"

"The Great Lady from the heavens as the story goes," Marie said. "Her plane ran out of fuel, crash-landed, and sank in the center of the atoll. Rescued, she took up with the inhabitants. And while trying to salvage items in the plane, she discovered the atoll had been severely undermined. For centuries, a rather unusual fish the Lekiniochians refer to as the flicker had honeycombed the coral that made up the base of the atoll. Daily tidal changes worsened the problem, slowly hollowing out a network of underwater tunnels. The Great Lady, after convincing the elders, prepared everyone for an evacuation. It's believed the Great Lady was likely Amelia Earhart."

"What? Earhart!" Gail's heart beat wildly. If such a thing had a shred of truth, the story would be a Pulitzer, for sure.

"Do you think there's any truth to this?"

"Lou does. He knows Jason enough to not push him on this issue. Says there is some sort of deep secret within Jason. But he does recall Jason acting oddly whenever Amelia Earhart's name popped up when someone dug into the folklore that surrounds her disappearance."

Voodoo Cruise

"Continue, Marie, is there anything that could prove this?" Gail asked.

"Well, I did some reading, and based upon where Lekinioch is, this so-called sunken atoll was within several hundred miles of where they figured Amelia's plane ran out of fuel."

If Jason has knowledge of this, Gail thought, *how to get it out of him?*

"Ruth said Jason goes to Lekinioch from time to time."

"Yes," Marie replied. "He'll spend many months on the Lekinioch atoll with what he refers to as his family."

"But why here? Haiti? Voodoo and all this sort of stuff?"

"It's Ruth . . . For years, she lived with her partner, a Smithsonian apiarist."

"Apiarist! What's that?"

"One who studies and keeps bees. It's very likely Ruth learned of Atabeira's secret many years ago, through her partner, and perhaps even attempted to conceive a child. It could explain why she ended up here. I don't know her that well."

"You told me Jason offered to pay my way on the cruise. Is Ruth his source of funding?"

"No, it's the other way around."

"Jason has money? How, he was an orphan!" Gail said, surprised.

"It's the one thing Jason doesn't share with Lou."

Gail recalled the crystal rosary. It was likely they were diamonds, she surmised, and likely the source of his earnings.

"Ruth said Jason was going to meet the captain tonight after talking with the village elders." Gail changed her questioning.

"As you obviously saw, the village isn't pleased with the presence of the *Sapphire Orchid*. Anchoring, invading once a week, because the Haitian government allows it."

"Are the Atabeiran elders threatening the ship somehow?"

"It depends on how strong your faith is in the power of the spirits summoned by the mambo," Marie said. "The mambo has been threatening to sink the ship via the black magic and has sent several warnings."

"Like what?" Gail asked, completely taken.

"If you follow the news lately, there's been a rash of incidents with cruise lines, such as rogue waves, engine breakdowns, et cetera. Do you think the sinking of the *Concordia* was an accident? The mambo's warning came the minute we set sail. It will happen during the flight of the frogs."

"Frogs! You mean the twister that splattered the deck the first evening?"

"Yes," Marie said.

"Are we safe?" Gail asked, concerned.

"I can't answer that until Jason talks to the captain tonight."

"How would Jason know?"

"That's what he was doing here, measuring the quality of the reef, meeting with the village elders who say there's no fish. I'm sure his meeting with the elders took place when we were at the temple."

Gail was shocked. Clearly there was a concern by others outside of Haiti. She was beginning to believe this could happen. It made sense.

"Don't you think passengers should be warned?" Gail asked.

"Not until Jason meets with the captain. If the cruise line agrees to leave the lagoon and never return then we are safe. If not, well, that's not good, particularly if you are a serious believer that voodoo can actually sink a cruise ship."

"How do you know all this, Marie?"

"Jason confides in Lou, likely the only person Jason trusts. And Jason knows he can't go it alone."

"But why reveal all this to me? Why did Ruth allow me to see the hidden orchids?"

"Because Jason has come into your life."

"What? I don't get it."

"You won't, until after the fact."

"Marie, you are making my head spin. It's been a long day."

"I agree," Marie said. "Let's just set this thought on the shelf for now."

Climbing three flights of stairs, Marie took Gail through the staff quarters. "Take the service elevator from here. It's quicker," Marie said.

As they waited for the elevator, Marie explained how she would set her up for tonight's encounter. If Gail decided to take Marie up on her offer, she was to place a bet for three consecutive spins of the roulette wheel where Fabrizio worked. First, bet on double-zero using a chip Marie would give her at dinner tonight; a special five-dollar chip with the *Sapphire Orchid* logo. The next two spins, a five-dollar bet each, would be her room number; first the number eleven, then on the second spin, thirteen. Fabrizio would then roll the marble in the opposite direction, acknowledging he would come to Gail's cabin. His shift ended at 10 p.m. "I will stop by your room at nine thirty to teach you how to take the honey," Marie told her.

The elevator arrived. Gail hadn't yet decided to go through with it. Particularly since she wanted to prove there was no witchery in voodoo, given the mambo said she'd conceive twins tonight. She was perplexed, close to the goal line, possibly having a child, and the part of her that made her a great and aggressive street reporter said, "Go for it. The timing is physiologically perfect."

Arriving at her cabin, removing the sacks she had carried the entire time, Gail lifted the contents and set the doll and decorated jug on the desk beneath the mirror. She searched in the desk drawer for stationery to make notes; to get down on paper the events of the day before she forgot. *How much crazier is this story going to get?* thought Gail. A

Caribbean village threatening to sink a cruise ship! An Amelia Earhart lead! Honey that magically made infertile couples fertile. She needed to make a digital record right away. Protect her copyright before she headed to dinner, while it was fresh in her mind. It was a story that must get told.

After a refreshing shower, Gail gathered her hurriedly scribbled sheets, tossed back on the same dress Ruth had given her, and headed to the ship's Internet room. She swiped her keycard to enter the empty room loaded with computer terminals. Swiped a second time to access the computer she sat at. Gail tried to log into her work email account, but couldn't login directly through Google. Instead, it redirected to the ship's browser to log through. She thought that odd. It included another advertisement to entice onboard sales, freezing the screen fifteen seconds for the ad to run.

A bit annoyed, she thought of the timing and type of ad. First, it was sexy lingerie, and now that they were two days into the itinerary, product sales and lovemaking lotions that lined the retail shelves in the promenade. "They've got this down to a science, don't they," Gail said as the ad ended and clicked through.

Referring to her notes, she typed a lengthy email, using her journalist writing skill, describing all she saw and believed was the true story of the *Sapphire Orchid*, including the village elders' threat to sink the ship using voodoo. She added that she suspected the goodwill nurses were actually planted to gather the life-giving honey for their infertile passengers. Gail reread the copy, then edited it as was her training, so it read concisely. The whole time, a fear came to her that Emmitt, her producer, would criticize her work no matter how well written. Though she didn't care for him at all, a story this big might get him to ease up. Emmitt was a great reporter in his own right; it was just that the camera didn't care for his looks. Often his misdirection was a frustration for the softballing of good news stories. She sent the email to herself as a form of documentation to certify ownership of the information, in case Emmitt hijacked it when she returned at the end of the week. She clicked enter. There was a delay, then the email shut down. Gail logged off and returned to her cabin.

Chapter 10

The entire time she readied for dinner with Vera, Gail kept returning to the desk. The decorated jug was bugging her. Was this stuff the for-sure cure to infertility? Why didn't anyone know about it? "Twins?" She lifted the doll that looked nearly identical to the one Jason gave her, except it was clearly female. "I'm to conceive twins within twenty-four hours, only if I sleep with Fabrizio!"

A bowl of fruit sat on the nearby refrigerator. Also a chilled ice bucket with a selection of juices and a bottle of rum. There was a complimentary note from Captain Lavaki, reminding her she was a guest of Emerald Cruse Line and a rather obvious statement that she reciprocate. The handwritten note reminded her of the underhanded things she disliked about her profession. She too was guilty of pitching softball stories to appease large advertising clients.

"I need a stiff drink."

She mixed the rum with coconut juice and ice, and the drink went down smoothly. With a second drink in hand she went out on the balcony briefly and watched as the island of Haiti and the *Orchid*'s return voyage through the spires of the Navidad Narrows, the sun setting behind the distant landmass.

Voodoo Cruise

Dinner time, she thought, coming inside. But as she dressed, she kept looking at the voodoo doll staring at her. It was an eerie presence. "You know what I'm going to do, doll? I've got a friend for you." From the nightstand drawer, she retrieved the doll Jason had given her and tied them together using the mambo's scarf. "Go ahead, the two of you have sex tonight."

She picked up the colorful sequined bottle that sat next to the paired figures and examined it for a third time. The three hearts; two were a glittering white, the third was black. *Me and my twins.* "If this stuff works, why don't I take some? Maybe it will allow me to relax enough to go to the casino. Maybe it's all physiological, a placebo perhaps, for the weak in spirit, a ruse." She wasn't sure what to think anymore and needed to know if voodoo was for real.

With her thumb and index finger she removed the fitted cork and held the opening to her nose. "What a powerfully sweet smell, like the honey of a thousand flowers."

As she inhaled, a cool rush of excitement spread across her body. "Wow!" Her sinuses cleared. She felt incredibly good and energized and a sudden arousal.

Fabrizio must be pretty good-looking, she thought, setting the bottle down, reaching for a brush to run through her hair. Marie was no slouch when it came to her selection of men. Her husband was handsome and Mediterranean. Marie had assured her the dealer was a gentleman, respectful, and would be everything she needed.

"No, it can't be." Then she thought for a moment. "The coca leaves, there's cocaine. That's it, nothing but a sweet-smelling drug that gets you high."

Like Pandora's box, Gail debated. *If it works, Fabrizio will get lucky tonight, and I will have twins.* How dangerous could this be? Each nurse, even Marie, used it. Marie said it made lovemaking with Lou incredible and passionate.

Gail pondered if she should experiment. Testing it could further validate the story she'd written, an experiment, taking her deeper into the subject matter, her own experience making the story more interesting.

"I'm going to do it! Fabrizio, look out!"

She poured a third drink—her anxiety still lingering. She dumped a shot of rum into an iced glass, filled it with fruit juice, and took a sip. "I needed this." Again, she debated. Should she? She was a skeptic and believed she had enough self-control. That if it affected her, she had the confidence she could manage whatever it was that took over her body. "All I've got to do is keep my legs closed, if I so desire."

Gail lifted the bottle with its glitter and heart-shaped design. Again, another whiff, the aroma making her feel great—confident. Marie had asked that she be present so she could give her the right dosage. That felt a bit intrusive. This was personal and private. She would administer it herself. How bad could this be?

Slipping her thumb through a hole near the neck of the jug, Gail tilted the bottle over her drink, holding it at an angle in case too much ran to the lip. Several seconds lapsed. Nothing came. She tilted the jug some more. It was like molasses. "Reminds me of ketchup." She tapped the end to move the viscous elixir along. Several sequins released and dropped to the laminated desktop.

"Hear it comes." The honey filled the opening and bubbled out, hovering above the rim of her glass. Gail waited for it to plop out. "Hmm, this shit's thick."

"Oops!" Suddenly, as the bubble touched the rim of the glass it oozed into her drink. Quickly, Gail lifted the bottle, leaving a trail of stringy molasses.

"Shit, how much was that? I'll just mix it well."

Using one of her pens, she swirled the drink for several seconds, dissolving the honey. Then she wedged the cork back in and set the bottle next to the bound voodoo dolls. "Here you go, guys, a toast. Why don't you two go at it while I'm at dinner."

Gail laughed. "Voodoo, fertility, a love potion, I don't think so!" she said, sampling the mixed drink.

"Yuck." It was too sweet. Her tongue curled and grew numb.

She took a second, much bigger, sip and waited.

"Nothing's happening," she said, smacking her lips, licking, feeling residue on her tongue.

A third sip.

"Huh, still nothing!" Gail finished the mixed drink. "That was a bust."

She looked at the desk clock. "Oh, it's time, I should get going. My stomach's empty. Gotta eat. Marie and Vera are waiting."

It took a few more minutes to pretty herself, but as she readied, there was a small reaction to the drink. She felt much better about her looks. Her mood was good and she thought fondly of Jason for some odd reason. She wasn't sure why, except that he held the answers to this incredible story.

Feeling sexy and a lot less intimidated, or perhaps just less self-conscious, Gail chose to wear a short, peach dinner dress with some tightness around her upper waist to increase her cleavage, in case Fabrizio was worth sleeping with. The hem of her dress stopped mid-thigh. Pleats allowed the sexy dinner dress to flair. *It's my Marilyn Monroe look, over the subway grate,* she thought, liking that she'd found it displayed that way in the onboard boutique with the famous Marilyn poster. "Let's show a little more leg."

She still had her beauty, and felt she could easily draw attention tonight, catch someone's husband sneaking a peek at the only unattached woman onboard.

"Take that, you horny males. I'm beautiful and single, bet some of you wish you were single again," Gail said, laughing, contemplating dinner expectations.

"At least I can say in my story that the cruise ship stores didn't skimp on quality. This is a stylish dress."

She slipped into thin heels that made her look tall and widened her stance. Then she traced on solid reddish-peach lipstick. Brushed her hair, checked its bounce, and splashed a dose of perfume. "It's the smell of orchids." Feeling good about her look, she left her cabin.

Soft music played in the narrow corridor, and again, the smell of chocolate and almonds. "I love that smell . . . mmm." She tried to recall the song. "It's Bocelli, from a movie. A tango. How ironic, the scene from *Scent of a Woman*, *Por una Cabeza*." She recognized the song. Argentine tango had taken off in Tampa as a trend. Vera recommended Gail take tango lessons as a way to meet men once her divorce was final.

Bocelli's golden voice, the artwork, the oxygenated air—Gail felt the best she had in a long time, enjoying the tantalizing ambience surrounding her. The elevator doors opened. She stepped into the all-glass car with several couples from other floors. Like her, the women were dolled up, perfumed, and undoubtedly ready for action. It was THE night, from what the blogs said, when most believed conception occurred. Light-headed, tipsy, Gail reasoned the alcohol was responsible. She needed it; all these couples were exceptionally well-dressed. Alone without a mate wasn't a good feeling; the alcohol was doing a good job.

The music changed to a purely instrumental version of *Scent of a Woman*. She wanted to dance. The quarters in the elevator a bit snug, Gail had brushed up against the husband next to her. *He's so muscular*, she thought. *So tall and handsome.*

Voodoo Cruise

As the elevator lowered, it passed the library. Gail turned to see if she could spot Jason. And there he was, neatly dressed, in his work chair, tapping away on his laptop. *If he's there after dinner, I'll go over and grill him, get his story, use every ounce of my reporter skill to trick him into telling . . .* Then she thought otherwise. For some reason, she felt compelled to seduce him. *You know what. I'll do what most woman do—seduce him, it's worth it. He's handsome, I'm sure I won't mind, even though we don't agree completely . . . Wait a minute,* she thought. *Not tonight, it's Fabrizio. I'm supposed to conceive . . . No, I can't do that . . . What do I do?*

The elevators doors opened. The couples shuffled out. But not before one of the husbands had paused to politely allow all the women to exit. *A real gentleman,* Gail thought as he smiled and said, "Ma'am, you're next." He voice was Texan and masculine. He had the build of a hardworking rancher.

"No," she said, "go ahead with your wife."

"Ma'am, I can't do that."

Gail knew why he couldn't. It was the cowboy's credo, politeness, respect for a woman. He wouldn't leave until she exited. It was why his wife was beautiful and loved him.

"Thank you," Gail said. But her mood, Bocelli's golden voice, she felt compelled to tango out of the elevator. Following the rhythm of the music, she clasped his hands and lifted them, as when the Argentine dance was about to start, and waltzed from the elevator with the tall Texan.

Though a bit surprised, he played along and danced politely into the lobby, spun Gail in a circle, allowing her to lean back, supporting her by the waist as she kicked her leg, dress flaring as she drew close. "Oh, excuse me," she said as the Texan let go, his wife eyeing him. But when her hands were freed, she embraced his broad shoulders and rubbed up against him, wriggling her body in a sultry, stimulating gesture, then gyrated her hips into his groin.

"Ma'am," he said politely, looking down at her, maintaining his composure. "You should stop."

Gail couldn't. She was a cat in heat.

"Get away from my husband," yelled the Texan's wife, who pried Gail away.

"Ma'am, may I suggest you dance with your husband next time."

The spouse snatched her husband's arm and angrily yanked him toward the main dining area.

What did I just do? Gail thought, flushed. *Must've been the drink, the great music, and lack of food.*

Gail gathered her composure. "I can't believe I lost control like that." Red-faced, she headed off to the Emerald Class dining.

"Lucky for me they aren't going in my direction," she said.

The Emerald Class bar at the dining room entry was the most opulent bar on the ship. Rich in design, it was where couples gathered, often sharing a drink prior to the maître d' seating them. Gail remained puzzled as to how she had behaved in the elevator. Was it the presence of the handsome man and great mood music? Having not danced in years, she contemplated if it was the three exceptionally strong rum drinks and the stress she was under, constantly thinking how she needed to conceive. It must've welled up inside; a psychosis of some sort. Then she considered if it was the honey. She didn't want to believe it was true.

"Good evening." Gail heard a familiar voice. It was Marie with Lou.

"Marie," Gail said, smiling.

"You look flushed. Are you okay?" Marie asked, holding hands with Lou.

Voodoo Cruise

"I feel fine," Gail answered. "Terrific, in fact. Thank you for inviting me to Atabeira. The experience was special. Did you bring the special roulette chips? I've decided to go through with it. Just as you said."

Marie could tell something was wrong. She sent Lou ahead to get them seated.

"Are you here with anyone?" she asked, concerned Gail was dining alone.

"Yes, my friend Vera is over there." Gail pointed to the far side of the dining room, where they sat last night, by the floor to ceiling windows.

Gail turned and asked the bartender for a glass of ice water.

"You look incredibly sexy, your dress, it's the peach Marilyn Monroe dress in the shop window. It suits you," Marie said. "I don't see how Fabrizio could resist."

"Yes, right after dinner. I'm hot to trot." She couldn't believe what she just said. The words leapt out, like she couldn't refuse.

Marie smiled. "Let's meet in your cabin before Fabrizio arrives. I'll help you with the gift the mambo gave you today."

"Oh no, that's not necessary. I've already helped myself."

Marie's face went into shock. "No! You didn't!"

"It was a bit too sweet, I must say."

"You may want to eat really fast," Marie said, concerned. "Soon you'll be drawn to any man. I hope you have great self-control. Oh my, Gail, your high beams are on."

Gail peered down at her chest. She'd worn no bra.

"They're standing proud. It's taking effect," Marie observed.

"I'll just have to deal with it," Gail said. "After all, I'm a sexy woman."

"Gail, how much did you take? I'm curious."

"I had a bit of a problem," Gail said as the adrenaline inside grew. Her eyes fell upon the ass of the bartender filling her glass with ice. She wanted to reach and attack him.

"The honey is very powerful. You should have only taken a half-teaspoon."

"How much is a glob?" Gail said, giddy. "It came out in a clump, like wad of bubble gum. But I mixed it very well. It was really yummy. But like I said, too sweet."

Marie's eyes grew wide. "Drink? Surely you didn't mix it with alcohol."

"Why? You said the mambo does it that way."

"Not on an empty stomach. It speeds the absorption and intensifies the effect. I'm worried for you, Gail," Marie said. "You should return to your room right now and I'll have Lou watch over you."

"I feel okay," Gail said, assuring Marie. "I don't think the secret potion is working all that well. I'm just feeling the effects of the rum. The best in years."

Gail left the bar taking the ice water, leaving Marie standing. Eyes wide, feeling sexy, Gail strutted into the dining room.

Marie went after her. "Gail, I think you should return to your room."

"I'm okay, Marie, really."

"Have it your way," Marie said, worried.

Marie split away and sat with Lou, but kept a close eye.

"Hi, Vera," Gail said, allowing the maître d' to seat her. He was handsome. She winked at him. Her mind raced. *No, I must control myself, the casino, Fabrizio. Trust Marie. Get food in my stomach, quickly.*

"Gail, where have you been?" Vera asked, as Gail sat next to her, allowing the maître d' to push her seat behind.

Voodoo Cruise

Ian sat directly across and next to the giant ocean-view window. On the horizon, the sun had set. The atmosphere was romantic. The busboys busy. Quickly, the setting across from Gail was removed.

"So, tell us about your day," Ian said, staring deep into Gail's blossoming cleavage, her breasts very much alive.

Vera followed Ian's stare. "Oh, my goodness, Gail!" she whispered in her ear. "You are at your ovulation peak, aren't you? Should have worn a bra."

Quickly, Gail drank the entire glass of ice water, hoping it would settle the intense arousal she was feeling.

Not far off, Marie kept a watchful eye.

It came upon Gail like an erupting volcano. A switch had flipped on. The feeling a woman gets when her mate has done the proper amount of tease and foreplay, arousing her to a point where she craves his insemination; a point of uncontrollable passion, a need to feed her incredible euphoria, the craving overwhelming. The Want. Gail grew flushed and a passionate sweat poured from her. She was ready in every way. Without notice, Gail stood and dove diagonally across the dinner table; forks, wine glasses, saucers, knives, spoons, and fresh-baked bread went tumbling. She latched onto Ian. Spread her legs around him and the chair, landing in his lap, facing him. She ripped open the top of her dress to expose her bare breasts; her chest heaving, hands gripping the back of Ian's head, coaxing him to suckle her.

The entire dining room gasped. People froze, even the waitstaff.

Vera screamed, "Gail, what are you doing!"

With Ian's face buried between her breasts, she started grinding her hips into his. She reached down between them to unbuckle his pants, wanting to have intercourse right on the spot.

"Gail, Gail, what's got into you, that's my husband. You don't like him. Get off him."

The busboys ran to the kitchen. The maître d' raced to the table and tried to separate Gail from Ian. But her legs were locked tightly around Ian and the chair, Gail undoing Ian's zipper. Two other men rushed to assist, their wives in complete shock. As the men struggled to remove Gail, she tried to yank off Ian's pants. The chair tilted on its hind legs and tumbled backward, Gail falling directly onto Ian, breast-planting his face as the two men latched onto Gail's shoulders.

But she twisted from their grasp. She'd gotten Ian's pants down and was working to remove his boxers. The men finally got a firm grip and lifted her off.

Kicking wildly, Gail knocked tables. Plates smashed. "Let me go," she said, spinning, wriggling, wrapping her legs around one of the men. She tore at her dress, ripping it more; her top fully exposed, legs around the man that worked to pull her off Ian, her hands reaching for his belt buckle too.

Now there were four men, including Lou, trying to restrain Gail. Tables overturned, spouses holding back their mates. Gail was out of control. Her hair a mess. Her beautiful, tattered peach dress completely removed, with nothing but her panties. Her legs and arms attempted to lock onto any nearby male. Finally, security arrived, and six men pinned her. They lifted her naked, twisting torso, carrying Gail out of the dining room.

"Take her to cabin 1113," Lou said. "I'm the ship's doctor and will tend to her."

"Go get Jason," Lou said to Marie. "She's overdosed. There's only one solution. It might as well be him."

Marie followed as six security guards wrestled with Gail—an out of control woman in extreme heat.

Using the inside crew stairway, they carried her up the stairwell to her cabin, shoved Gail into her cabin, and slammed closed the door. It'd taken six men, scratched and bruised with torn clothes, to subdue her.

Voodoo Cruise

Carrying Gail's tattered dinner dress, Marie burst through the double doors and raced down the corridor and found Jason in the library. "Jason, come quick. We need you. It's Gail. She's taken too much of the honey. It's not pretty."

Jason slapped closed the lid of his laptop.

"If we don't do something she's going to hurt herself," Marie said, frantic. Jason followed Marie back though the double doors.

"She's overdosed," Lou said as Jason arrived.

"How did she get her hands on it?"

"Blame it on your mother, Marion, and Marie," Lou said. "She and Marie felt sorry for Gail."

"My mother!"

"Yes, she tipped off Marion, who set her up."

"The reporter doesn't have the personality to be trusted with such a thing," Jason said.

"Nothing we can do now," Lou said. "But if we don't act quickly, she may hurt herself. She's taken quite a bit."

There was a considerable amount of commotion coming from the other side of the cabin door. There was squeaking of the mattress springs and the sound of a tumbling chair.

Jason reached for the doorknob, cracked the door, and peeked inside. Gail was naked and spread-eagle, humping the pillows. Sweat poured out of her. She saw Jason and raced for the door, trying to wedge her foot through. Jason slammed the cabin door shut just before Gail's foot got there.

"She's taken entirely too much and will harm herself," Lou said. "Can someone unlock the cabin next to this one? Go through to her balcony and make sure she doesn't jump overboard."

Immediately, a security guard stationed at Gail's cabin went into the next room and opened the divider that separated the balcony from the adjoining room. He stationed himself, wedging his boot in the track to lock the thick glass door. Fortunately, the blinds were closed.

"It's that powerful, Jason. She'll think she can swim ashore and find someone. She must attempt to conceive, or she will kill herself trying. You must go in there," Marie pleaded.

"No!" Jason objected. "Ask one of the crew members or a security guard."

"No, you are the most familiar to her. It wouldn't be fair. I don't think anyone on the ship would comply. She's got the black magic inside her. You must go save her life. The longer she waits, the worse it will get. She won't last the night."

Jason shook his head. He knew what Marie said was true. He'd seen it before, and why he hated all that was going on with the *Sapphire Orchid*. It was bound to happen; and here it was, with a woman desperate to have some real substance in her life. Overdosed, she would tear at her body until she was penetrated. It had been a long time since he made love to another woman. He'd been celibate, focused on his humanitarian projects, his orphanage, his foundation. But when he carried Gail in his arms at Alligator Alley and argued with her, he felt something, a familiarity and warmth, her need for him. But he was afraid and kept his feelings contained, a Chuukese trait, kind at heart. He came from another world she was totally unfamiliar with, and he feared the difference was entirely too great for their lives to come together as one.

Jason never imagined such an act to help someone in need. Marie came to Jason and rubbed his arms. "Relax," she said. "Help this poor woman. She's alone in the world. Don't let her die of a broken heart. It's unjust. Help someone for just this one time, instead of an entire world. We aren't even sure if she'll conceive given the size of the dose she's taken. It may have the opposite effect in some medically unexplained way."

Voodoo Cruise

Marie kissed Jason on the cheek like a mother, draped Gail's dress across his forearm, placed his hand on the doorknob, and pushed it down for him. She opened the cabin door and gently nudged Jason inside.

Chapter 11

Jason lay there with Gail wrapped tightly within his arms. He could not recall the last time he felt the warmth of a woman next to him— her shallow breathing, the perfect beauty of her naked body, so close, her heartbeat at a satisfied rate, skin as delicate as butterfly wings. He wanted to wake her and make love one more time, when her mind was right. But that would be a mistake. He did it for her safety. She was vulnerable, just as the children in the Tortola orphanage he cared for, supported by the considerable wealth he had access to.

She now knew too much about Atabeira's secret and the incredible strength of the genetically altered orchids, and the selective behavior of the bees that harvested the nectar. Ruth's life partner, a Smithsonian scientist, had discovered Atabeira and the hybridization of orchids. It was Ruth who'd educated Jason on the chemistry of the honey and its powers, and the danger of taking too much. Marie Battar was well aware, after witnessing Gail's extreme overdose, that only Jason would understand the danger and would do something to save this woman's life.

Reluctant to release her from his arms, Jason could feel the surge of the ship as it sailed for Tortola. The sea was heavy this morning. Dark clouds had rolled in. The weather would not be good today. Across the cramped cabin, bound voodoo dolls sat below the mirror. They were face to face, the scarf holding them in an embrace, the same way he woke. Next to the dolls was Fréda's gift, the sequined bottle, the cork stuffed in top. His eyes focused on the design of the bottle. He wondered why three hearts. What was the symbolism?

A believer in voodoo, gazing at the bound-together dolls, Jason shook his head. It was karma, his destiny to be with Gail. Raised in a non-westernized culture, Jason carried a strong belief in the actions of the spirits. Little did anyone know his role on the ship, except for Marie, Lou, and Captain Lavaki. This morning, before he left to tend to his orphanage in Tortola, he would meet with the captain and inform him of the elders' decision: the *Sapphire Orchid* must never return. The elders reminded Jason of the black magic brought to the *Concordia*, a demonstration of their power, and of the rogue wave that violently tossed another cruise ship off the coast of Antarctica, and the disabling fire in the engine room of a passenger vessel in the Gulf of Mexico, just this past Saturday.

The power of the black magic—was it enough to sink the *Sapphire Orchid*? Yesterday, he met with Atabeiran elders and informed them the fringe reef was dead, suffocated by the turbidity in the lagoon. And it didn't help matters when the *Sapphire Orchid* arrived and tethered, when the captain ordered a broadside blast from its electric propeller, stirring the bottom, sending a milk-filled wave toward the village. It was a defiant and deliberate act by Captain Lavaki, payback for the frog-filled twister that splattered his ship two days ago. The elders had sent a warning—the twister full of frogs. The *Sapphire Orchid*, if it were to come again, the mambo would summon the black magic and prevent any ship from forever destroying the fragile life-giving ecosystem of its reef.

Jason's greatest fear was of the captain, a nonbeliever with a Greek-size temperament. Jason did his best, pleading to the elders not to let the mambo release her black magic—not kill the passengers as the collateral damage. But this time, in a private meeting, the elders' decision was final, regardless of the well-being of their village or passengers. Atabeira had grown frustrated by the rule of the Haitian government that threatened not to protect their rainforest should the elders not comply with the condition that they share their life-giving product with the cruise line for the badly needed cash Haiti received to support the poorest county in the Caribbean. There was no easy solution.

The elders had heard this all before. But their Taino tribe had been wiped out by disease centuries ago. Then nearly every child was killed in a landslide while at the central school. Atabeira had brought itself back from the brink, thanks to the life-giving rainforest and the genetically modified orchids. But left with the decision to kill their reef, or their rainforest, which was most important? It was the reef and the ocean that gave them life. The elders had given the mambo the go-ahead to sink the *Sapphire Orchid* and informed Jason of their decision.

Jason slid his arms from underneath Gail. *How beautiful she looks.* She slept soundly and wouldn't remember it was him. Their lovemaking last night was passionate and felt right—a fondness for her stirred from the moment he'd given her a hard time on Alligator Alley—testing as he often did to determine a person's quality, their resolve. But was she capable of coming into his life? His mission, his wealth, the Atabeira's secrets she could never convey; for if revealed, it would destroy the village and the children he loved and cared for. She was a spitfire, but could she handle the cultural change it would require to join him on his life-long mission to do good for orphans like him?

Jason slipped from bed. He threw on his shirt, but could only find one of his Italian-made shoes. He went over to the desk and untied the voodoo dolls. Reaching into his pocket, he produced the rosary-like necklace that never left his side. He removed two stones from the necklace and buried them inside the torso of the Jason doll. He returned to Gail's bedside, leaned over, kissed her on her cheek, and took in the completely satisfied look on her face. He allowed himself a moment to enjoy the sight of her, as a man would . . . Quietly, he left the cabin with the click of the latch.

Gail felt herself in a free fall. *Wham!* She'd rolled out of bed and smacked the floor. Dazed, her head spun as she sat up. "What happened?" Her cabin was in complete disarray. Bed sheets crumpled and wrinkled, mattress cockeyed and not centered on the box spring. The desk chair toppled. Her peach dinner dress torn and left in a heap. Her undergarment hanging from the corner of the small TV on the dresser.

"What the hell happened!" Gail couldn't remember a thing, except sitting at the Emerald Class bar, receiving a glass of ice water. Back in her Philadelphia days she'd gotten stupid drunk with Richard. It was a great night, the night she thought she found the right man to marry. And she could only recall how the room was when they made love for the first time.

Slowly, coming to her feet, she waited for the room to stop spinning. "I need fresh air." Gail drew the veranda curtain. She lugged open the balcony door. "Oomph." The salt air rushed in. There was the familiar hiss of the *Orchid* cutting the ocean. She rubbed her eyes and let the fresh air fill her lungs. The sky was cloudy, the Caribbean dark from the lack of sunshine. In the distance, she saw islands. "That must be Tortola."

There was a knock. "Just a moment," she said tossing on a robe. Her bedspread had been partly pushed up against the door. She kicked it aside. It was her morning coffee, sitting in the hallway. "Thank goodness. I need this bad." But just outside the doorway she spotted a security guard sleeping in a chair.

Huh! she thought. *What's he doing outside my cabin?*

She brought the tray to the desk and set it in front of the dolls. "What?" she said, seeing the separated dolls and loose scarf. "What the hell happened here last night?"

Gail spotted the sequined bottle. *Oh my!* The lady in the elevator, screaming to let go of her husband! That was all she could remember. How embarrassing! It must've been the rum and that she'd not eaten all day.

Frustrated, dizzy, she struggled to recall last night. The conversation with Marie, instructions on how to place her bets at the roulette wheel. She couldn't recall if she ever made it to the casino.

"Shit! It really happened!" Gail could tell, the way a woman often feels the morning after, a bit sore in the right place.

"Why can't I remember what he looked like? It had to be the sugar in the honey and the rum in the drink. I must've skipped dinner and gone directly to the casino. Was I that desperate?"

She surmised she was too drunk to know what happened, but could tell from the stirred-up cabin the result of her passion. "Did I enjoy any of it?" She could tell by how her body felt; she must've made love to someone last night. Marie made good on her promise to deliver a Latin lover. Was he handsome? Was he intelligent? I really should know who he is. That way, if something happened, she would not have to bear the eternal guilt of explaining she did not know the father of her child.

Gail tossed the spread back onto the bed. Underneath was a shoe of a man. Italian-made, expensive, a light brown. "Huh, size twelve! Nice size. Might explain why I'm sore." She shrugged, pushing off the thought she'd made love to a man she would never know, and for the entire rest of the cruise she would suspect any crew member she passed with such a shoe size.

Voodoo Cruise

Taking the coffee pot, Gail sat on the balcony. She collected her thoughts and assembled the pieces of the puzzle in her head, the reporter in her rearranging the story. She had emailed it to herself last night to protect it. What part of the story to cut to meet the time constraint, how much word count? What words to use to be concise and impactful?

After draining the entire pot of coffee, Gail showered, dressed, and decided it best to eat. She'd lie by the pool, hydrate, and rest until the ship arrived in Tortola, hoping she would remember more as the day went on.

Gail opened the cabin door. The security guard was awake and stood outside at eye level. "Excuse me," Gail said politely.

"Sorry, Mrs. Stroud, you are to remain in your cabin, captain's orders."

Gail attempted to step past. The guard politely blocked her. "Orders, Mrs. Stroud."

"But, for what reason?"

The guard stood firm, inching Gail backward through the doorway. "I'm not to discuss anything. Just doing what I'm ordered, Mrs. Stroud."

"I'm not sick. Why am I being quarantined?"

"All I know is you are to meet the captain once we are in port." The guard pulled the door closed.

Gail was at a loss for words. "I'll call Marie."

She lifted the cabin phone and punched the front desk button. "Marie Battar, please." But she was rebuffed by the operator, given the same reason as the security guard.

"Can I speak to Jason Applegate?" she said, thinking he had clout.

"No, Ms. Stroud. I've been advised that until I receive orders, no calls are to leave your room."

Gail grew angry. "You have no right to detain me. Wait until I get on dry land," she yelled over the phone. "Your cruise line will pay dearly for this in the news."

There was silence, then a click on the other end.

Gail sat on her bed and considered the mess in her tight quarters. Was it because she was caught with a crew member? Did a steward catch them in the act? Did whoever she slept with tell a different story to protect his job? Gail was at a loss.

Chapter 12

Captain Nickoli Lavaki was bold, and Jason knew it. The tough Greek sailor would likely not heed what he was about to say. For this was Nickoli's vessel, his charge and his ocean. The *Sapphire Orchid* brought incredible profits and paid a hefty stipend to the Haitian government to fund an impoverished country, a stipend that was never enough. However, he expected something else, a male heir, and he'd not yet succeeded in that endeavor.

The captain left the bridge after tying up to the Tortola pier and arrived in his conference room at the end of the narrow, wood panel corridor with portraits of three generation of Lavaki captains. His mood wasn't good because one of his five mistresses, Sherrita, the smartest, most dominant and unpleasant, had given him a hard time last night. And for a short period, she refused to have sex with him as per her schedule.

Because of her intellect, Sherrita was privy to Nickoli's most private thoughts. In bed, after she had capitulated to his need, the seasoned captain would often vent, discussing intellectually his concerns. It was how he dealt with the heavy responsibility of piloting the *Sapphire Orchid*—navigating the dangerous Navidad cut, the most stressful part of each voyage. His lover, an educated lawyer and once famous Spanish flamingo dancer, had argued with him about the voodoo warnings—knowledge he shared of the black magic threat to his ship and the curse put on him by the mambo, preventing conception of a male heir. The captain had grown weary of the negative pregnancy tests and told Sherrita not to bother him with any more results until the news was good.

Jason was waiting when the burly seafarer entered. Nickoli, at six feet five, was as broad as an Armenian hard coal miner.

"Captain," Jason said, not wanting to waste time. "I met with the Haitian government and the board of directors of Emerald a few days ago in Washington, DC."

"And?" Nickoli asked, his mood miserable.

"You know the Atabeirans threaten to release black magic. The coming of the frogs, as the mambo indicated, will signal the *Sapphire's Orchid*'s final voyage."

"Bah, I don't believe in such myths. My mighty ship can't be stopped." Nickoli took a seat. "I take it by final voyage, you mean the sinking of this vessel."

"Captain," Jason replied. But before he could continue, Nickoli cut him off.

"It's a threat. And no puny village has such power. I've seen many strange, unexplained things in my life at sea, such as you say the invasion of frogs. Voodoo is a myth, a superstition. You know that, Jason, you've lived with Polynesian navigators, and no doubt know through their stories, the superstitions of the sea."

Jason knew he wasn't going to get anywhere by arguing the century-old seafaring mysteries. It was his knowledge that Nickoli had another reason for intimidating the village. He had five mistresses onboard and was desperate to sire a son.

"Captain, the ship is killing the fringe reef and jeopardizing the village food supply. When you docked and tied off, you sent a burst of turbidity through the entire lagoon. That was not necessary." Jason wasn't afraid of Lavaki and scolded him.

"It was a message to the mambo to release her curse, if you believe in such things."

"Apparently, you do," Jason said.

"We give them plenty," Nickoli replied, deflecting from why he had stirred up the waters. "The reef is dead. It was dying before we came. You and I know that. So does the Haitian government. They all need our money. The head tax they charge us is ridiculous." The captain preferred to use his height as a form of intimidation. He stood, as did Jason. "Besides, how do I keep my mistresses pleased if I don't give them the honey anymore? I'll be the most miserable, virile Greek captain on the seven seas."

The captain was not budging. But Jason had to say his piece. He hoped the mambo would do as he pleaded with the Atabeiran elders—damage the ship in a way where lives were spared. For the honey brought life, and to take many lives and the ones about to be conceived conflicted with their own intent to give life for the past five centuries.

"I heard you were called into action last night with that reporter woman you wanted onboard for all the freebies she's charging up." Nickoli winked, passing Jason a big-bearded grin. He was like a proud father, supportive of his son's sexual conquest.

Jason responded. "You know there are no freebies. I'm paying her bills from the consulting fees you pay me to prevent the mambo from bringing the black magic to your vessel."

"Huh, you mean Emerald Cruise Line is paying you. You are paid to put everyone's mind at ease, the ones that believe the voodoo, so the company can make money. Look at the size of this vessel. Do you think some African descendant that summons spirits can do anything that would hurt my ship?"

Jason didn't care to argue. They'd been at odds for a while. Jason was doing what was asked by his adoptive mother, Emerald Cruise Line, and the Haitian Embassy, negotiating.

Nickoli grunted. "You are a good mediator, Jason. But Atabeira is westernized, sneaking their honey aboard, not everyone in the village is a saint. Especially that Marion. She's the source for the honey we need for our passengers, because of all the babies she wants us to bring into the world."

Jason was clearly aware. It was Marie and Lou and Marion who were responsible. The cruise line paid handsomely to anchor there. And Nickoli's observation was the sinking of the ship would likely not happen in any manner, purely from a commerce point of view.

"Your girl, the reporter, I'm throwing her off in Tortola. It's for her own good."

Jason did not overreact. Gail had created quite a spectacle last night. He expected Nickoli would remove her. It was best for Gail to leave anyway; otherwise, the captain would quarantine her. Because remaining onboard, it was likely all eyes would fall upon Gail the entire itinerary, risking a confrontation by passengers about her behavior, fearful it would happen again.

"As you know, Jason, we have sophisticated ways of monitoring passengers for security reasons. The reporter sent an email last night, documenting the secrets of the *Sapphire Orchid* and Atabeira."

The captain, still standing, leaned over the solid wood conference table and slid a copy of the printed email.

Jason read it. "This makes me uncomfortable, for sure," Jason said. "But it's what she does, her livelihood, just as you and generations of your family as mariners. We all live a purpose. It doesn't surprise me. And perhaps, if her story gets out, maybe it's the voodoo that has summoned her here, before the black magic comes and sinks your ship and your family reputation."

The captain gave Jason a hard sailor stare. "She won't be telling the world her story," Nickoli said.

The captain walked over to a TV monitor and touched the screen. It activated, showing video clips of security cameras from several directions. The video he selected showed Gail dancing in the elevator. There was audio of the Texan's wife demanding Gail to get away from her husband. The next clip was the most revealing; Gail entering the dining room, leaping across the table, Ian's chair flying back. Stripping, her naked breasts, clawing not only Ian's pants, but the security guards that wrestled her down.

Jason simply smiled. "Looks like all of our secrets, yours, mine, Emerald's, and Atabeira's, will remain intact."

"She leaves the ship in an hour."

Jason came from around the table and shook hands with Nickoli. He wasn't one to judge someone's purpose in life, either Gail's or Nickoli's. Ruth had done a good job raising him. Such things as he saw on the video were trivial, an opportunity for changing one's life. It was the Chuukese in him; everything was a matter of fact not relevant to the next sunrise—island style, no drama, we'll get through this, just as the Haitians, somehow miraculously dealing with their severe hardships for generations.

"You know I will not be on board, Captain," Jason said, leaving.

"But of course, go take care of your children at the orphanage. Do you want me to send you supplies?"

Nickoli smiled. He regularly sent food, and on occasion visited. Often, the captain played for hours with the children. It was how he dealt with the absence of a child of his own.

"Goodbye, you tough Greek, Godspeed," Jason said, wishing him well.

A knock came to Gail's cabin door. Two security guards asked Gail to come with them. "You are to meet the captain."

"He's going to get a piece of my mind," Gail said, angrily, having sat nearly an hour and a half watching thick clouds roll in, a heavy drizzle keeping her from the balcony.

The guards escorted her through the ship's innards, but not downstairs, which was where a bevy of twenty-four-hour activity took place. She went up one flight, the metal staircase changing to a plush carpeted landing. There was a wood panel corridor with paintings of captains, all with a full head of hair and thick beards. The guard opened the conference room door.

The burly captain was waiting, sitting at the endcap of the polished conference table. The maître d' and the female officer who had escorted Gail onboard at Fort Lauderdale sat at opposite sides. Gail was furious, but somehow, after knowing she would meet the man in charge, she managed to gather control. She would use her reporter wits, then get even when back in Tampa on live TV. Perhaps a sixty-minute segment on the cruise ship industry and the environmental impact on the private islands they controlled. For the past hour, as she waited, she considered if she should threaten to expose the truth behind the *Sapphire Orchid* and the Atabeira village. But what stopped her were Jason and the heartbreak of couples who couldn't afford costly infertility clinics, but could afford the cruise. The Atabeira village would get overrun by her revelation, and then the inevitable exploitation of the life-giving sweetness.

"Good morning, Mrs. Stroud," Nickoli said, his accent thick and solid. "My most sincere apologies for detaining you."

The big sailor, his shoulders broad, leaned forward and set his elbows on the thick table. "I'm Captain Lavaki. Have a seat. I trust you had a restful sleep."

Voodoo Cruise

Before continuing, he waited for Gail to sit at the opposite end. A measured, righteous grin buried was beneath his beard.

"Good morning Nickoli," Gail said firmly, suspecting this man loved confrontation. She deliberately did not call him captain, using his first name as a disrespectful act. Every ounce of her emotion wanted to charge and claw his eyes out for imprisoning her.

"Do you know why I detained you?" he asked.

"No," Gail said angrily, bouncing her knee, twisting her shoe against the leg of her chair, a vision of her cabin when she woke, her undergarment and torn dress scattered.

Nickoli shoved a piece of paper to the female officer, who brought it the length of the tight room to Gail.

It was the email she sent last night.

"You deny my right to free speech?" she said, a rage boiling within.

"You aren't in your country," the captain said boldly. "It's my vessel and my country. I am the dictator."

Speechless, she knew there was no law she could summon for protection.

"I take it my story never left your ship."

"Exactly," he said, combing his fingers through his beard. "Emerald has quite an investment in this vessel. So do infertile women like you and the children yet to be born."

Clearly, this confident man was well-practiced in conflict, Gail thought. This was his command. *Control your anger,* she reminded herself. Find his weakness, a chink in his armor, a way to outmaneuver and break down the dominance of his presence.

"When I return to Tampa, I will have my freedom. And certainly, you wouldn't think of throwing me overboard until then."

"Miss Stroud, I'm a reasonable man and an admirer of beautiful woman such as you. I wouldn't want to deny any man the opportunity to make love to you. For it would be a sin for such beauty not to provide the greatest pleasure life brings us men."

Grinding her teeth, Gail became undone. "Chauvinist pig," she blurted.

"Yes, a chauvinist, but no pig. But my Sherrita might agree with both when I'm with another mistress making love to bring me a Greek son. But you, too, are of breeding quality and in a hurry to do such."

"What! Don't be ridiculous." Gail had no idea how to get control of this conversation.

The captain signaled for the maître d' to go to the monitor. They watched as he tapped the screen. The twenty-second video clip began.

"So what, I danced in the elevator. There's no crime." Gail's mind whirled. She had only a vague recollection of last night. And a notion that Marie had hooked her up with one of the casino staff. Her mind raced. What happened? Was there a video of the casino, placing the bets as instructed by Marie? Of her cabin, engaging in sex with the dealer? *Oh, my God! No, this can't be happening! My career!*

"Show her the good one, Mauricio," the captain instructed.

Gail cringed as Mauricio touched the scream.

The video began with her entering the dining room, something she had no memory of. Then, as she witnessed herself lunging for Ian, she gasped and wanted to crawl under the table.

"Ian!" she said. "Eeooh, I did that?" Gail wondered if the video was doctored, but quickly dispensed the thought—not in such few hours.

She watched as she tore off her dress, her bare breasts on display— onlookers' eyes wide and focused upon her. She grew beet-red, embarrassed with all she exposed in the classy dining room; nude, with nothing on, when security guards wrestled her away.

"You drugged me," she said. "I can make that accusation to your bosses and the cruise line."

Voodoo Cruise

"Go ahead," Nickoli said. "The video is more believable. At least half of the world will not believe you. You will be naked on the Internet for all eternity for all men to enjoy and fantasize over you, and your children to witness should you be so fortunate to breed."

The video ended. Gail felt defeated. It was likely the video would go viral, given how well-known she was in Tampa. There would be no job interviews. Her producer would be the first to play it; ratings would soar. Aging television anchors such as her in regional markets were disposable. There were many pretty broadcasters on the ladder rungs below, eager to take her spot.

"Mrs. Stroud," Nickoli said. "I must ask you to peacefully disembark my vessel immediately. The items you purchased onboard, we are keeping. I've ordered your personal belongings delivered to the dock."

Nickoli stood to indicate it was time to remove Gail from the ship.

"What? You can't do that," she said, standing, trying to get eye to eye with him.

"Watch me," Nickoli said, his presence ominous and growing impatient. But before he could leave, the conference door burst open. It was the second officer.

"Captain, a storm."

"So?" grunted the captain, angry at being interrupted for such a trivial matter.

"A tropical depression has formed with no warning at all."

Though there was no window in the room, the second officer pointed in the direction of the stern. "Black clouds on the southeast horizon, sir."

"Calm down, young man," the captain said, gathering his temper. "Haven't you ever seen the heavens open up?"

"Miss Stroud." The lady officer signaled Gail to leave by escorting her by her elbow.

Gail wanted to stall, to witness the concern of the second officer.

The female officer directed Gail out. But not before Gail heard the words "tropical storm" and "the itinerary needs to change."

The captain quickly departed, the second office trailing behind, both heading toward the bridge. "Our passengers pay good money for us to make sure they are safe and have fun, and the weather is always good," the captain was saying. "Head north, avoid the rough waters so our guests don't get seasick and mess up my bathrooms. We don't have enough staff to handle that."

A moment later Gail found herself in a small elevator with two security guards. "Can I return to my room?"

"No, captain has cleared your room. You are no longer a passenger and must leave immediately." The guard handed Gail her purse. The pair escorted her from the elevator to the pier, exiting from the starboard stern. Her belongings, stuffed in a clear plastic bag, waited at the bottom of the metal ramp.

"Plastic bag! Couldn't you have provided more hospitable luggage!" Gail grumbled as she walked down the ramp and collected her belongings.

"It's about to rain cats and dogs," the security guard said. "We are doing you a favor."

Gail spun the bag to verify the clothing Jason had plucked off Alligator Alley was mostly there. The voodoo dolls, once again knotted in an embrace, were squashed against the plastic, the size twelve shoe apparently left in her cabin.

"I wonder where Jason is," she said sarcastically. "According to the dolls we are to be together."

Chapter 13

Infuriated, a vindictiveness raging inside, Gail walked the entire distance of the pier and the towering *Sapphire Orchid*, clearing the bow just as the heavens opened. A wind-whipped deluge erupted. Her hair went straight. She'd no umbrella and no help from the ship's crew. She was left alone on the dock, except for a hurried staff preparing the *Orchid* for the unexpected departure.

Tour buses had not arrived because the only vessel in port decided not to let passengers disembark. Gail heard the captain's announcement, explaining the decision: "Due to impending inclement weather," his deep Greek voice echoing, "the *Sapphire Orchid* will return to Atabeira."

"Lucky them," Gail said, drenched head to toe, the leather on her flats struggling to hold from the water that splashed at her feet.

The rain was relentless. The thick ropes used to secure the *Orchid* had been cast off. The massive steel structure edged from its berth. *What to do next?* she thought, searching for some cover. "How to get to the United States?" In the driving rain, she unknotted the plastic bag and dug through her clothes looking for a something to put over her head.

Then she realized something; she had no cash. "I'm flat broke!" There wasn't a soul around.

"There must be an embassy, or government office, or police station. Perhaps in the center of town?"

The rain beat down.

As she held the bag over her head like a sack of grain, despair overcame her. The thought of how her husband had financially cleaned her out arrived. She had no cash. She had no child.

She came to an octagonal tourist information booth that provided some limited shelter. *Where from here?* she thought, every inch of her dripping wet.

Listening to the horn blast of the *Sapphire Orchid* signaling its goodbye, Gail saw in the distance a strip mall, where she could dash to make her way to Road Town.

As she headed off in the driving rain, tears rolled from the corners of her eyes. "Where have I gone wrong in my life?" The dream that kept her going each day, the notion somehow she'd become a mother—Gail sobbed, the deluge making no difference anymore. She splashed sadly through the parking lot. The glue in her soaked right shoe gave way, the leather lost its grip, and the shoe came apart. As she began limping, the crushed shell gravel that made up the parking lot cut her foot. Mud splashed up to her knees. Her progress was slow. Crying, Gail felt she could not go on anymore. She broke down and started bawling. She was alone in a world that had caved in. It was difficult enough living with the choices she made. But what she witnessed of herself in the dining room, not remembering, was the final straw. "Ian of all people," she cried. It had likely destroyed her friendship with the only person she could trust, Vera.

Stranded, broke, and embarrassed, she had no doubt someday the videos would make it to YouTube. That was how things worked in the age of Internet media. Her career was finished.

Voodoo Cruise

The sky started to flash with lightning. Gail, in a limp, raced toward a row of stucco retail stalls at the corner of the lot. She dropped the plastic bag. It split and her clothes spilled out. She squatted to shove her belongings back, but the plastic ripped more. Tears flowing, hands trembling, on the verge a complete breakdown, she heard a voice, as a man stepped from around the corner of the building.

Gail's breathing immediately seized.

"Here, let me help you with that," the man said.

Gail looked at him, frightened. He was short, with black hair.

He helped Gail to her feet. "It's okay. I'm here to help you."

"Who are you?" Gail asked, eyes swollen, her face blotchy.

"I own this little jewelry store. Why don't you come inside and dry off?"

She was hesitant.

"My name is Milan. But you must wait a minute. I locked my keys inside."

Gail watched as he skillfully used a tool to pick the lock on the metal barricade that protected the unit. Shoving back the collapsible gate, he jimmied the latch to get inside. "Come and get dry."

Gail obliged.

"What are you doing out here?" Gail asked, cautious, sniffling, watching as he wasn't looking for the keys he locked inside. She suspected he was breaking into the place. But she needed him to help her, give her money, and she'd immediately leave if he'd tripped some sort of silent alarm.

"I was about to asked you the same question," Milan said.

"The captain tossed me off the cruise ship."

"Why?" he asked.

"It's a long story. How about you?" Gail queried.

"I have to take an expensive ring to St. Thomas. I forgot it when I left the shop yesterday."

"Thanks for inviting me in, but all I need is some money to get to the airport."

Milan inspected the shop; all the jewelry was locked in a safe. Not saying a word, he went behind a glass counter and crouched in front of the safe and started turning the dial. "I'll loan you some in a minute, as soon as I open the safe."

Gail grew nervous. She wanted to run. But she had no shoes and wouldn't get far.

She saw a suitcase. "Does that belong to you?"

"It was left by a tourist. Go ahead and use it."

As he continued to work the safe, Gail took her wet clothes and repacked them. Cautiously, she edged to the doorway. She heard the click of the safe.

"Ah, we have it. This safe always gives me a hard time."

Milan repeated why he was here. "There's a gold ring that needs resizing. I promised my best customer, across the channel in Saint Thomas, I'd have it resized by tomorrow."

He removed a small cash box. "I'll loan this to you if you give me your contact information."

"That's nice of you," Gail said. "Let me write it down on one of your business cards."

Milan walked over to the emptied cash register and pulled a card from atop the drawer.

Gail scrawled fake contact information. "I work in Tampa, and when I get home, I'll wire you the money."

"Good," he said. "Call this number on the card."

Gail thought for a moment. The name on the card must be that of the owner, and it wasn't Milan.

"I don't know you that well. I'm giving you only a hundred dollars. That should be enough to get you to the airport, a night's stay in a hotel, some food, and enough to contact whoever you need." He looked at the card. "Tampa? I doubt I'll see this money again, but you appear to be an honest woman. I'll take a chance."

"I'll prove you wrong. You'll get this back," she said, backing away, stashing the cash into her soggy pocket. She lifted the old suitcase and left the store, still suspecting he was robbing the place.

Initially, Gail started to walk inconspicuously beneath the awning like a tourist, along the closed units of the deserted marketplace. She turned at the corner unit so she wasn't in Milan's sight. And as soon as she could, she became invisible, racing back into the driving rain, limping across another large lot, but paved this time, heading toward town. At midway, as the deluge persisted, the headlights of a red pickup raced toward her. "Oh no, police! They will find the stolen money on me."

The small truck fully separated a large puddle. Gail veered away, but it was clear the truck was heading for her as it pulled alongside. Nervous, Gail walked briskly, diverting her direction. But a voice called her name as the window rolled down. "Gail, it's me, Jason."

She stopped and turned. Her eyes wide and in a state of shock, she was desperate to get out of the drenching rain. Gail opened the passenger door and climbed in, setting the suitcase at her feet. Jason wore raingear and at first glance she couldn't see his face.

"Can you take me somewhere I can get some help?" she asked.

Jason pulled back the hood and chuckled. "We meet again."

Again, Gail expected a personality clash, but noticed a softer demeanor. There was no provocation or inflammatory statements. She wasn't in the mood for it anyway. It would not have been a good thing for either of them—her raging anger for men buried within. Another man added to the list, Captain Nickoli Lavaki.

"I take it you had some issue on the ship," Jason said, not revealing what he knew.

"Yes, I screwed up," Gail confessed.

"How?" Jason asked, not driving anywhere just yet.

"Email—but why am I telling you this! You know more than me about the ship."

Jason nodded. "Yes, I do. There's lots, including the fact passengers are in danger."

"Danger? Why don't you tell someone?"

"What do you think I've been doing? Commerce has gotten in the way, once again. Just as it has for centuries."

Gail knew what he meant; the deeper meaning.

"I'd sit here and talk, but I must get to the orphanage," Jason said.

"Orphanage?"

"Yes, that's partly why I'm here."

"That explains the van at Port Everglades."

"Van?"

"Yes, from my balcony, I saw you load children into the passenger van. And oh, by the way, why did you offer to pay my way onto the ship? You don't like me!"

Jason smiled. "So, you think the guy that has now rescued you twice in one week doesn't like you?"

Gail's jaw dropped. She was speechless. He had a point.

"You're soaking wet. How about we get you to a dry place and square away your troubles? And I'll tell you a bit more about what's going on. But you must promise me it will be off the record."

Gail wished she had an alternative at that moment. But she didn't. "Off the record, agreed."

Jason released the brake. The way out took him by the retail shops that Gail had come from.

"I think one of those stalls is being robbed," Gail said. She pointed to the door that Milan had broken into. "I was in there because I thought he was the owner. He'd broken into the safe."

Voodoo Cruise

Jason stopped, reversed, and pulled to the door and shined the headlights inside. "Whoever you saw, he's gone. But you might not want to get involved, the police will detain you if you are trying to get back home. Besides, the inventory belongs to the cruise ship company. They own many of the stores these days. Much of it is overpriced and of little value."

"You know," Gail said, recalling what Milan looked like, "he looked like the guy I saw when we left Fort Lauderdale. He seemed most interested in watching the ship and what you were doing. I couldn't get a good look from the balcony, but when I saw the vanload of children drive off and you disappear, he appeared to be the same guy that left immediately after."

Jason shrugged his shoulders, not seeming to care.

Gail wiped the moisture dripping from her forehead. Not a single part of her was dry.

"I'm a fortunate person," Jason said, as he drove off. "I've been given the means and responsibility to care for people."

Driving through the dead streets of Tortola, Jason revealed a piece of his life to Gail. Of how Ruth found and raised him. That he'd no memory of his parents. But he did learn who they were. His father was a navy captain and taken time off to sail around the world on his catamaran. His mother was a schoolteacher. He shared the story of Atabeira, which matched up with what she'd already heard. And his belief that this sudden tropical storm was black magic to tempt the ship back to Atabeira. He shared his conversation with the dogmatic captain, his rising frustration and refusal to listen.

"Don't you want to warn the authorities?"

"You are a newsperson; would you believe it if I told you?"

"Probably not," Gail said. "But I might run the story anyway."

"What I asked of the mambo is no one gets killed."

"And what did she say?"

"She gave me one of those possessed grins and rambled on in a Creole I couldn't understand. But my read was the black magic she brings will be as needed, to prevent any ship from entering the lagoon forever."

"Does that mean sink the ship?"

"I don't know," Jason said. "The frogs were a final warning. There were several previous warnings, the latest on Sunday. It was likely the mambo who stopped the engine on that cruise ship in the Gulf of Mexico, sending a message."

"I saw the newscast. The television in the Fort Lauderdale terminal went black a few seconds into the report. But how do you know it wasn't just a mechanical problem?"

"That's just it," Jason said. "You don't know. How do you know there is an afterlife? Yet, such a belief is prevalent worldwide."

"I get your point," Gail said, her mind working as a reporter. "It ties to the fact that no one will believe a tiny Haitian fishing village can sink a mighty cruise ship."

"Exactly!" Jason said.

The pickup splashed through the grid of Road Town, winding its way along a back street and up the side of a substantial hill. A virtual river ran along the berm, washing onto the roadway at every sharp curve. Gail could see the storm didn't bother Jason. He was in his element. "I'm not sure if the rain will break," Jason said. "The mambo wants the *Sapphire Orchid* back in Atabeira. It's unlikely she'll allow this storm to relent until she's sure they are heading her way."

Gail couldn't believe what she heard. How could he deduce all this? "Why doesn't the mambo wait until the ship returns on the next itinerary?" Gail asked, with the inquiring mind of a reporter.

"Why do you ask so many questions?" Jason said.

"I'm trained that way."

Voodoo Cruise

"Voodoo is about the timing of nature. Such as the rogue wave that struck a cruise ship in the South Atlantic many years ago. The rogue was to occur at a specific moment in time, regardless if the ship was there or not. The ship could have stayed at its last anchorage thirty minutes longer, thus missing the formation and collision with the rogue. What was it that drove the captain's decision to position his ship as such? Karma! The *Concordia* was about a captain showing his lover a better view. What was it that put the girlfriend into the *Concordia* captain's life? Tragedy can be natural, human, or mechanical. The twister you saw would have happened at that exact moment regardless of the ship's presence. The mambo has her ways of affecting the timing of things. Likely, the natural events she knows are coming. She'll use it to do what she believes must be done. That's why she's calling the *Sapphire Orchid* to Atabeira. Something's about to happen. She wants the *Orchid* there for that reason."

"Jason, where were you last night?" Gail asked, the idea striking her. Gail wondered if it was Jason's shoe she found in her room. "Did you go to the dining room?" She was concerned if he was aware of her behavior last night. Did he see her naked? She was sure Marie or Lou might have said something. Because, from the videos, Gail could tell that Lou and Marie had followed her out.

"No," Jason lied. "I was in my cabin. It'd been a long day; communicating with Emerald's executives to get their captain and company to cooperate—but to no avail. I've done my work. Time to move on to my business on this island."

The road topped out after one last push up a steep incline, floodlights illuminating the area as they arrived. A one-story schoolhouse with several structures linked by a covered walkway sat near the center of the tabletop plateau. The place looked much like a summer sports camp Gail attended in the Poconos Mountains of Pennsylvania when she was a teenager.

Children arrived from all directions, a variety of skin colors pouring from every building, greeting Jason's pickup in the driving rain, not bothered by the weather. Jason handed Gail his raincoat as they left the pickup. Dodging the battering deluge, they raced a short distance to a covered walkway. The orphanage director, a well-fed Caribbean woman, waited beneath the awning.

"Welcome home, my second son." The big woman was polite and kind, the temperament of a patient and loving mother.

"Gail this is Principal Pearl."

"This is a first for Jason, a beautiful woman at his side?" Pearl said, broadcasting a warm smile.

Gail blushed. She wasn't comfortable with the observation. In the television industry, there was never enough beauty for the camera. Extreme physical criticism was the norm, with plenty of suggestions for beauty enhancements.

"Pearl, she's a stranded traveler," Jason said.

"That's too bad, son. Helping a stray I understand, but taking a wife to bring your own children into the world is what's right for you."

Gail waited for Jason to react to her suggestion. But as she watched, Jason quickly turned his attention to a young child clinging to the principal's skirt, lifting the child into his arm. "I have many children, as you can see, Pearl. Our friend here will be staying the night and traveling home in the morning. Can you help her get settled?"

Pearl took Gail by the hand. "You'll shower in the girls' dormitory, while I find dry clothes." The motherly principal walked off with Gail.

There's no warm water, Gail thought, as she showered. *I'm in the tropics, why would we ever need it?* she considered.

Pearl returned with a single-piece dress that fit her rather well, showing her figure. It was colorful and displayed a large toucan bird design. She also brought a pair of sandals.

Voodoo Cruise

"Let me take care of your hair, my darling," Pearl said, guiding Gail to a chair near one of the bunk beds. "I will make you Caribbean beautiful."

"How nice, thank you!" Gail couldn't believe how pleasant the woman was.

"The dress belongs to one of my teachers. She is young and with bosoms as wholesome as yours," she noted, as she sat next to Gail on the bed and began to brush out Gail's knotted hair.

Gail felt safe here, and amazed that Jason had something to do with this place.

"You came with Jason?" Pearl asked, initiating a conversation.

"Yes," Gail answered, understanding the question phrased in a manner that required further explanation.

"You come from the *Sapphire Orchid*, don't you?"

"Yes," Gail said enjoying the attention she was getting. Several of the girl children had gathered to watch.

"Where is your husband?"

"There is none."

"Ah, like the children, you are orphaned in love."

Gail nodded as a tear filled her eye.

"We will make you look like a young island girl, with braids and beads to make you pretty for Jason."

"Jason!" Gail grew stiff.

"He needs a good woman. And you are the first he's brought here. He must like you."

"I doubt that. It's all a horrible accident."

"Nothing's an accident," Pearl said. "He takes care of the children. Only good things come to such a person. You are delivered by the hand of God."

The lady finished the length of a braid and continued, stripping out another section of Gail's thick brown hair. "Aren't you a believer in God?"

"Ah . . . well, yes, when I was a child, but I have gotten away from it."

"God never abandons you," she said.

Gail had to think about this. An hour ago, she was bawling her eyes out in the pouring rain. Now she was sitting in a comfortable place, high on a hillside, cared for by a rather nice lady, prettying her up just as her stylist doddled over her at the TV station. In that thought, she saw why Ruth lived in the Caribbean. Life was simple, people focused only on daily essentials, no television. There was little stress in their lives. No motivation for materiality.

"Let me put flowers in your hair." She slipped two hibiscus flowers into the braids.

"Turn around."

Gail felt she was back in the studio with her adoring makeup artists.

"Allow me," the principal said as she put lipstick on Gail.

"Finished." She held up a mirror.

Gail was delighted with what she saw. "I look so different. Not like on TV."

"Let's go see Jason," Pearl said.

"What, ah, I'm not interested in him. Or, he's not interested in me. You've got this all wrong."

"So do I, you say? A woman of my age and experience?" Pearl laughed. "It's no matter. I know men. It's every girl's right without a husband to look beautiful and ready for love."

"What is Jason doing?" Gail asked.

"He's meeting with teachers and caretakers and paying bills; doing the not-so-fun stuff."

Voodoo Cruise

Gail was speechless. This was a side of a man she'd not known. Was there such a man on this earth? Much of her married life was amongst a different class of people, though some well-intentioned. Not much discussion amongst her Tampa social circles about truly humanitarian efforts. Jason was authentic, with little personal time for anything else. Explained why he wasn't married and not a part of her world.

"Exactly," the principal said.

"What?" Gail said. "I didn't say anything."

"You didn't. I can see it in your spirit and in your mood."

It dawned on Gail that these people didn't live with television. Their people-skills evolved differently. Reading someone's mood might not be all that difficult, given everyone lived as a cohesive community.

"You'll need an umbrella," Pearl said.

They went out on the porch. Pearl opened the oversize umbrella with multicolor panels and laughed as they both tried to fit beneath. "Let's go see Jason."

Briskly, they hurried across the soft grass, shortcutting to the adjacent building, giggling like high school girls. Inside were children. She guessed they were age seven to ten mostly, and well-behaved, happy, and obviously well cared for. There was plenty of staff.

It was lunch time.

Where does Jason get the funds to support such a venture? Gail wondered, the reporter in her resurrecting her curiosity.

"Wait here," Pearl said.

Seconds later, she returned with Jason from an office located behind the cafeteria kitchen.

There stood Gail, looking beautiful. She could feel it. Her hair done as never before—the tight knots of the braids whispering she was beautiful, lipstick, thick and rose red. And her dress, tight around her waist and colorful. She glowed.

Jason's eyes grew big as his gaze traced Gail's figure. His cheeks grew flushed.

"You look stunning," Jason said. "The Caribbean look suits you."

It was the first time in a long time she'd heard she was stunning from someone other than her makeup team. From a physically fit and handsome man, the compliment served to reduce her defenses—a wall built from difficult times and ignorant people who had surrounded her for years. For the first time, she realized how jaded she'd become, and that the world was entirely different outside of her work routine. That in fact, she was merely a reader of information on air, and not a liver of her life.

There it was, the rawness, the comment Jason had said to her on Alligator Alley—a reader. Gail smiled glowingly as she realized what he meant and instantly forgave him. His provocation was simply an observation from an entirely different and legitimate cultural perspective, nothing more than his thought on life. One that focused on awareness, simplicity, sustainability, and realism. Like the lives that surrounded her in the cafeteria, in need, but very much alive.

"Thank you for that compliment, Jason," Gail said, crisscrossing her feet, standing at the typical camera angle that made her appear thinner, showing the length and curve of her frame.

"You clean up well. Pearl did a great job."

But there was something else in his look. Gail couldn't quite pin the expression. Like they'd been closer than she knew, a fondness, or resolution that comes after making love. Jason's smile was warm, wanting, and affectionate.

"Lunch?" Jason said, his face still a bit flushed.

"For sure," Gail answered. She'd not eaten all morning.

What a journey, she thought as Jason escorted her down a long cafeteria table to open seats at the end.

"So, you are a humanitarian," Gail said. "How did I miss that in you?"

"It's been my purpose in life. I have, sort of a responsibility."

"Responsibility?"

"Off the record?" Jason asked as a way of reminding her, the requirement for his openness.

Gail nodded and batted her eyes, "Yes, but of course."

Jason paused for a moment. He was considering. "You know what, I'd rather wait. I'm not ready to discuss it. Perhaps later."

"I guess I have no choice," Gail said. "I can only hope you will let me inside your head as some point."

"I'm sure you'll find a way," Jason said. "There is a ferry to St. Thomas early in the morning and an eleven o'clock flight to Fort Lauderdale. I'll see you get home safely."

"That's kind of you, Jason, I'll pay you back when I get back to the States." Gail had no choice but to accept his generosity. In the same thought, she wanted to ask how he earned a living. How he funded the orphanage. No doubt asking would be too personal yet. She didn't want to offend him, given she was in his good company and heading back home. And she wanted it on the record for when she arrived home and researched who he was. But for now, she figured Ruth helped him, or perhaps funded much of his efforts.

They spent the afternoon hours with the children and the teachers. Jason asked Gail to tell them a bit about herself and her job.

Gail relived her career, particularly the 9/11 incident. After all these years, it was still difficult to convey. She'd shown a side few people knew.

Raining in heavy cycles much of the afternoon, it finally let up after dinner.

"You know, I don't have to go home right away," Gail said. She'd taken the entire week off.

"You might want to get back as soon as you can. Tomorrow's flight might be the last if this storm gets worse. Possibly this may become a hurricane. I'm staying here for a few more days, then off to the Pacific."

"Why there?" she asked as Jason escorted Gail to the girls' dormitory for the evening.

"Got some business to tend to."

Jason didn't add any more.

"This is where we part," Jason said, as they came to the porch steps.

"I want to thank you for everything you've done, Jason. I was wrong about you and wish you well."

Gail affectionately lifted to her toes and kissed him on the cheek. "Goodnight."

"It's likely once you go inside the girls will ask you to tell them a story."

Gail froze. Think up a story all by herself? Not rely upon a teleprompter?

"Pearl is usually the storyteller, but it would be nice to give her a break. I'm guessing she'll ask you."

"Can I read them a book? I'm a pretty good reader," Gail joked.

"You know what?" Jason said. "That'll work. There are some children's books in back. And if you want to dig a bit more into who I am, I suggest you read *The Missing Night* to them."

Gail turned and entered the wooden, dormitory-style building.

Chapter 14

In the girls' dormitory, there was pleasant chatter. The older girls tended to the youngest. For Gail, it was an incredible sight, a kinship amongst these alone children. She questioned again where Jason got the money for all this; the mountaintop facility, well staffed and well kept.

A young child about the age of six approached and crawled into her lap, holding a book.

"Can you read us a bedtime story?" the child asked.

She was a beautiful, a dark-skinned girl, her permanent teeth just starting to grow in.

"How can I resist?" Gail answered. Several children, obviously accustomed to being read to, gathered on the floor with legs folded, forming a semicircle at the base of Gail's bunk.

The book the child handed her was thick, the font larger, with artful renderings at the beginning of each chapter. "How much am I supposed to read to you?" she asked. "To read it all would take all night."

"All of it," another child replied as she crawled onto the bunk and curled up next to Gail.

Gail thumbed through the book. On the back cover was a gold, circular emblem embossed with "RJA Foundation." A clue to Jason's wealth, Gail thought. Some sort of charity in Jason's and Ruth's name. The same emblem she'd seen in his Jeep.

"You should know I'm a pretty good reader," Gail said to the gathered girls. "I read every day." Gail had to pause. There was that word, reader. She considered if Jason was well-read.

"I read lots when I was each of your ages," she said to the children, all eyes fixed upon her. "I love words. And the first thing I do when I read a book, I look to see who wrote it as respect for the creator of so many words."

The book cover was a black-and-white drawing of an island atoll with a bright light shining from the center, like a beacon into the nighttime sky. "The title of the book is *The Missing Night*," Gail said. "Oh, it is the story Jason asked me to read." She looked for the name of the author. But there was none. *It must be self-published*, she considered.

"Let's get at it," she said to the anxious eyes of those waiting to hear her lift the words from the pages.

"Chapter One," Gail read to the children.

"From the crystal blue core of the Upitao atoll a brilliant light beaconed, as if the tallest waterfall in the world had inverted and shot a cascade of sparkling diamonds up and into the navigator's nocturnal sky. Colorful light-spears radiated an entire prism in glowing octagonal, pentagonal, and hexagonal shapes."

Gail paused. "Oh, how descriptive. Just like the book cover." She continued.

"The Polynesians that relied upon the nighttime beam to travel their equatorial waters said the Pacific had swallowed a star—the light's source, legendary, and a mystery—never known, and forbidden because of its unexplainable, almost routine appearance.

"For a generation, the beacon appeared eight days after the blue fin tuna stopped biting, exactly at the rise of the full moon. Two days prior,

a school of broadback black manta rays would arrive with white-tipped wings that spanned eight meters. But the mantas stopped short, at a breach that nourished the atoll. The mantas refused to enter. Instead, they circled as sentries, stationed at the deepest part of the breach, warding off a gathering of sharks that grew in numbers as the sunset began."

Again, Gail paused. She looked out upon the children and thought for a moment how great it would be to bring a child into the world, or perhaps adopt several of the children at her feet.

"The coming of the bright light was a mixed blessing to the atoll's village. Fishermen complained the absent blue fin left their trolling hooks barren for too many days—even the swarming hungry sharks refused to snack. The women of the peaceful village that occupied the equatorial side of the island complained because the nighttime brightness made their sleepless children cranky, fidgety, and whiny. And the frigate birds and cockatoos that chirped a litany of lullabies from breadfruit limbs had mysteriously fled to the Mortlocks, a two-day travel when the trade winds blew firm, creating a noticeable absence of song.

"For the inhabitants and wildlife of this pleasant, self-sufficient island, the Missing Night, as the villagers called it, was as if God had deliberately decided to skip to the next day.

"But the beacon made up for its cyclical annoyance, because for some mysterious reason, the island's taro grew taller, meatier, and more plentiful. The breadfruit and coconuts that tossed in the wind and shaded the central pathway tasted sweeter, and ripened much faster. Spiny lobsters, chased by a rising column of plankton from the atoll's seemingly endless depths, scurried from the deep blue into the clearness of the grass shallows, behaving as lemmings, gathering at the lip of the shoreline. As if they could breathe, they seemed to want to claw from the grasses and scoot across the crescent that housed the village, then

scuttle along the mud footpaths of the taro patch to escape across the chunky coral beach into the tumbling ocean breaks of the southern shore.

"To ward off the sleeplessness that came with the missing night, the villagers toiled in shifts to harvest the taro, shuck the coconut, mash breadfruit, and trap the gather of lobsters. And when the curvature of the setting full moon drew tight and starved, and the silhouette of the ripening dawn started to live, the beacon's radiance weakened and accepted death, allowing the self-reliant Upitaoans to sleep once more."

Turning the page, looking at the children, Gail saw in their eyes a hunger for affection.

"And—then it began—with the death of the full moon—big, black-eyed flicker fish, with large glistening, crimson scales and translucent fins, with exploded stomachs, floated from deep beneath the column of plankton. The atoll's caldera became thick with dead fish. So thick, it bound and halted the cutting keel of any canoe that ventured forth. And before the warmth of the saltwater degraded the black-eyed flicker's buttery meat, the circling mantas would strip off in pairs, glide through the breach and into the abyss with wide-open lobes, vacuuming the plankton beneath. And when they were belly-full, the mat of flickers disturbed and tossed; the graceful broadbacks returned to their duty station to allow for another pair to feed.

"It wasn't until every manta had feasted that they broke rank, opening the atoll for the gather of short fin makos, great hammerheads, silver tips, white tips, and black tips—sharks of the Austronesian Pacific. The grainy skins jetted through the breach in such mass the channel looked like the jet-black stream of an inking octopus. For hours, the seawater boiled. Sharks bit and chomped and leapt and shredded and swarmed the dead flickers, crowding each other, until finally, the *atoll was returned to its natural state, clean and clear and crystal, reflecting a blessed turquoise blueness—the color of God's eyes."*

"This sounds like an interesting story. What do you think, should I read some more?" Gail asked.

"Yes," the girls said in unison, enjoying the motherly tone and practiced pace of Gail's storytelling.

"Okay, just a bit more and it's bedtime."

"Chapter Two . . . Mau Palu, a young boy, lifted the anchor attached to a coir rope in the bow of his grandfather's canoe and flung the rusted weight over his right shoulder. Cautiously, he snuck from the family hut into the splendid glow of the fading beacon. With a brisk trade wind kissing his olive skin, he followed the central pathway through the coconut grove toward the open beach that led to the breach. The soles of his youthful feet, tough and thick from climbing coconut palms, gripped the gritty, washed over coral. Gingerly, he made his way across the maze of trickling channels that laced the hardened beach. With the lapping Pacific on his left, Mau made his way, another one hundred meters to the breach. He paused, as all Polynesians do when they approach the sea. Read its mood, the angle of the chop across the lightening horizon, the height of the tide, which said something wasn't quite right with the atoll. He watched the dorsal fin of a palm-size red snapper squiggle in a panic through a crack in the draining coral, escaping—its behavior frantic, odd. The Pacific, rushing across the atoll's barren beach to Mau, seemed a bit more powerful, one layer thicker than the last full moon.

"Gazing across the dwindling glow of the bright light as dawn arrived, Mau recalled one of a lifetime of stories passed along by the elder navigators who populated the islands of Micronesia."

Gail paused and looked up at the ceiling, contemplating. *Did Jason write this story?*

She continued. *"Soon, dawn, the youngest sister, will awake, thought Mau. If she's pleasant and smiles the yellow glow of the sun, the sea will be calm at least until noon. If she's cranky and fire red, storms will arrive just after the afternoon apex.*

"Shouldering his anchor, Mau became guilt-ridden. He was about to defy a generation of elders and Upitaoan Law: do not disturb the mystical light. He would die if he entered the water before the bald crest of the full moon was swallowed by the Pacific horizon. The elders warned the beacon opened to the earth's core, collecting evil-doers for all eternity, and he too, would be sucked down with them should he swim before the bright light sleeps. But the curiosity of a self-reliant child could wait no longer. Mau sensed something was not right with the atoll. What was the truth about the light that inhabited his perfect island? Why was the tide talking to him differently than he learned? He heard the elders whisper their concern; the island was sinking.

"As the horizon became morning, and the radiance of the bright light sank in the depths, Mau waded to the lip of the breach, the long rope trailing behind. Soon, he thought, peering into the channel that nourished the atoll, two broadbacks will pass.

"Slipping his hands through a pair of braided loops, he fed out the anchor, allowing it to drop but not hit the water. He rocked the anchor back and forth, building momentum until it spun like a propeller. Slowly, he worked to change the apex until the anchor swirled overhead, feeding rope until the radius measured the drop of a free-falling coconut. His arms strained as he waited for the broadbacks to appear. And on the final rotation, before he was about to quit, the hook at its maximum length, the torque taut, a pair of mantas entered the channel.

Mau released, letting the anchor fly toward the awakening day, skipping in front of the second manta, quickly sinking. He slipped his foot into the bottom loop and dove off into the channel alongside the passing manta just as the hook of the anchor snagged the pectoral fin. Mau gripped the loops as the coir pulled taut with a sudden jerk and rapid acceleration. The tightened loops bound his wrists and feet as he trailed behind the giant submarine bird within its slipstream."

Gail found herself captivated by the story. "Wow, let me catch my breath. Do you like the story?"

Wide-eyed nods came from the enthralled listeners.

"The ocean swished and swirled as Mau's swimmer's body towed along. Beneath him, Mau could see the fading beacon was barely visible. He clung and waited for the manta to dive and disappear as it'd done many times before. And as he'd practiced, Mau took his last breath of air.

"With the curve of his grandfather's anchor tightly secured, the broadback broke from the ocean as if it knew how to fly in the thinness of the air, then dove straight and swift and steep and down. Mau said to himself to count what he practiced; one minute, with one minute to return to the surface.

"As he descended, the depths grew bright, so bright Mau pulled onto the manta's back and lay with his head close, using the manta as shade. He could feel plankton flick at his body. Deeper and deeper Mau fell, clearing his ears and slowing his heart rate as he had practiced—until abruptly, the manta rolled and the anchor dropped free.

"Hands bound by the loops and dragged by the weight, Mau tumbled downward, unable to free himself. But he did not panic, for he knew it would mean death. And he reminded himself of his grandfather's great teachings: Upitaoans are descendants of bold navigators who are brave and fearless and venture the uncharted. It explained why his young heart felt compelled to discover the origin of the bright light.

"Into the brilliant vertigo, Mau descended. The light blinding, he could not see. The seawater sparkled as if the sun sat outside the window of a grand cathedral and beamed its most brilliant illumination directly through its multitude of magnificent stained-glass windows. There were sounds, like the distant clatter of bottlenose dolphins. Clinks and clicks, which grew louder and thicker and blended. Is there a bottom? he thought as the anchor pulled him deeper through the dizzying light. He'd reached forty-five seconds. A fear entered his thoughts as to the consequences of discovering the unthinkable and that he'd get sucked into the vortex of hell. But suddenly, the coir rope, with its tight nooses, loosened. There was a smashing crunch, like the anchor had crushed into a bed of brittle clams and broken coral. He felt as if a thousand bees started to sting him. His arms and legs and knees and feet felt blistering pinches all over his skin, as if he'd been entangled within the tentacle snares of a large jellyfish. Without any swimming goggles Mau was unable to see the stinging things that surrounded him.

"Quickly, Mau freed his hands and feet. He was holding his breath and knew he would soon pass out if he didn't quickly return to the surface.

"Once again, he slowed his heart rate. His blood was nearly depleted of oxygen. He struggled to control his thoughts. But it was his fear that any moment he would be sucked through the blistering brightness by whatever was on the other side, and perhaps it would be God himself, angry that his secret had been revealed and soon the entire earth would know.

"Panicked, Mau swam for the surface as fast as he could, until finally, for what seemed an eternity, he reached the surface.

"With a deep and endless inhale, Mau, desperate, re-oxygenating, tried to catch his breath. Buoyed by the saltwater, he flipped onto his back and rested, his lungs hungry. The morning sun was coming on bright and strong. His arms and legs and backside bled from skin slices *no longer than one centimeter. Did he discover the thorns at the gates of hell? Or an impenetrable layer of glowing jellyfish that sealed in the sinners, sucked into the molten earth core, captured for the eternity as described by the elders?*

"As Mau contemplated his failed attempt, as the saltwater stung the cuts and slices on his bleeding back, something bumped and tickled along his calf. A dead big-eyed flicker fish surfaced and bobbed next to him. Within seconds more appeared and surfaced until the ocean was thick and full with dead flickers. He tried to swim toward shore but couldn't; the layer of fish was too thick.

"I'm bleeding, thought Mau. Once the mantas are done feeding, the sharks will come and trail my blood.

"Kicking his feet, he tried to shove the flickers aside and swim in the direction of the village. But when he looked across the endless layer of dead fish and saw dorsal fins entering the breach, slicing and feasting sharks at the outer edge of the flickers, his mind raced in another panic. It will be the great hammerheads that will eat me. They're aggressive and devour humans.

"Mau bravely prepared himself for death, as the mass of flickers slowly devoured. Mau watched as the lifeless eyes of a juvenile shark darted past, breaking the surface, scooping mouthfuls of dead flickers. He tried to remain still, but knew it was futile. The blood from his wounds would excite and draw the sharks en masse.

"He looked below. A mako rising from the royal blue deep sighted him. With swift dorsal twitches, the speedy shark darted toward him. Mau rolled onto his stomach and swam with such swiftness the shark missed.

"Treading water, Mau searched for the next attacker. Strike him on the nose, Mau remembered of the teaching of the elders. Don't panic, for the mako will sense your fear. Strike the snout to make him disappear.

"Three whitetips jetted in from different directions, but ignored him. Instead, each scooped nearby flickers, nearly colliding as they competed for the same drifting fish pods. Which one would not care that he's not a flicker? Mau thought, panning the chewing sea.

"Suddenly, in the glare of the climbing sun, the towering sickle-shaped dorsal of the great hammerhead knifed through the flickers. Mau studied the widening and trailing eddies that followed the big fish. The tailfin serpentine pattern. The slipstream swirls were powerful, forming miniature underwater cyclones, indicating the hammerhead was old with a broad beam and many rows of teeth. Plenty big to swallow me whole, he thought.

"Squinting, tracking the approaching hammerhead, Mau contemplated how to ward off the attack. At twenty meters, the rake of gnarly teeth opened and readied, plowing the seawater. Mau flipped to this back. Jam my feet exactly within the margin of its eyes, at the most sensitive spot, so, the force of my heel is blunt and powerful.

"Mau recoiled his legs and thrust as hard as he could into the hammerheads snout, above the many teeth expecting to devour him.

"Abruptly, the mighty shark retracted its serrated incisors and veered. Mau sucked alongside the aged giant. Quickly, he latched onto the tall dorsal and towed in the direction of the crescent for several hundred meters, until the great hammerhead rolled and dumped Mau off.

"He wants me for himself, thought Mau, clearing the raft of dead flickers, swimming to keep the hammerhead within sight. The great predator will circle in figure eights and toy with me, like killer whales do with the black seals. But not for very long.

"Mau watched as the mighty hunter made a wide berth, sizing him up, tasting his blood. The voice of his wise and kind grandfather spoke within his memory. Stay vertical. Hold still and straight as a squid and drift as a turtle to confuse them. Predators are wary and patient and *sure and final. Keep them unsure, so they get bored and leave. As the direct and chosen descendant of great navigators, you, Mau, must know how to survive in the open ocean. Warding off a predator when you abandon your canoe is what every child of the atoll must learn. And if you are to confront the greatest and hungriest and mightiest, you must be agile and ready to strike them at the spot they are most vulnerable and prepare to die as a brave warrior.*

"As the great hammerhead circled, it seemed the other sharks had dispersed, perhaps warned through sonar that Mau was solely the hammerhead's meal.

"The final strike will occur at the widest turn, thought Mau. When the figure eight doubles in size. The hammerhead will cut off halfway around at nearly ninety degrees and with one great, swift flip, jet toward him with such force Mau won't feel any pain. And as taught, Mau watched the great fish open its distance, signaling it was ready to strike. A flash of its lethal eyes, a twist of his tall tail arched nearly in half to leverage against the sea. Mau closed his eyes and waited for death with the bright sun beating down, wondering if he would join the source of the beacon during the next full moon for defying the elders."

Gail paused. "I hope the shark doesn't eat him."

She read on.

"It seemed as if God had brought him the shade that suddenly arrived, shielding the sun so his soul could lift to the heavens just as the great hammerhead struck. There would be no pain. Just the freshness of the air as he felt his body removed from the sea. But pain quickly arrived, not of the tear of the hammerhead's teeth, but of a gunwale, scraping against his back and the grip of a man beneath his armpits. And the smell of breadfruit, coconut, and cinnamon blended with the smell of caught fish, the perfume of every canoe hollowed from the breadfruit tree. The sun and salt and bark made his body sting and scream in pain. Mau was staring directly into the village chief's eyes.

And he saw the scorn, that again he defied the order not to pursue the great light. Behind the chief were the strongest men in the village, stroking the water with their long paddles. Their muscles strained and twitched as their lean backs churned the ocean, trying to slow the high speed that the canoe had attained while it raced to rescue Mau. And just in time it had."

"Oh my," Gail said, exhausted. "I must stop."

Two girls had nodded off, and the child who sat next to Gail had heavy eyes. And as Gail let out a yawn and coaxed the girls to bed, it was time for her to sleep. Tired, she closed the book and lay back. *Who wrote this great story?* she thought.

Chapter 15

I trust you slept well," Pearl said, waking Gail. The dormitory was empty. "No one let you know it was time for breakfast, did they? With all the ruckus, I'd thought the girls would wake you."

"Me too," Gail said, sitting, stretching, her hair still in braids.

"You needed your beauty sleep. There is time to shower and pretty yourself for Jason. He will take you to the ferry."

It took twenty minutes for Gail to get ready for her travel back to Tampa. Twenty minutes was all it ever took, given how early she left for the news station. The bandwidth of time had been engrained.

While Gail stood outside beneath the walkway canopy waiting for Jason, Pearl arrived.

"Don't you look as fresh as a springtime bloom," Pearl said, carrying a nylon satchel. "I have something better than that tired suitcase." She handed Gail the satchel.

"Twice, I had to lug my belongings around in plastic bags. It was embarrassing," Gail said, laughing. And it was in that release of laughter that she realized she took life entirely too seriously. Why should she care what other people thought? It was in her immersion of her television career, the day-to-day time-constrained task to deliver news in a manner that produced profits, that she lost herself. Emmitt was a product of that same culture. He was bitter and jealous because more people watched TV longer when a woman served as an anchor on the morning news. Tight outfits, a cleavage shadow, crossed bare legs on a stool or interview couch, bold and solid dress colors. It was all about profits and not the quality of the content.

"I guess I'm going back to my daily reading," Gail said, as Jason arrived and opened the pickup door for her.

Jason walked around and tossed the satchel into the back.

"It's all I can do before I move on to a better and more satisfying career, likely as an English teacher as my mother would have wanted," she continued.

"Did he hear a word that I said?" she whispered to Pearl, joining her at the window.

Pearl leaned her head into the window and whispered. "He did not hear what you said because he was captivated by your beauty. Believe me, I know Jason, his mind was elsewhere."

Gail didn't bother Jason. He was deep in thought. She sat mostly silent, contemplating what she had shared with the children. The story she'd read—was there truth to any of it? Why was he heading to the Pacific? Did it have to do with his wealth?

Arriving at the ferry and the small collective of buildings that lined the waterway, Jason smiled. Gail could see that look in his eyes again. Like he'd been intimate with her, and liked what he saw. "Men!" she said, sensing he found her attractive. But it felt good coming from a man who didn't carry much personal baggage.

The timing was good; the ferry was about to depart.

"I want you to have some travel money," Jason said, handing her two hundred dollars. "You tend to get yourself into crazy predicaments. I'm hoping not, but just in case, here—to help you out. Also, I'll return the jewelry store stolen money for you."

Gail started to tear up. She came close and looked in his eyes. Kissed him on the cheek and gave him a loving hug. And as she did, she felt his arms wrap and hold her tight. Her heart beat wildly. She grew warm and felt safe and could have stayed in his arms forever. Then there was a flash in her memory. Jason in her cabin, making love, passionately. Gail pulled back and looked at him; was it Jason and not Fabrizio? And just as she tried to get her head around the memory, it vanished with the blast of the ferry's horn, signaling its departure.

Chapter 16

The rust-stained, dual-hull ferry cut through the steady chop on its journey from Road Town to Vessup Bay. Entering the cabin lined with wood benches, Gail braced as a strong wave slapped the port side. She counted five passengers, all sitting up front near the restroom. Not in the mood to talk, she headed down the narrow center aisle to the last row and slid to the back corner. Gail pictured why Jason lived much of his life around such island communities; likely traveling on ferries like this one. He was heading back to the Pacific. What was that all about? she thought again, positioning the satchel in a way to cushion her back.

She headed home to the wreck of the life she'd left behind. What was supposed to be a relaxing cruise had ended. It was the "reader" comment Jason pointed out that affected her most. Defending it, forming a prejudice against someone who had a different perspective on life. Her bias had evolved over the years; her judgment clouded. She was deep inside a funnel. Good journalists do not allow their opinions to enter their stories. Jason was a person who did good in the world. He lived in the absence of television and its influence. The media was her world— her fashioned thoughts, perspectives, and the tendency to inflame facts to drive ratings. Her life a compromise, she went on this cruise to trick someone into making her pregnant. What kind of person was she to deny the father? Should she have done it with the knowledge there would be a child out there that belonged to him? In retrospect, she had evolved in a way that wasn't good, something her parents would not be proud of.

As the ferry fought a headwind and tossed side to side, Gail thought of the Atabeira village and that she might conceive twins. Given what she witnessed on the security video that caused her to get tossed from the ship, a conception could have easily happened. The potion was strong. She was careless and ignored the advice of people who befriended her. The super-sweet honey was a chemically loaded female aphrodisiac.

As she quietly pondered the mystery of the video, Gail questioned why she couldn't remember anything—carried off to her cabin by six men. She didn't remember what happened in her cabin, though she was naked when she woke. Then the thought occurred—had Marie arranged for a midnight visit? The video and her body certainly told she would have done the deed. But Marie had told her she would have no memory, one of the traits of the potion; perhaps genetically engineered to protect the young women who came back from wherever they went, not wanting to know what may have happened as a child grew within. In her reporting career, in the housing projects of Camden, she reported on fourteen-year-old pregnant girls delivering babies they had no clue they carried for nine months. How could they be so naive? Was she also naive, given her current predicament? She so desperately needed to speak with Marie. She would know who she made love to that night. Gail feared all the guilt that would come with not knowing the father of her child. Tossed from the *Sapphire Orchid* so quickly. Not allowed access to Marie, who knew who entered her cabin two nights ago.

The ferry wrestled with the heavy seas, the cloud cover closed in and low. The arrival of another heavy squall; the ferry deliberately angling to cut across the waves, surfing the backside of each crest. A short, dark-haired man had come from the bathroom. "That makes six passengers," she said. And as he sat, Gail instantly recognized him. It was the jewelry thief.

She hunched in her chair, hoping he wouldn't see her. But it was the green cap he wore that alarmed her. He definitely was the man at the Port Everglade terminal spying on Jason. What was he doing on this vessel? Was he following her?

The crossing took longer than expected. The ferry arrived in the calmer waters of Vessup Bay. Soon it would dock, thought Gail, trying to figure a way off without Milan seeing.

As the engine slowed, Milan came to his feet. But instead of preparing to disembark, he came down the center aisle, walked its entire length, and slid across a row of seats directly in front of her.

"You clean up well," Milan said, greeting her. He pulled from his top pocket the card on which Gail had scrawled her contact information. "You forgot to write your last name on the card, so if you don't return the money I loaned, I can contact you."

Gail sat frozen. It was the green hat, years as a street reporter, she could sniff out a villain. Coming to greet her, getting her name wasn't why he stopped.

"Ah . . ." She didn't want him to know her real name and said the first thing that came to her head.

"Applegate."

It was a mistake and she couldn't take it back.

Milan cocked his head. It seemed he was shocked by what he heard. "Applegate! Are you the wife of the Applegate that operates the orphanage?"

As the ferry collided with the berth that allowed it to slide in and dock, Milan slid across the slick bench but caught himself. Gail came to her feet and tried to put a distance between them, pretending she was in a hurry and needed to disembark.

"Uh, no," she uttered, at a loss for words, heading for the aisle and the opening that led outside.

Milan was close behind.

Gail thought quickly. "He's my brother."

"Brother?" Milan asked, becoming aggressive, reaching to pull on her shoulder to slow Gail. "I'd heard he was an orphan."

"Yes, you are correct. Jason's mother adopted me also," Gail lied. She needed to end this conversation, a diversion, something that would stop this man's pursuit.

"Did you ever find your keys?" she asked.

"No, someone must've stolen them. I changed the locks. But I did find the ring I needed to resize. That's why I'm on the ferry. Taking it to a jeweler, so it will be ready for my client this afternoon."

"That's nice," Gail said as both stepped onto the ramp that led to the marina. "I must go. I will send your money as soon as I get home, Mr. Milan."

Quickly, she raced to a cab waiting at the top of a steep grade and said to the driver, "To the airport."

Gail was nervous. This man was no good. He was tailing Jason, and now her, trying to learn something.

The modern airport came as a shock to Gail. Bright lights, well-dressed people, small retail stands, and franchise food concessions. Her ticket was waiting. Jason had called ahead and booked her flight. But what surprised her was the ticket. It was first-class.

She'd never flown in such luxury and for the entire flight to Fort Lauderdale and the short hop to Tampa, she thought about this man who cared for her, wanting to know more about him. He didn't convey the attitude of someone with an accumulation of such wealth. Philanthropic individuals, at least the ones she reported on, were older, knowing their great wealth would do them no good six feet under. But for Jason, to possess such wealth, his poise and generosity, to buy her a first-class ticket, puzzled her. He could have saved that money and spent it on his kids. It was that small fact the investigative reporter in her keyed in on. There must be a tie to his travel to the Pacific and the island Ruth had discovered him on.

Chapter 17

Papua New Guinea, Manus Island
Two and a half years prior

In the cramped prison bus, his wrought iron shackles having had three links removed, Milan Petrovich struggled to stand. Imprisoned for twenty-three months on Manus Island in Papua, New Guinea, this was the first time he had left the prison located somewhere deep in the central lowland jungle. His only chance to live longer was as slave labor onboard a Japanese tuna trawler. If he worked the tuna catch, the prison would keep him in better health, where life expectancy was just short of three years. Milan had survived bouts of malaria, dysentery, lice infestation, and near starvation. And now, finally, the opportunity to live a bit longer by working the trawler.

The stench was of urine—prisoners not permitted to relieve themselves properly. Milan's entire torso ached. This, his first journey, he hadn't earned a seat on the overcrowded bus; forced to stand for the torturously long ride from the mud-rut jungle to where the trawler would slip into the port in the darkness to pick up the shipment of prison laborers.

The bus headlights went dark, the knock of the diesel slowed, then silenced. Not a single prisoner made a sound, except for the clank of their chain links. As the bus door cranked opened, the tribal language he'd gotten used to hearing ordered them along. One by one, prisoners stepped from the rot, each taking a deep breath of the fresh, nighttime salt air.

Milan followed—head low, making no eye contact with the guards or deckhands that waited onboard. There was clatter on the plank-boards and the complaint of corroded hinges. Up a ramp, more racket and more orders, but this time in Japanese.

A deckhand grabbed Milan by the elbow and shoved him the length of a bench fastened to the starboard gunwale. Twice he fell, unable to keep in step. At mid-bow, where the last prisoner was seated, the deckhand shoved Milan to the bench. And as the bus emptied, the three-slat seat filled. A bucket was passed along. Each prisoner drank a ladle of water. A pot of rice was passed. And as he'd done a hundred times, he scooped a fistful and mashed it into his mouth before the prisoner next to him fought him for it.

There was a rapid instability, then the biting smell of exhaust as the vessel left the mooring, listing severely port side. Milan clutched the bench as the trawler made way for the dark Pacific. For Milan, the journey was as described by cellmates who worked the tuna catch. His work onboard would be the worst job.

As Milan often did, to hold stable his mental state, he recalled his memory of a great, luxury-filled life, living like a prince in the south of France—a thief, scouting the vulnerable and wealthy who frequented Monaco. He was most interested in married women and the fine jewelry they adorned. His greatest asset was his smooth-talking tongue, a talent that hadn't yielded him much success in prison, except for now, an opportunity to escape.

Voodoo Cruise

Milan stole diamonds of the world's most exceptional quality. But two years ago, when negotiating the sale of an eleven-carat, point-cut diamond, he met his demise. What puzzled him was the secrecy of the arrest. Whisked away with no trial, no lawyer, no opportunity to contact anyone. This bad fortune came when the black-market contact that certified the authenticity of the stolen gemstone refused to facilitate the underground sale. Word spread among the illegals of Milan's possession. The diamond was a rare Utopia stone—closely tracked and sold exclusively by just one Jewish distributor. Milan's contact ratted him out, because if he too were caught, he would be swept off and never heard from.

To survive this hell, Milan often went into a near catatonic state, living in the memories of his past. The heist that put him here, he regretted. It was an Arab woman. Beneath their modest clothing, they adorned themselves in the world's most expensive jewelry . . . Tailing his victim for weeks, sometimes months, he sought ways to discover the jewels concealed beneath their hijabs. The best way to catch a glimpse was when these women exited modes of transportation, from a limo to a hard surface. His location of choice was as an employee of a five-star hotel as a doorman. When he opened their limo door, their hijab would slip off their shoulder. And as they stepped to the sidewalk it would unravel, the wind exposing their neckwear. And once he had his next victim, he'd tail her. If she was vulnerable to his gift of gab, he would befriend her while her husband engaged about his business or recreation. A sheik who was unfaithful provided the most vulnerable prey.

Lifting the Utopia diamond was a rather simple heist. While the sheik was with his mistress, Milan was servicing the jealous wife in the same manner. He slipped from her hotel room after lifting a gold necklace with a locket as its centerpiece. Hidden inside was the rare diamond. Within hours, as he often did, he sailed off into the Mediterranean in his catamaran. An accomplished sailor, it was on to Sardinia, down and around the boot, and onto the countryside of Bosnia, his homeland, to lie low.

Milan slept sitting up. The prisoner next to him yanked Milan's dirty shirt made of rough canvas and jolted him to his feet. The ship's stern had suddenly illuminated with bright lights. Startled, he had no idea what time it was or how long he slept. Or if it was a good rest.

A short Asian man pointed to markings on the trawler deck, assigning work locations. The line dwindled until it became Milan's turn. He was directed mid-ship, near where a crane slung the tuna nets. A Japanese deckhand, slightly smaller than him, wielded a long, thin knife. This was his workstation. Milan looked around. There were two tubs on either end of a thigh-high table. At the center, where he stood, sat a plastic mushroom barrel. Bolted to the table was a meat grinder with a feeder pan fastened on top. Though Milan couldn't understand the commands he was hearing, it was clear that whatever went into the first tub was processed using the grinder and dumped into the second tub.

By the time the deck was fully staffed, daylight had arrived and the trawler got busy, maneuvering to signals directed from the crow's-nest, the vessel leaning as it cut hard, working a school of tuna—Milan stumbling, the width of his shackles too narrow on the unstable deck.

The purse seine that dragged in the ocean grew smaller as the netting pulled to the stern. There was a boil as prisoners gaffed yellowfin tuna and slung them onboard. On each side of the gaffers, men wielded rifles. A flipping yellowfin slid across the wet deck to Milan's station. The knife-wielding deckhand stomped on the head to stop the slide of the large tuna. He jammed his knife between the tuna's eyes, stunning it— the hard-meat fish vibrating in a catatonic state. Coming to a third-world squat, he inserted the knife into the belly and cut off the intestine at the base of the rectum. Using his free hand, he lifted the crimson gill cover, jammed in his knife, and made a precise cut. Then he yanked out the intestines, gutting the yellowfin in less than twenty seconds.

The Asian lifted the bloody mess by the gills and nipped out the heart. It bounced to the deck and rolled to Milan's feet. The man barked an order and pointed to the mushroom barrel. Milan picked up the beating organ and flipped it into the barrel. The gut cluster was tossed past him into the first tub. More orders barked, the giller motioning to turn the grinder crank. Milan reached into the tub, gathered the innards, and dropped the mess into the top pan. As he turned the crank, a meaty mash squished through holes into the second tub.

As the yellowfin catch processed, Milan's arms and back ached, the table too low even for a short man. But he'd heard stories of prisoners that complained or were not productive tossed overboard. Which explained why the shackles were never removed. By the fourth tuna, Milan was covered in a splatter of blood and guts. The rocking of the vessel made the pain in his body worse. His rest came only after the net was raised and readied for the next school of tuna.

The giller, Milan's master, came over, and with the point of his long knife pricked a heart out of the partially filled plastic barrel. With swift slices, he cut it into four pieces, then slid his knife under one of the pieces and offered it to Milan. Mr. Gill Gut, as Milan named him, encouraged him to eat. Milan took the piece of ruby protein, swallowed it whole along with the remaining pieces. He offered Milan a wet towel to clean the blood that covered him.

By late afternoon, they finished a third catch. This first day was a successful hunt. That night they steamed north and did not fish the second day, as if they were heading to a deliberate location. That second night, as they slept, the trawler stopped and pulled anchor beneath a full moon. At daybreak Milan was ordered to his spot and for the next two days they caught tuna. Mr. Gill Gut, as was accustomed, had finished his last tuna and again offered the heart, then went below deck. But for Milan, there was more work; the unprocessed tub was a quarter full.

His arm aching, he considered jumping overboard and killing himself, the work too grueling for any human. He reached into the tub and lifted another dangling mass. The tuna's stomach was full of fish. It happened on occasion, though most tuna vomited their lunch in the seine due to the trauma of their capture. Dropping the gut into the grinder, Milan turned the crank, and as the mass in the tuna's stomach chewed, the crank seized. Milan reversed the handle and turned again, but with greater force. A mesh of fish flesh and pieces of brilliant crimson scales squished through. But again, the crank jammed. It'd struck something hard. A third attempt, and again a hard jam. Milan unscrewed the plate that held the stainless steel grate in place. He reached into the throat of the device and scooped the remaining portion of the swallowed fish.

"Shit," Milan said, feeling a sharp object. It sliced the tip of his index finger. Using his other hand, he picked out the fish and tossed it to the low table. The object that nicked him had lodged in the fish's cavity. It looked like a piece of glass.

How did this get inside a fish? he thought.

Smartly, without spending time analyzing the solid piece, fearful the sharp item would get discovered, possibly having value to slice someone's throat, he slipped it into the pocket of his soiled prison uniform.

Milan went back to the low table and analyzed the chewed fish. The upper body was intact. Its scales were large with a rainbow reflection. Cautiously, he dug into the cavity and found two more pieces just like the one that cut him. The fish head had gigantic black marble eyes with crimson irises. *What an unusual fish,* Milan thought. He lifted the fish to toss it into the top pan. Briefly, the sun appeared through the towering cumulous clouds. And when the light struck the scales, they shined like a thousand blinding prisms. He tossed the fish into the pan and destroyed it, turning the crank.

As he was finishing his work, dragging the tub to where he'd dump the mush into the hold, it began to rain. To clean the blood on his arms, head, and legs, Milan stood in the downpour, head up, open mouth, catching the rainwater. And as the drenching subsided, he went to his spot on the bench, working an escape plan.

That night, the sounds that came from the commercial fishermen in their quarters indicated they were pleased with the good fortune of the catch. Lying on the deck, Milan watched as a full moon appeared once again, illuminating the calm sea. He held the objects he'd found up to the moonlight. They glowed. He had an inkling they were diamonds and was certain they were the blood diamonds that had put him here. The cut, a point cut, was the exact dimensions as the Utopia stone, a perfect crystal. How incredibly unbelievable was this? He checked to see if he was dreaming or hallucinating. Diamonds were found deep inside inactive volcanoes. The atolls of the Pacific were once volcanoes.

It was on the seventh day, after Milan was sure Mr. Gill Gut had taken a liking to his labor, that he executed his plan. Disciplined, Milan worked, challenging Mr. Gill Gut, processing the intestines faster than he could remove them from the tuna. Competing, smiling in gestures and nods. But he had a dilemma; how, as a prisoner could he bribe his captor? Perhaps the man wasn't smart enough to know all he had to do was take the diamonds from him. Perhaps he would feel an obligation for not being any trouble, so he didn't have to toss him overboard, which happened to several prisoners as a demonstration if they didn't work hard. As the day ended, Milan debated. He could see land and an anchored ship waiting at the entry of an atoll. Some sort of resupply or transport ship, he thought.

The entire night, Milan, with the remaining prisoners in chain-gang style, tossed the processed tuna catch from the hold to the waiting ship. If it was not for him eating the tuna organs, and the protein it provided, Milan was sure he would have collapsed and been tossed overboard in shackles.

Daylight came. Curled in a fetal position, Milan couldn't recall when they'd finished offloading the catch. A bare foot jammed his side to wake him. Mr. Gill Gut brought him breakfast, a reward no doubt for his hard work as a sign of respect. It was a mix of fish and garlic. And like a scavenging dog, Milan ate. His provider watched in curiosity. Milan handed back the empty pot lid that served as a dish. But his master didn't leave; he started talking in Japanese. Produced a photo, showing his wife and five children; a gesture to the fact that he too was a slave, driven by the need to provide for his family.

This was the opening Milan was looking for, an opportunity to reward Mr. Gill Gut for keeping him alive. They'd lost nearly a quarter of the prisoners. Milan dug in his pocket and handed him the brilliant stone, and pointed to his children in the picture, saying in French, "For your family."

The man eyes grew wide as he inspected what appeared to be a gem. Though unsure as to its authenticity, or if he truly believed it was real, it was the kindness the fisherman understood; an acknowledgment of his personal challenges and why he believed Milan worked so hard for him. Mr. Gill Gut closed his calloused hand around the gemstone and disappeared below deck.

For the remainder of the day the ship remained anchored at the mouth of the atoll. The processing ship had left to whatever port it came. The sun baked the trawler deck and prisoners that remained alive. Water passed along twice. Milan had crawled beneath the bench to shade himself. It must be some sort of day of rest, he thought. Tired, he slept until darkness came.

Voodoo Cruise

It was a waning moon when Milan woke. But when a large cloud drifted to block the partial light, the trawler deck was as black as a South African mineshaft. That's when he felt a tug on his ankle. It was Mr. Gill Gut twisting a wrench, undoing one of Milan's shackles. He slid the bolt back into its hole so not to leave any pieces onboard. Politely, he tapped Milan on the calf and disappeared.

As with the scoop of rice gobbled before he lost it, Milan didn't waste a moment, crawling on his stomach to the stern where the net hung over the side. The shackle dragged from his left leg. Milan was careful not to make it rattle. He leaped and clung to the net that dangled, then laddered down and dropped into the warm Pacific.

The ocean was at rest. And each time the partial moon illuminated from behind a drifting cloud, Milan stopped swimming, fearful he'd be spotted. Treading water, he used the moonlight to determine where the shoreline of the atoll they'd anchored near might be by gauging the angle of the stationary trawler. And when the darkness came again, he swam clumsily, the shackle a problem.

The current of a rising tide at the mouth of the atoll had aided his swim. Nearly two hundred yards away from the ship, he could hear the lap of the sea strike the hard coral. Milan swam toward the sound of the beach wash. "Oomph," Milan murmured as the coral scraped along his stomach, protected by the tough fabric that made up his prison shirt. His hands toughened and calloused, he crawled across the jagged surface. Several times the shackle caught. Working within the deeper crevice, he finally made it onto the sand. And like a nesting sea turtle, he squiggled a trail beneath a full moon in the direction of a grove of coconut palms.

Reaching the cover, he rolled like a playful child into the shadows. Milan then rested. He lay there nearly an hour fearful the ship would be alerted—the discovery he was missing, search party let out. Standing, convinced he would not be seen, Milan made his way deeper into the darkness of the grove, cautiously listening. He came to a mud path that led through a taro field. The plants were tall and thick and leaning. Stepping off the path, he separated the taro stalks and made his way, finding a place where he could lie down and sleep, comfortable he wouldn't be discovered in the thickness.

Milan woke to a cluster of horseshoe crabs that had crawled onto him. The sun had risen twice. He'd slept for two days, the taro providing shelter. He had heard voices, again in an unfamiliar language, but had drifted to sleep several times. Covered in bug bites, welts, and scabs, hair full of lice, he tried to stand. Grabbing the shackle that dragged, using the taro to stay upright until the blood flowed properly in all his limbs, he worked his way through to the path and back to the coconut grove. Panning the outer reach of the atoll, where the break in the reef was, he saw the trawler had left. Milan showed no emotion. He was free, but the hardship that he'd survived had taken a toll.

Walking the path back through the taro, the shackle dragging, Milan came upon a thatch hut. He continued, the trail widening just as he came to a two-story block home.

At least I'm not on an island of cannibals, he thought. More huts and cinderblock homes appeared. A child spotted him and raced from his sandy front yard, leapt over a fence made of muddied shells, and followed Milan. The child smiled and said nothing. Neither did Milan.

Ahead was an open area, a grass field and what looked like a schoolhouse. The child raced ahead without saying a word. But as he traversed the field, several other children came running from different directions, gathering around the stranger. They weren't a bit intimidated, even though his ankle was shackled.

Why would they be? thought Milan. *There's no way off this island.*

From inside the schoolhouse, a Caucasian woman emerged, led by a child. Her hair was tied off her shoulders into a thick pretzel braid. She wore a deep blue muumuu, and smiled as Milan approached.

Voodoo Cruise

She laughed and so did the curious children. "You look lost."

Milan, understanding her English, replied in French. "I was thrown off the trawler. They expected me to drown." Milan hoped to draw sympathy.

The beautiful teacher answered him in French. "You are a prisoner from the tuna trawler?"

"Yes," Milan said. "How do you know?" She nodded to his clothing. "Bodies wash ashore. Fortunately, you aren't one of them. They take our tuna. The vessel is no friend of the Chuukese."

"Chuukese, I'm not sure where that is," Milan said, sitting on the ground and holding his bolted ankle cuff to provide some relief, children all around.

"Lekinioch Island, Micronesia, ninety kilometers north of the equator," she said.

"You are a white woman, and French speaking." Milan observed, curious as to why she was here.

"I'm a Peace Corps volunteer. I speak several languages."

"In the middle of the Pacific?" he questioned.

"It's the most remote assignment. My name is Mariel."

"That's a beautiful name," Milan said.

"Thank you," she said. "Let's get you clean and out of those clothes and that shackle."

Mariel spoke Chuukese to the children. It seemed she was giving instructions.

The children gathered and escorted him behind the schoolhouse to the water's edge. There was a collapsed seawall about fifteen feet out. They led him into the water and encouraged him to strip his clothing. Milan removed the two diamonds from his pocket and rolled them into his palm, clenching his fist to conceal them. Nudity wasn't an issue to the children or to Milan, a Frenchman. He disrobed and was handed a bar of rough soap. A few curious adults had arrived.

Mariel brought Milan a pair of shorts, a T-shirt, and a wrench to remove the shackle. She fed him breadfruit and dried fish, apologizing for the lack of food, explaining the atoll was fished out.

As he ate, she explained the island people. It was embedded in their culture for people not to walk alone; that was why the children came to greet him. No one ever walked alone. The volunteer indicated it could be a bit unnerving, because you had no privacy.

As Milan learned where he was and about the people around him, he debated exposing the diamonds that came from inside a fish. These westernized natives, descendants of the Polynesians, likely might have some knowledge. It was likely the diamonds came from nearby.

Should he reveal the stones to Mariel? The Chuukese had no loyalty to the trawler. Though he was a thief, was their culture such that they'd not suspect him as someone evil? Or was it even relevant, given money had no value here? If the diamonds did have value, he may need to barter them to get off this remote place and safely back to Bosnia. But if he could locate the source, giving them away would be the price he must pay.

Sitting on the schoolhouse steps, he reached into the pocket of his clean shorts and produced just one stone. The sun struck the gem and shined with an incredible brilliancy; colors of the rainbow, a prism. The brilliancy of the diamond was incredible, like it had found its home and wanted to celebrate the return.

Mariel said, her eyes wide, "How beautiful!"

Suddenly, she grew guarded and opened her distance.

"No, I found these stones inside a fish," Milan said. "I did not steal them. I was a doorman in Monaco and kidnapped and taken prisoner for no reason, a mistaken identity." He went on to tell a convincing story of his imprisonment, the tuna trawler, prisoners tossed overboard, and discovery of the stone inside a fish. It was when he described the fish that Mariel's shoulders relaxed.

Voodoo Cruise

"Your story is plausible," she said. "They talk of a big-eyed fish with large prism scales that chase schools of anchovies. To digest the anchovies, the Chuukese say the fish will chew on the reef and swallow sharp shells and snap their bodies in a way to chop up the anchovy in their stomach as a method of digestion. The Chuukese call them flicker fish. That's all I know," the pleasant Peace Corps volunteer said.

Milan debated. How should he proceed? "Is there someone that can tell me more?"

"Yes, Grandfather can."

"Grandfather?"

"Yes, Grandfather Mau. He's an elder and holds the stories of Lekinioch and the Pacific."

"Can I show him the diamonds?"

"Of course, but you'll need an interpreter."

Milan noticed how incredibly beautiful this island was. As the sun rose, a firm trade wind awakened and swayed the shading coconuts. On occasion, he'd hear the thump of a fallen coconut. The ocean that occupied the caldera of Lekinioch was rich with seagrass. And further out, a deep blueness. The inhabitants came out of curiosity to inspect Milan and seemed pleasant. Mariel explained all the Chuukese had such a temperament, and were known culturally as the smiling people. For Milan, it was as close to heaven as he could imagine.

They walked the central pathway to the thatch hut Milan had come across when he exited the taro field earlier.

"This is Grandfather Mau's place. Our elders prefer traditional living," Mariel described.

Removing her flip-flops, Mariel invited Milan to enter. "Let's meet Grandfather."

The grandfather, holding a wooden hand tool, had finished repairing a fishing net. Mariel spoke Chuukese for several minutes. It appeared she was explaining how Milan came upon Lekinioch.

Grandfather gestured Milan to sit on a stool made from a tree stump. Mariel sat on a floor mat with her legs folded and spoke some more.

She spoke to Milan in French. "This is Grandfather Mau. He is the eldest and wisest man on the island."

Milan smiled at the elder, noticing the hands of a worker and deep-wrinkled, weathered face.

Mau passed him a toothless grin.

Milan opened his hand to reveal just one stone. He could hear Mariel explain in Chuukese, her expression assuring he'd not stolen it. There was no reaction from Mau. He pitched back in his handmade chair, fashioned without the use of nails, the joints bound with twine. To the right, next to him, was an anchor and coiled rope. Mau looked up at the thatched roof as if he was drawing upon a memory. Then he looked over at the anchor; it provided for a memory also. The elder rubbed the sides of his arms, which appeared to be scarred; a memory. Whatever it was bore a relationship to the anchor.

Mariel waited patiently, for deep thought was the expectation of an elder, summoning the story the crystal clear stone was part of.

Minutes passed.

Why didn't he examine the stone more closely? Milan thought. Perhaps he didn't have to. Or was it not relevant? Milan was thrown.

Grandfather Mau leaned forward in a hunched posture and spoke.

Mariel interpreted. "This and many more brought the bright light. The trawler had fished around a sunken land during an arriving full moon. If what you say is true, it came from a flicker. The flicker chew on the stones beneath the reef that once formed the sunken island. This island was special in that its atoll was filled with many of these, the same shape and clearness. For centuries, the flicker came to feed on the anchovies before they spawned. To digest their food, they'd gnaw at the base rock, releasing the diamonds locked in the volcanic stone. They swallow three or four, then contort their bodies rapidly, relying upon the sharp edges to break down the swallowed anchovies. Unfortunately, when they spawn, the flicker die just as they say of the salmon, and the stones sink to the bottom of the sea."

"Bright light?" Milan questioned

Mariel interpreted.

Even the elder had the Chuukese smile. It was clear he was contemplating a fond memory. He spoke to Mariel this time, telling his story.

"I lived on the sunken atoll. A great lady had saved us all. It was the most beautiful place on earth. The fish were plentiful, the lobster healthy and easy to snatch from the grasses. At the coming of the bright light the flickers came in great numbers. And when they died they would fill the entire lagoon, only to be eaten by the coming sharks that would leave the atoll clean by sunset. I am the last of the elders from the atoll."

He sat back in his chair and seemed lost in his fond memory. Then he quickly dozed off, the release of the memory emotional.

Mariel stood and spoke in French. "Milan, it is time for Mau to rest." Though he was asleep, she bid Grandfather goodbye, kissing him on his shoulder.

"I must return to my Chuukese family. There are many chores," she said. "As long as you remain here you will be taken care of and will be asked to help with the cutting of the taro and gathering of coconuts."

They were escorted once again by the children, who brought him rice, a plate of Spam, and water. Milan was to sleep on a mat made of weaved palms inside the schoolhouse. Mariel explained no one slept on mattresses due to the lice, rats, and bedbugs.

As the day ended and everyone left him alone, Milan inspected the room. It seemed well stocked for such a remote schoolhouse. The desks were of good quality. There was a library on the far wall. Each book had a gold seal with the name of its donor. In fact, so did the many of the school books that were in a supply cabinet. He inspected the shiny seal, embossed on a math workbook: RJA foundation. Milan opened a book. There was an inscription: Donated by the Ruth and Jason Applegate Foundation.

Chapter 18

Nickoli Lavaki angrily commanded his officers to the bridge. He was known for such a temperament. He wasn't happy. Though no one's fault, it was the meteorologist he blamed.

"Why wasn't I informed about this sudden change in weather earlier?" He pounded his fist on the console. "This tropical depression came out of nowhere, whale shit!"

"Sir, it can't be explained. The storm formed overnight to our east as we arrived in Road Town," the Greek first officer explained. "There was no warning of such weather from Fort Lauderdale. NOAA didn't see it either. The tropical depression had blossomed offshore from a cluster of thunderstorms and rapidly intensified. It's expected to become a category two hurricane before we arrive back in Port Everglades."

"We must sail west to avoid it," the navigator said, sitting at the far end of the console. "If we continue with the itinerary, we will not make Port Everglades by Sunday to disembark. And you know how important it is to anchor in Atabeira two days into the next itinerary," informed the officer.

"How many days late?" Nickoli asked.

"Maybe two, most likely three," the officer replied.

"We can't go in circles in the Caribbean waiting for the storm to clear out, passengers will be barfing everywhere. Best bet is to return to Atabeira and remain on the north side of the hurricane. Let it chase us back to Lauderdale. Returning to Atabeira is best for passengers and Emerald's wallet."

"Captain, sailing west along the south shore of Haiti, then north around the horn, will provide for the calmest seas," the navigator indicated.

"That's the long way around. How many hours?" Nickoli asked.

"At twenty-five knots, likely forty hours. We'd reach Atabeira just before dawn in two days."

"Set your course for Atabeira," barked the tough Greek, confidence in his voice.

Nickoli knew well that Emerald's site selection and the construction of its private island was a calculated decision. Atabeira was perfect for such situations. A protected cove and a day's sail from Florida at top speed provided great flexibility. The peak demand for cruises was during hurricane season. Logistically, it made sense because studies showed eighty percent of hurricanes that formed in the Atlantic passed south of Atabeira, or weren't fully formed when they struck. For the captain, the protocol was to head back to Atabeira taking the calmest seas.

However, there was another reason why Nickoli wanted to return to Atabeira. He'd grown frustrated with a secret of his own; that he had not yet realized the sole reason why he piloted the *Sapphire Orchid*. The Greek had not yet sired a son. Delivering a male heir to continue his bloodline of seafarers was paramount. To be the male heir that ended generations of prominent captains was an embarrassment and a life failure. But after several years in charge of the *Sapphire Orchid*, a son had not been born. Nickoli paid handsomely for the five women in waiting, one for each of the remaining nights of the itinerary. The thought of voodoo gnawed on Nickoli. The most disturbing, a curse put upon him by the mambo. She had delivered a voodoo doll with its genitals gouged out. A gesture that made him bitter and defiant. Nickoli wanted to demonstrate to the mambo he was not afraid of her black magic. This time, returning to Atabeira, he planned to detain the village elders, personally threatening to stir up the turbidity so much that he'd kill their reef forever if the curse was not removed.

As the *Sapphire Orchid* sailed west and north to avoid the storm, the Caribbean settled. The sky cleared. It was time to administer the Atabeiran honey. It was Lou and Marie's job to assure safe distribution of the sweetener. Gathered from the supposed volunteer nurses, it was on the captain's orders when the love potion would be secretly distributed. It happened first in the dining rooms in the form of a delicious dessert for the women. The busboys were ordered to report names of the couples whose spouses did not consume the dessert. This explained why some passengers did not conceive—calorie-fearing wives missing out. However, with those couples the staff would attempt alternatives.

So, it was in the dining rooms that this life-making honey made its way, the greatest attention given to Emerald Class passengers, since the price to dine there was twice the rate, with the honey delivered for the next four nights. Not a single complaint came from the males.

For Nickoli, management of the honey was important. Sailing in calm seas helped. Fewer people became sick, which improved the odds of conception.

Chapter 19

Deep into the night, Atabeira was peaceful—the entire village asleep except the mambo. Dressed in her white ceremonial outfit and carrying a staff taller than her, she left her simple home and walked through the village to a pond on the south side. Stepped into the water knee-deep and started to chant, stomping her feet, smacking the surface with the staff. Though it was dark, a thickness gathered and surrounded her feet. The mambo released from beneath a scarf tied around her waist, a doll, dressed as a sailor. Two needles protruded from the groin. The mambo pinched the round head of each pin and remove them. She tied a rock to the doll, and using the tip of the staff flicked it far into the pond. And the moment it sank, in the thickness surrounding her feet, emerging from the murk, were thousands of red-eye frogs. En masse, they crawled across the sand, an army on attack, disappearing into the lap of darkened lagoon.

Quietly, in the dead of the night, the mambo walked the empty streets to the temple. Minutes later her drummers arrived and the temple came alive. But no one else came this time. As the mambo lit candles, the temple filled with the scent of beeswax. She removed her sandals and shuffled her bare feet, turning in tight circles, dancing in sync with the drumbeat. For nearly an hour, she danced around the blue pole that rose through the center, candle flames flickering. The intensity of her dance remained constant as sweat poured from her large body, until finally the spirit came and entered her.

As the drumbeat grew louder, the mambo became tense, her dance rigid and dramatically different, a shivering stomp of the earth as if she was working to bust open the ground. And as she raised the staff and touched the center pole, the drumbeat ceased. There was dead silence as the staff lifted high into the air, then struck down onto the altar, shattering the decorative tile. The mambo stared at the ground, as if she were watching the energy travel to the earth's core . . . Then suddenly, the earth answered. There was a blur. A tremor, then the earthquake. The village shook. The broken tiles rearranged . . . Then there was quiet, as the mambo collapsed to the ground, the spirit departing.

For the first time, Captain Lavaki would enter the lagoon in darkness. He timed it that way. Nickoli ordered his first officer to steer the *Sapphire Orchid* into the Navidad Channel. It was four o'clock in the morning. By sunrise, after navigating the narrow passage, they would be at anchor in Atabeira once again. He looked forward to this moment, a chance to put the mambo on notice that he would not be threatened. He would turn the clear blue water into a slurry, suffocating the reef, making the mambo pay for the curse she'd cast upon him. And he would not relent until the mambo acquiesced.

Out of the corner of his dark eyes, he watched his underwater cameras, but relied much more on his feel of his vessel—the sonar ping, the subtle pulse of the electric motors, the soft nighttime chop of the Caribbean. This was what Emerald Cruise Line paid him to do, move the giant hull amidst underwater outcrops into the cove where Christopher Columbus harbored on December 24, 1492. No other cruise ship dared such a maneuver. The next forty-three minutes would require absolute focus.

The Navidad Channel was the product of a split in the seafloor formed by collided tectonic plates millions of years ago. On both sides, beneath the surface of the mean tide, was a knife-like ridge of basalt the entire length of the cut. At two-thirds, the cut narrowed to six meters on each side of the *Orchid*'s hull. As long as the ping of the sonar spoke at a rapid but comfortable interval, Nickoli was calm. Though he had all the technology to aid his navigation, he was old-school, as were his father, grandfather, and great-grandfather, all named Nickoli.

At a quarter mile to the vertical spires, Nickoli opened the top of his thermos and poured coffee into the thermos lid. But as the black liquid poured from the steel throat and dropped the short distance to the metal cup, Nickoli's eyes widened. The cup began to rattle—the seafloor suddenly disturbed.

Dropping the thermos, he raced to the broad window of the bridge. Off the starboard bow, a twister had formed and moved with the cautious pace of the ship. And, as when he started the voyage, the tornado tossed its contents, frogs, pelting the bridge, smashing at the thick plate glass, splattering reptiles, decks quickly becoming covered with leaping, creepy creatures. And as quickly the disturbance arrived, the twister dissolved into a mist.

A sailor's voice announced a tremor had occurred on the seafloor, confirming 6.5 on the Richter scale. Nickoli's mind raced. *Throw the* Orchid *into reverse, impossible.* His only choice was to continue and exit the narrows.

A second tremor. Again, a voice called over a speaker, "Four point nine."

Nickoli, in his steady, confident gait, left the bridge and went outside to the starboard bow. He mashed across the deck littered with slimy creatures, ignorant to what it meant. The ocean air smelled disturbed, the sea nervous. *Something's askew,* he thought. Two officers followed, but kept a distance in case he barked orders. It was Nickoli who lit the search light and illuminated the dark water ahead. He could hear the seafloor grumble and could see a slump in the black surface. It was the kind of divot made when the seafloor changes elevation. A wave of about seventeen feet had formed from the energy released below. It crashed over the edges of the channel and rolled like a miniature tidal wave into the darkness away from the reach of the light.

Nickoli returned to the bridge, the sonar ping annoying. "Turn that damn thing off!" he ordered. "Clean those damn windows."

It was in that command that the second officer, disturbed by the twister, threw the wrong switch. Instead, the *Sapphire Orchid*'s stabilizers, used to hold the ship steady in a rough sea, extended. Quietly, with every nervous eye distracted, it was only when the stabilizers were nearly all the way out and about to crush against the basalt that Nickoli stepped to the counsel, shoved the second officer aside and to the floor. He flipped the switch to return the underwater wings back into their tuck. It was too late. The giant fins of the *Sapphire Orchid* struck both sides of the basalt, ripping back, tearing off, striking the starboard turbine where it attached to the ship, snapping it off and sending it falling into the bottomless depth of the Navidad Channel, descending like a wounded helicopter.

"Call general quarters," the captain ordered.

Immediately, throughout the entire vessel, the staff became active and anxious. A recorded announcement called for everyone to wake and proceed to their designated muster stations. Staff, well-trained, banged on cabin doors and took positions to direct passengers, informing groggy souls not carrying life jackets to return to their cabin and get them. Many couples, fearful of being left behind, didn't care to wear additional clothing—women and men in underwear, some wearing their mate's, hurried by the panic. Couple after couple filled hallways and followed verbal directions.

Nickoli, in his mind, imagined the damage beneath his mighty vessel. "Port thruster twenty-three degrees," he said, ordering a correction to the increasingly cockeyed axis of the vessel, the only remaining electric motor working. The officer at the control, warning lights blinking, turned the dial to adjust the lone prop to move the *Orchid* parallel. And with hard eyes, the bearded captain stared boldly into the nighttime darkness, looking at nothing, seawater entering its hull. "She's going to strike," he called to the crew that surrounded him. An order in several languages blared through every speaker on every deck and galley. "Prepare to brace! Prepare to brace!"

The captain set his big hands on the console. "Do as you see me."

Nickoli counted. "Four, three, two . . ." There was a prolonged scrape, and then the buckling of thick steel. The captain's expression did not change. No fear in him at all.

"Be silent, I want to hear all of it," he ordered. The sound of earth colliding with manufactured steel plates. Buckling ribs. The rate of deceleration would tell him how badly the structural integrity of the hull would be compromised. A jolt versus a crunch, mentally measuring how long the collision lasted . . . Seven seconds . . . A pause. A drift. Another five seconds and a jolt of enormous proportion. The bow had struck to the port side of the Navidad cut, grinding the rock formation below the black surface. The collision swung the stern starboard against the knife edge of the channel, cutting open the hull two-thirds back of mid-ship. A rock gutted the *Orchid* and snagged a rib and lodged, listing the ship, twisting the massive white hull longitudinally. Inside, and everywhere, there was crashing of furniture, glass, china, and every loose item. Passengers tumbling. And as Nickoli in his mind analyzed the impact, he viewed that as good; a wedged bow and stern would prevent the

Voodoo Cruise

White Lady from sinking too quickly, evacuation by tender not compromised.

Nickoli cursed every nautical command imaginable, tossing aside any of his crew that didn't follow his directions quickly. His concern was to seal the flooding compartments and protect the onboard souls. In his mind, he imagined which doors to close and demanded it done.

As trained, sailors responded as practiced—the captain's voice, firm and confident, headstrong, bellowed throughout the breached cruise ship. The *Sapphire Orchid* listed, no doubt seawater filling from somewhere. Orders executed perfectly, the predawn evacuation of the ship had begun, summoning passengers, lifejackets checked. The injured, triaged and treated. Though there was fear, since passengers were moving along, loading tenders, inboards starting and quickly separating from the vessel, floodlights illuminating the ocean surface, most remained calm. It took thirty-nine minutes to completely disembark the *Sapphire Orchid* with only Nickoli remaining with his mistresses and Marie and Lou.

And when he went to gather and send them all on their own private tender, it was Sherrita who told him the good news that all five of them were with child, having learned from Lou moments ago their tests were positive.

An hour passed, the sky lightened. Nickoli checked every compartment himself, assuring no single soul remained. He retrieved from his private quarters a half empty bottle of Scotch handed down from his great-grandfather, grandfather, then father, for the day an heir would certainly come. He tucked it under his arm and walked the empty corridor to the bridge. Beneath him, he knew much of the hull had given way, the ship not designed to sink properly—a top-heavy hotel atop a cargo vessel was all she was. Nickoli heard the popping of the meticulous welds, and could feel his vessel contorting—the demons of the ocean eating and having no mercy. The structure misaligned in the channel. Nickoli poured the Scotch into the cap of his thermos and sipped the two-hundred-year-old ferment. It was smooth and perfect.

Dozens of lifeboats headed off, as ordered, to the Atabeira lagoon four miles away. There was no emotion from Nickoli as he stood at the bridge. The only person onboard, he must listen to the sinking of his vessel, for it was important to know how to salvage it. How it would twist and fold and buckle; to know if possible, the removal of the cruise ship from the channel.

The electricity went out. The *Sapphire Orchid* was dark. Nickoli left the bridge, for he heard the edges that held the plate glass in place pop. The bridge would soon be swallowed. All this, the fault of engineers, the fault of the vessel's size, the fault of the consumer. A Titanic, its own weight would crush it, not the sea. And as the stern sank and the bow pitched, Nickoli made his way to the very tip of the steeply angled bow, holding the rail to keep from slipping into the sea. The helicopter pad was at forty degrees. The sea had consumed the mid-ship, gurgling its way toward him. An ocean gulp and a surge of seawater came, as he straddled and locked his legs within the railing. He was about to sire an heir and would not be denied as the Caribbean came and washed all around. Amidst white foam and sounds all too familiar to the unnatural event, Nickoli felt himself lift as the stern sank deep, lodging, releasing an echo, the bow elevated in a way, becoming a beacon.

The sinking had stopped. There was no more metal bending or glass breaking, just the debris. Nickoli knew the depths of these waters and its outcrop, for they were deep enough to swallow the *Orchid* entirely. And as the sea calmed, the debris floated, and the sky whitened, Captain Nickoli Lavaki, the bottle of Scotch in hand, legs locked, was wedged on the only area of the *Orchid* that broke the surface.

Chapter 20

Gail arrived at her Davis Island residence via shuttle from the Tampa International Airport. Overwhelmed the day she left for her cruise, Gail had forgotten to stop her mail; the stuffed mailbox was a vivid reminder of her financial crisis. Her husband's overdue credit card statements still came—three of them under her name. An IRS second lien notice against her home sent certified, awaited her signature at the post office. She tossed the satchel to the floor, showered, and collapsed to her bed. For most of the night she tossed, bothered by the vivid reminder, her life a mess. And the strange events that led her to return home early added to her confusion.

Unable to sleep, Gail decided to go to the TV station, a second home, source of comfort, and emotional support in some respects. It was four o'clock in the morning. Using the remaining cash Jason had given her, Gail took a taxi. Only a three-minute drive.

Entering the WKMC station through the rear parking lot, she saw only the interns and newest hires had arrived and were fully caffeinated. She apologized for the surprise, explaining she left the cruise ship in Tortola—the only single woman onboard was the heartbreaking reason given. "It was unnerving and I could no longer take the hard stares," Gail told arriving friends in the control room.

Though she despised Emmitt, this morning he was unusually friendly. He was breaking in a new female reporter; undoubtedly her eventual replacement. This didn't bother Gail much, as she was guilty of similar aspirations. It was likely he'd soon turn his jealousy to the new young one—his journalistic skills not relevant, the root of his anger, competing against the eye-appealing requirement of a viewer's morning news consumption—a slim woman, dressed in a tight, bold-color dinner dress, with lots of curves and a hint of a sexual tease.

Gail settled in her dressing room. It was a mess, the way she had left it. For the next thirty minutes staff trickled past her door, all surprised to see Gail, especially the young female anchor hungry for airtime. It was partly the reason Gail came, wanting to know how much time she'd have before they replaced her with someone who didn't require as much makeup and body contouring. She had bills to pay and would need to start looking for another job quickly, should the station replace her sooner than expected.

Emmitt told Gail she looked horrible and should go home. Gail wanted to kick him between his legs. And if she had a mambo of her own, she would have brought the black magic.

At exactly 5:30 a.m., the production staff gathered to review prepared video packages for the 6 a.m. news. Gail enjoyed sitting on the sidelines for once, an observer, watching the nervousness of the beautiful and youthful substitute anchor.

As Emmitt laid out the news timeline, Gail watched. Was he going to mess with the new girl, or give her softball stories to make her look good? How much influence would he have over dress color, makeup, shape of her chest? Emmitt was an overall cranky person with a bad gambling habit. His decisions were often based on the degree of his morning misery, or the degree of financial loss at the Let It Ride table at the Hard Rock Casino. As the meeting progressed, Gail could see Emmitt's eyes harden at the breaking news bulletin just handed to him by an intern—which wasn't entirely unusual, because just about anything qualified as breaking news these days. He turned his head and looked at Gail in a manner that'd she'd seen when a great story arrived. It was that "hard news look," the Great Story expression that suddenly consumed a good journalist. Was the substitute about to get a big break? Gail thought. Was the new girl good enough to make the story dramatic, a skill Gail had honed her entire career?

"Aren't you supposed to be on the Love Boat?" Emmitt said, holding the sheet of paper.

Gail didn't know what to say. It was a seven-day cruise, but here she sat in her chair in the conference room. Did the cruise ship company secretly send him the video? Was Emmitt holding onto it for the day he surprised her with it? A video to end her career?

He started to ask her rapid-fire questions, which allowed no time to respond. "How did you get back so quickly? What port were you dropped off? Why did you leave the ship? Were you thrown off? You're broke, how could you afford a last-minute plane ticket?" All questions Gail would ask if she were the reporter. Emmitt had worked the neighborhoods of East Houston. Though an asshole, he was a great investigative reporter in his own right.

Gail had never considered the consequences of coming to the station. Television was her life. It was all she had, and she had never contemplated that she'd be on the receiving end of a good reporter's grilling. A valid lie had to come quickly. But Emmitt was as good as her in her Philly days, and felt he deserved her anchor spot. It was the simple fact that she had the capacity to form a great early-morning white smile, a cleavage, and read the teleprompter exactly as written at a word rate that packed as much news as possible before the next commercial.

Gail thought quickly; something that would buy her time. *Give him a piece of the truth.* Like she did to hold viewers through a commercial break, a teaser. *I know the secret of the* Sapphire Orchid *and why women conceive.*

In the long pause, she'd obviously conveyed there was nothing she could say to lie her way out of answering his questions. The entire newsroom was quiet. They all wanted to know how she got off the ship and back home so quickly. But to Emmitt, holding whatever information led to his rapid-fire questions, her lack of a response told him this was a great story and Gail was a big part. He'd get to the bottom quickly. What he held in his hand, it couldn't wait. He wanted to see her face contort one more time, making her pay with the notion that she'd be dead right now if the news was correct.

At the head of the table, Emmitt leaned forward and slid the printed bulletin down the length—past emptied coffee cups. Two people had to pass it along before the bulletin reached Gail.

"Read that," Emmitt demanded. "Out loud."

"Breaking News," Gail said, conveying the words in her smooth television voice. "The *Sapphire Orchid* sa . . . sank—" She coughed and gasped. "My God, Vera!"

"Read it," Emmitt said. "I'd like to know if you can do it on air."

Instantly, she knew what he was getting at. *Me! . . . Reading this on television, my emotions tumbling. . . how I would react to a near-death experience!* It was raw and virile, given she was on the *Sapphire Orchid* less than forty-eight hours before it sank. He could work this for at least two weeks, upping advertising rates, solely because the viewer had a direct connection to the sunken *Sapphire Orchid.*

"Go ahead, Gail," Emmitt said in a respectful, supportive manner. "You can do this."

Voodoo Cruise

This was one of the many parodies of Emmitt. Though he was a bastard, this type of intensity was what they both lived for. He tossed aside his jealousy when it came to such raw journalism.

"Gail," Emmitt said, softly this time. "I know you can do this."

"The *Sapphire Orchid* sank in the notorious Navidad cut, off the coast of Haiti . . ." she read.

There were gasps in the newsroom. All eyes fixed on Gail. She was present, in the newsroom, and not at the bottom of the Caribbean.

But what set Gail apart from other reporters was her character and how it carried in front of the camera. She came across as sincere and likable. Genuine.

She finished the next two sentences. "There are few details to go on, except to say a distress call was put out sometime around four o'clock a.m."

"News travels fast, doesn't it?" Emmitt said.

Gail's hand shook as she held the paper. Vera, what about her friend, did she make it off alive? For Vera to die without Gail ever being forgiven was disheartening. When would all this bad luck stop?

"Gail, do you want to go on the air and report this story as it unfolds?"

It was a moment of reckoning. To not go on meant she wasn't a reporter but a reader.

The answer was simple. "Yes!"

"Five, four, three, two . . ."

"Good morning, this is Gail Stroud from WKMC TV Channel 5 Tampa Bay. This morning, we bring you exclusive coverage of breaking news. The *Sapphire Orchid*, owned by Emerald Cruise Line, sank in the Navidad Narrows off the coast of Haiti this morning. What most of you don't know is that I was on the *Orchid* less than forty-eight hours ago. It's frightening to think I would still be on the ship had I not elected to return to Tampa early."

Gail paused, a compulsion coming over her as Jason's words echoed that she was a reader, she'd not been a true journalist since leaving Philly. "What most of you also don't know is that I've been unable to conceive a child." She spoke off the top of her head. Emmitt, in her right ear, said, "You go girl, honesty" . . . "For some unexplained reason, infertile couples on the *Sapphire Orchid* conceive at an unusually high rate. But as my viewers learned on-air last month, after I booked my cruise on the *Sapphire Orchid*, troubles in my personal life played out. So I decided to make the best of my time on the cruise, without a mate, to investigate the life-giving mystery that surrounds this ship."

Gail could hear Emmitt coaching her, saying, "Take your time, we are about to go viral, people are turning on their TVs. Give us more, sweetheart."

Sweetheart! . . . "But now isn't the time to tell you what I've learned about this special ship. It's more important for you to know the safety of the passengers. If everyone made it off safely." Gail paused. File footage of the *Sapphire Orchid* rolled on the green screen. "I was fortunate enough to meet someone we can go live to as soon as we make a satellite phone connection. Be patient, folks, as we try to contact an American who lives near where the *Sapphire Orchid* sank and likely saw it happen."

Emmitt spoke in her earpiece. "Great call, Gail. Let's go to commercial break. But how the hell are we going to pull off what you just said? What if no one picks up on the other end?"

As they cut to a commercial everyone in the station cheered. It was a great story. Calls were arriving from major broadcasting stations, requesting to link to her broadcast.

"Gail," Emmitt said. "You got two minutes. Get your person on the phone. CNN will broadcast you live."

Gail was prepared. Ruth had given Gail her satellite phone number, written on a slip of paper. Fortunately, it was in her purse, which an intern rushed to her from her dressing room. Dialing, she prayed Ruth would answer.

It took nearly a minute to make the connection. She was on speakerphone. "Ruth, this is Gail."

"Hello, Gail, Jason called and told about your mishap on the ship."

Shit, Gail thought, *everyone in the newsroom now knows there was an issue. Crap.*

"Ruth . . . news about the ship. What can you tell us?"

"I'm at the dock now, surrounded by passengers that got off safely," Ruth said.

Emmitt tapped Gail on the shoulder.

"Ruth, sorry to interrupt, we are about to go on the air. Would you mind telling the world what happened?"

Everyone in the newsroom held their breath, without knowing the news. What if thousands had perished?

"Okay," Ruth replied. "It's mostly good."

Emmitt stood off camera and counted using his fingers . . . Four . . . Three . . . Two . . .

"We are live on satellite phone with Ruth Applegate, an American living in Atabeira, Haiti, near where the *Sapphire Orchid* sank just before dawn. Thank you, Ruth, for taking my call. Can you tell us where you are and what you know?"

"Yes, I can. Atabeira is about four miles from where the *Sapphire Orchid* sank. In fact, I can see the bow sticking out of the water."

"You said the news is good. What can you tell families and friends who might know people on the cruise ship?"

"They are all safe and alive, every single soul, thank goodness. Some are injured, mostly bumps, bruises, and broken bones from the jolt, striking the side of the Navidad Channel."

"Really, can you tell us how they were able to get off the ship safely?"

"I was awakened by an earthquake. Then, a second tremor. I couldn't sleep, so I went out on the porch. You remember, the one we sat on just two days ago. I could see the *Sapphire Orchid* all lit up. It was unusual in that we weren't expecting it back."

"Ruth, did you see it sink?"

"Yes, it sank slowly, which was good, because there was enough time for everyone to abandon the ship. I heard the captain calling general quarters. A few minutes later, a warning to brace for impact. The lights flickered, but remained on for a considerable time. The ship listed, then slowly sank, stern first. It took nearly an hour. Every water taxi in the village went to help. By dawn everyone was off except the captain."

"That's great news," Gail said, looking directly into the camera, a stock photo of the *Sapphire Orchid* as her background. "But you said the captain stayed onboard?"

"Yes, I can see him through my binoculars. He's perched on the bow with ninety-nine percent of the *Orchid* underwater. All I can see is a portion of the bridge and the very tip of the bow. I think he's drinking from a bottle."

"Thank you, Ruth. Concerned families can rest easy, and so can I."

"You're welcome, come see me again."

Emmitt cut to the new woman reporter and the local news.

Instantly, the station telephone lines lit up, all from major news outlets asking to schedule Gail for interviews.

Gail went back to her dressing room, shut the door, and locked it. She buried her face in her hands and sobbed, emotionally drained, relieved everyone made it off alive. But there would be questions from reporters savvier than her, asking her relationship with Ruth. Her only answer would be the truth. But should she reveal Jason, the black magic, and her advance knowledge the *Sapphire Orchid* was in peril? How could she say the sinking was because of the cruise line's presence in the lagoon? Was it believable? She feared the worst, the release of the video, and must manage the story in a way to protect her career.

For the remainder of the morning, Gail did live interviews. Her staff generated footage of the lagoon, the *Sapphire Orchid*, and the geology of the ocean with plausible reasons why it sank. A tremor and shifting of the seafloor. The most interesting fact was that Christopher Columbus's *Santa Maria* ran aground in nearly the exact spot.

CNN was the first to interview her.

"Ms. Stroud, what an incredible breaking story and the worry you prevented by getting information so fast regarding the safety of the passengers."

"Thank you, Breanna," Gail said to the reporter.

"But I must ask, you were at the exact spot, Atabeira, prior to the ship going down?"

"Yes, I was on the *Sapphire Orchid* two days ago."

"What incredible luck for you to be off the ship! What made you decide to leave? Were you investigating a story? Did you learn something that no one else knew? Perhaps the sinking?"

This was the decisive moment. If she evaded the answer, the next interviewer would key off her answer. It was the moment where she had to tell her story, but instead of saying why she was thrown off, she told the same lie she told her station—the experience wasn't for her. Most people knew about the mystery that surrounded the *Sapphire Orchid*; the information wasn't hard to find. The story had been out there for many years. So, her answer was exactly that. She'd booked the cruise and planned a badly needed vacation. The story of her jerk husband was already public, so it could be pieced that she went alone after discovering his improprieties. Gail explained she snuck off to Atabeira because she felt there was a story here. She met Ruth and explained to the reporter who Ruth was.

The story of the sinking of the *Orchid* would run for a few days, with reports as passengers arrived back in the United States. And, as was the case of the *Concordia*, the news cycle would end, and the story would die after several weeks.

It was mid-afternoon when Gail arrived home again. She ignored the pile of mail sitting on the kitchen table. Exhausted, she collapsed and didn't wake up until after dark. She turned on the living room light and saw the satchel sitting where'd she tossed it. Gail deliberately left the TV off and her phone on vibrate. She must collect herself.

Crawling from the couch, she unpacked, and came across the voodoo dolls. And she wondered: Did the mambo really sink the *Sapphire Orchid*?

Gail held the handcrafted figures in separate hands. What an uncanny likeness of her. She inspected the area where the mambo inserted the pearls. *Twins,* she thought, recalling what Marie had informed her about what the pearls meant. *Different genders? Impossible! I don't feel pregnant.*

Holding the Jason doll, she felt something against her thumbs. "Ouch!" It was a sharp object embedded the same as the pearls, in the torso fibers.

Her pricked finger bled.

"What is it?"

Sucking her finger, Gail went into the bathroom and retrieved her manicure kit.

She inspected the doll. "What's in there?"

Using a cuticle tool, she inserted the narrow metal end between the fibers to dig out the object. Wedging it free, she stared as it flicked to the tabletop. It was a stone. A piece from Jason's rosary, one of the crystals. He must've put it there.

Inspecting the doll, she saw a second crystal lodged.

Voodoo Cruise

"Are these diamonds?" She went to her jewelry case and produced her tiny engagement ring and compared them in the light. "I never knew how cloudy my diamond was, almost yellow."

She debated. Were these diamonds? How much were they worth? But her real confusion came from the thought Jason had access to such an item. *He must sell these. It's where he gets his wealth. But, to give them away? Why me? Is he trying to help me, just as he does his orphans?*

Into the night questions raced in her head, repeating until she slept.

The next morning, the *Sapphire Orchid*'s sinking continued to generate newsworthy content. There were plenty of uploaded cell phone videos of the sinking ship, passenger interviews, in-depth discussions regarding the mysteriously high rate of conception. Speculation, talking heads, so-called experts claiming the wreck had wedged in the Navidad Channel a certain way, making it impossible to refloat.

By noon, the phone calls and emails had subsided. Gail assigned one of her staff to deal with anything else that involved her for the day. She wanted to visit a jeweler in Ybor City, a person she trusted, to determine if the stones Jason gave her were in fact real. A person she'd wanted to do a story on for some time, Saul Levine. At seventy-seven, Saul had reached a point in his profession where he selected the clients he wanted to work with and never discounted his price. A gemologist turned hermit, he became globally known for his expertise in grading diamonds and was often used as a resource for expert opinions in the valuation of estate liquidations.

Saul regularly loaned jewelry for Gail to wear at the galas she attended as part of the public presence she had to maintain. A kind and generous man, up in years, he worked alone on the second floor of his Ybor City jewelry store, located on a side street off Centre Avenue. Gail thought Saul's life was interesting, having worked in Jerusalem for many years before coming to the United States. She routinely bugged him to do a story on his life work, but Saul kindly refused, saying anonymity was a lifestyle he preferred.

Saul took a daughterly liking to Gail and gave her back a pair of diamond earrings Richard had pawned in his last-ditch effort to win all that'd he lost before Gail found out.

Gail took the trolley from the Channelside District to Ybor City. Clutching her purse, she walked the two blocks to Saul's brick building that backed to railroad tracks. She entered, climbed the narrow inside wood stairway, and knocked. The door showed no sign someone earned a living there.

Old, it took Saul several minutes to answer. Gail was aware of the time lapse, because on two other occasions, she'd left before Saul answered. Turned out, if he was working on an item, an uninvited guest would be second in line. He did not answer the door because the work of his paying customers came first.

"Hi, Saul," Gail said, greeting him with a warm smile.

"You're lucky you caught me, I just finished my sandwich and was about to work on another setting."

Short, bent over from arthritis, Saul lifted his eyes to look up at Gail. "Did your husband pawn another piece of jewelry?"

"No, Saul, not this time. I'm here for another reason. Can you look at two stones given to me as a gift? I was told they are crystals, but have a hunch they might not be."

"Come in," Saul said, slowly making his way back to a workbench that'd seen better days.

A brightly lit fluorescent light hung above the table by just a few inches, concentrating the bright light.

Gail handed Saul the stones, bundled in a soft brown cloth used to clean her reading glasses.

Voodoo Cruise

Saul opened the soft cloth and studied the contents for several minutes. Showing no emotion, he got up from his stool and went to the far corner of his flat. With his right foot, he guided a stepstool to the base of a bookcase. High up, there appeared a collection of dust-covered journals—a personal inventory gathered over the years.

"Have a seat. I believe I can help," Saul said, stepping from the stool, carrying a journal with newspaper clippings shoved within.

He twisted to his side as if his spine had fused. "These are in fact diamonds, very precious diamonds."

Saul opened the journal. "They are unique in that they do not require to be cut. They are uniform and perfect in shape and dimension."

Gail's heart felt as if it leapt into throat. "Diamonds!" Speechless, her mind raced. "What would cause them to be identical? Aren't they mined as unfinished stones?"

"Most are," Saul said. "Except in cases where there is extreme heat. Like when a meteor strikes the earth. I'm familiar with this particular stone, but this is the first time I've held the remarkable gem."

Gail came to his side. The journal held paper-clipped photos of the diamonds that lay on the table.

Saul set one of the diamonds next to the photo.

"Here it is." He lifted his head and smiled. "You have in your possession the most flawless diamonds known to mankind. Read."

Crouching, speed-reading, Gail gathered the content quickly. "Utopia diamonds, no one knows where they come from?"

"Exactly," Saul said. "They surfaced about eleven years ago from a distributor in Jerusalem that prides itself in secrecy."

Saul smiled. "I must ask how you came into possession of such a rarity."

Gail gave him the *Reader's Digest* version as Saul listened.

"You do know they are priceless. You can receive a pretty penny for each."

"Really!" Gail said, surprised.

"You must keep them in my safe. If the wrong person knows you have these, your safety can be jeopardized."

"Really!"

"These diamonds are what I consider the rarest known to mankind. They are truly special and sought after by wealthy people."

"What should I do, Saul?"

"I can liquidate them for you, and no one will know where they came from."

"I desperately need the money. I think that's why he gave them to me."

"I would love the opportunity to sell them. And you know, of course, there would be absolute confidentiality."

Gail knew Saul's integrity, and was keenly aware his commission would go to local charities.

"Please do, Saul. How much do you think you could get?"

"For each diamond, half million, maybe more."

"Wh . . .What!" Gail nearly fainted. Such money would pay off her house and set her straight again. But why did Jason do such a thing? She'd had him so wrong, and didn't see the person beneath. She misjudged him from the very beginning . . . Or was he a thief like Milan?

But the bigger, lingering question was, once again, the mystery deepened. Clearly, Jason was the provider of the diamonds. And she, in possession of such great information. Why did Jason trust her? Was it time for the source of these diamonds to be revealed?

Chapter 21

Yaakov Kirshenbaum's cab dropped him off at the corner of Centre Avenue and 5th street in Ybor City. He regretted wearing his wool pants as he arrived in Florida, forgetting the thick summer humidity, and that it rained in August. Each pant leg sopped the wetness as the cuffs dragged in puddles that filled the imperfections of the cobbled brick walkway. It'd been an exhausting flight from the Tel Aviv diamond district, but not in any way unusual; travel like this was common. His life, like Saul's, was devoted to the appreciation, and in his case, the gathering of the finest gemstones on earth. His travels typically took him to the expanse of the African continent, deep into the throats of volcanic plugs, often a tireless and gritty journey. But as always, time was of the essence, before word leaked of such a rare discovery. The Utopia diamonds were the most sought after in the globe, amongst those who could easily afford them.

It was Jason who had informed Yaakov. He'd released two more precious stones, but not in the normal manner. He asked Yaakov to keep an eye out in Tampa, for the diamonds would surface soon. Fortunately, this find was relatively easy. Gail had selected a reputable and knowledgeable jeweler with impeccable integrity.

There was no wait at the top of the enclosed staircase this time. A knock, and Saul's voice called, "Come in, Yaakov."

Yaakov entered the flat that had not seen an improvement in forty years, except for the security cameras. Saul, slipping from the low stool of his jeweler's bench, met Yaakov halfway. The aged gemologists greeted each other, exchanging a mutual respect and politeness not often seen in the US, and got down to business.

Saul handed Yaakov the small cloth with the diamonds.

"Paragons," Yaakov said.

"Yes, a gift so worthy one could give it to God." Saul said, sitting back on his stool, bracing his hand against his well-worn workspace. He half-turned to Yaakov, his right hand shaking from Parkinson's.

"These diamonds seem to not be of earth minerals," Saul observed.

"You would think, but they are of this earth," Yaakov said, taking a seat on the same couch Gail had sat, not fully sitting back, but at the edge of the faded and squashed cushion; his briefcase close to his laced, travel-weary black shoes.

"What can you tell an old jeweler about the journeys of such a rare diamond?" Saul asked. "It's likely I will never set eyes upon such quality again."

"There is no greater quality on this earth," Yaakov said. "I assure you."

Saul smiled. He knew that.

"Out of kindness and trust, men such as us would appreciate knowing the journey of these precious stones. For there is never a normalcy that surrounds such brilliance. The discovery is believed to be a gift from God."

Saul waited patiently, knowing Yaakov had a duty to share the story; they were of the same breed. Yaakov was confident Saul would keep the secret of the stones that came from Jason, the only person who knew the location of the source.

"In this case, my friend, these are truly an expression of the heavens, delivered directly from the hand of God. The money goes to charity, and the poor children of the world through a delightful, youthful, and giving young man."

"Where did the name of the stone originate?"

"It's named after a place on earth that is as close to heaven as you can live. A place that once thrived but no longer exists. The diamonds come from a sunken atoll in the Pacific, near the equator. But no one is sure of the exact location, except the young man. The atoll, when it existed, was filled with natural riches, a place they say the angels came to vacation. The taro grew thick and tall, the breadfruit was sweet and hardy, and coconut palms snapped at the weight of their treetop bounty. Massive schools of tuna, so thick, would leap into boats, and the red snapper and shrimp, its flesh like sweet butter.

"Legend says that the bottom of the atoll glowed at every full moon, shooting a beacon toward the heavens. The inhabitants, Polynesians, were peaceful people and not in want of anything, living beyond a hundred years. It was in the length of their age and the story of their tradition, they passed down the secrets of navigating in dug-out breadfruit trees that the tale tells of the diamond."

Saul listened, but his face grew puzzled. "The atoll is no more. This young man, how did he come across the stones, and why him?"

"I know little of the man, except he was found as a child on an island in the region where the diamonds are believed to originate; raised by descendants of those that occupied the sunken atoll. I agreed only to represent his diamonds if he would assure me they were not stolen. He's by nature an honest lad, likely because he'd not westernized until his later years. His home is the island of Lekinioch. An elderly man he calls Grandfather Mau raised him. The grandfather had escaped as the atoll was sinking, and had told Jason the location, and that the diamonds were plentiful at the bottom of the submerged caldera. The grandfather was special in his own right, having discovered the diamonds on one of his dives. It was this discovery that led to the salvation of the sinking island's inhabitants."

"Does your effort do any good?" Saul asked.

"Yes," he replied, "all goes as I said to impoverished children of this world."

"Is that the wish of the person that has such incredible access to this limitless wealth?"

"Yes, and the world is fortunate to have such a person of control. For if anyone knew the location of the diamond's source, greed would take over. Only sadness could ever come from such desire."

"Agreed," Saul said. "But Tampa and the young lady that delivered them. I know her. She is a good woman. Why her?"

"The gentleman often does acts of goodwill. She, too, was in peril and he felt the need to cure the unfairness that happened to her."

"Hmmm, she's a beautiful woman. Would it be that he has an interest in her?"

"I've only met this man once. It was to negotiate the trust between us. I can't answer that."

Saul asked one last question. "Who are the purchasers of these diamonds?"

"A charitable firm that doesn't want them exploited. Most are held like items stored in the Vatican vault, so precious and pure, rarely are they sold. Because they are the clearest ever known, they also serve as masters in GIA clarity ranking."

Saul leaned to set his elbow on the table, taking pressure off his spine. "I must agree."

Yaakov lifted his traveled briefcase and set it on the workbench. "Before I leave, I must mark these stones. He lifted from his case a device. "Do you have a wall socket?"

Saul pointed to an outlet, where the fluorescent light was plugged.

Voodoo Cruise

Yaakov came to the table and set each diamond into the clamp and etched, using laser, an invisible inscription that registered the stones.

"When we come across one without an inscription, that's when we get concerned."

"How often has that happened?" Saul asked.

"Only once that I recall. We traced one such unmarked diamond to a laborer on a Japanese fishing trawler. The fisherman was interviewed. It came from a coworker who had fallen overboard. The trawler had worked the same area where we believe the source of the diamonds came from. It would be serious should the source ever become discovered. I understand there is a mighty number and would surely destroy the world market for diamonds; for as you know, we control to keep prices stable."

Chapter 22

On his way to the TV station, Emmitt Stooch stopped by Toccolano's Bakery on Swann Avenue to pick up an order Toccolano's owner promised for running a story on the now popular South Tampa bakery's grand opening of a second location in the Oxford Exchange. He specifically requested cream-filled Long Johns with coconut cream icing, Gail's Philadelphia favorite. Today was her last as the morning news anchor. The station had promoted Gail to the anchor position for the six o'clock news.

When she arrived for her final early morning broadcast, the station was dark. "Where is everybody?" she questioned.

"Surprise!" the news team said in unison, flipping the lights on and off, greeting Gail as she held a fresh cup of coffee.

"I don't know what to say, thank you. I could not have done any of this without you. We are a team."

Since she had paid off all her debts, including her mortgage, with the sale of the diamonds Jason gifted, she found she'd been a bit emotional lately, crying for no reason at all. Vera had forgiven her after Gail shared what she'd learned on Atabeira, telling her the story of Jason and his gift. She had plenty of money, paying off the IRS lien, buying a new car

Voodoo Cruise

and upgrading her wardrobe. The fact she felt better about herself showed in the way she came across each day in the newscast as a solid reporter, not relying on the teleprompter as much. But it was her breaking news story, the sinking of the *Sapphire Orchid*, that afforded her greater notoriety. She was nationally known, the station winning an award. Gail an anchor, a second seat at the evening news desk because of her strong viewer following.

"Long Johns, who brought them, my favorite!" Gail said, smelling the fresh-baked dough, immediately devouring one. "Mmm . . . it's still warm. I can't resist. I'm having a second."

"I brought them for your last segment," Emmitt said. "Thought you'd like to end your broadcast doing a dessert story."

"When I worked in Philly, I remember the smell of early morning bakeries. Toccolano's is as close as it comes to authentic South Philly pastries."

"Enjoy, there's plenty," Emmitt said.

As they prepared scripts and arranged the newscast, Gail found she'd eaten four so far. "I better stop, the cream inside is too rich. I'll get sick."

She sat in her makeup chair and said to her overly attentive stylists, "Make me beautiful, guys, one last time. And can someone hand me a drink of water? I was a bit of a pig. I need to wash this down."

"How about a tall glass of milk?" Emmitt said, handing Gail a filled glass.

"Thanks, Emmitt."

Gail and Emmitt had gotten along well for the past three weeks. Ratings were up, and he was breaking in the gullible new girl. What surprised her most was that he didn't seem at all jealous of her moving to primetime.

"Burps! Excuse me," Gail said as her hair was sprayed. "Did they change the brand of coffee we brew in the morning?"

"No, Gail, it's the same morning mud. But you know me, I'm a tea drinker, never touch the black stuff, it's not good for the skin or your television teeth," her stylist remarked.

"My stomach's been queasy in the mornings lately, I was wondering if it was the coffee."

"You know, you've been drinking quite a bit lately."

"I know. Maybe if I cut back my stomach will settle. Burrrp! Oh, excuse me again. I got donut breath."

"You're excused. Let's make your face look exceptionally great for the camera one last time in the morning. I'm going to miss you, Gail. The new anchor is a twit."

As she took her seat in front of the camera and the glare of lighting, Emmitt spoke to Gail through her earpiece. She finished her sixth Long John. "Let's make your last early-morning broadcast a memorable one . . . Ten seconds . . . oh, oh . . . Gail, you got cream filling on the tip of your nose."

Gail went into a panic. If she brushed her nose, it could smear and there wasn't enough time for someone to wipe. Her lips puckered, her eyes rolled trying to locate it on her nose. Her stomach tumbled.

"Just kidding, Gail," she heard in the earpiece. "Four, three, two . . ."

"Emmitt, you're an asshole."

"Oh shit," Gail heard in her earpiece. What an opening! They'd gone live and the microphone broadcast the sentence.

"Good morning and sorry for that opening remark, this is Gail Stroud from WKMC Channel 5. Today is my last broadcast. But I'm not leaving you. Just going to get some extra hours of sleep in the morning. You'll all see me on the six o'clock news. I hope each one of you tunes in.

"In today's news, the City of New Port Richey, after nearly thirteen years, announced the opening of the historic Hacienda Hotel. The city itself was once the home of the silent movie industry and stars such as Gloria Swanson and Thomas Meighan. Renovations cost over eight million dollars and the building is expected to contribute significantly to the city's already thriving downtown district."

The video feed from New Port Richey lasted three minutes. All Gail had to do was a few more short reads of the prompter, which, since her trip, reminded her of Jason each time the script ran. She wondered where he was, if she'd ever meet him again.

The minutes ticked off. A five-sentence piece about the cost overruns of the downtown Tampa light rail—a commercial break—the morning traffic report—lots of weather—another short piece from Gail, this time only four sentences—the sportscast. Finally, she was ready for her closing segment on Toccolano's Bakery. She'd eaten too many Long Johns, but they were fresh, she was celebrating the last of having to deal with Emmitt. As she waited for commercials to run, her stomach became more unsettled.

"Does anyone have some Tums?"

But what she heard in the earpiece was something entirely different. "Guys, I've lost our piece on the bakery, it's been deleted."

"What!" Gail said, concerned.

"Quick, we got less than sixty seconds; get another story," Emmitt's voice was heard.

"Are you sure you've lost the story?" Gail asked.

"Yes," a control room technician said. "The computer dropped the video."

"Okay, everyone, let's keep our wits about us. Get me another foodie segment, quick," demanded Emmitt.

"Thirty seconds. Are you going to be okay, Gail?"

With her hand pressed against her stomach, she didn't answer.

"I got another segment," Emmitt's voice came over her earpiece.

"Describe it to me," Gail asked.

"It's on a food truck, you know like the Taco Bus."

"Okay, that'll work. Put up the script."

"Fifteen seconds."

"Good God, I need something for my stomach."

"Gail, the segment is ninety seconds. Can you last that long?"

"I have to."

"Here comes your script."

"Three, two . . ."

"You remember the Florida State Fair and the deep-fried Twinkies, or last year's favorite, the deep-fried Oreo Burger. Well, a Hudson, Florida man is taking his deep-fried treats on the road. Calvin Snooks, owner of Everything Crispy & Fried, has a new item on his menu." Gail paused briefly as she read ahead, before the words were to depart her lips. "Deep-fried beer-battered geckos." Her stomach tumbled. Her throat jumped, releasing a burp.

"Oh shit," she heard in her earpiece. "Keep reading, Gail. We'll be going to the video in any second."

"Yes, you heard me," Gail read the words. "The critters we see racing about our pool lanais and crawling along our stucco are now a traveling delicacy, yum yum." Her mind raced. *Who the fuck wrote this piece?*

"Mr. Snooks says that the challenge to frying up these reptilians is when you dump them into the vat of boiling lard. It must be done fast, so that they don't have time to lose their tiny tails. He says most don't, but for those that do, you can eat them just like a curly fry.

"Burrrp!"

She heard in her earpiece, "She's about to puke, folks, get to the fucking video."

The camera switched to the video feed of Calvin at the fryer in his food truck. "You reach right into the bucket like this and scoop them up alive and drop 'em in the batter. You see? They can't escape because they's stuck in the goop. Then yin's pick 'em up and drop 'em into the grease."

A sizzling sound was heard. Off camera, Gail's expression was one of a seasick sailor.

"Hang in there, Gail," she heard. "Composure."

"It takes a few seconds. Scoop 'em out and set them on a paper towel to let the grease soak away. See, the little rascals are frozen in time with their eyes wide open, just as the dried-up dead geckos we see sometimes when we move the 'frigerator to clean."

"Gail, we are back to you in five seconds."

"But the best is when you bite into them. Ya see, the stomach's contents stay nice and mushy and blend well with the crunchy taste." Black goo squirted out when John bit into one. "Oops, got some on my shirt."

The camera came to Gail. She was flushed, sick, her eyes big and round. "Zoom in," Emmitt ordered.

Gail's cheeks filled as her stomach erupted. Projectile vomit, white cream and bits of dough and shredded coconut headed straight for the camera lens.

"Camera two," Emmitt called. "Get a side shot."

Gail heaved, a successive series of white vomit spewing from her mouth like a fire hose, covering the anchor desk, the open laptop, and her bright yellow dress. Emmitt's voice came. "Find some chunks, and zoom in on the dribble coming through her nose."

Gail signaled, knifing her throat to cut the shot. She could not say a word.

"Okay, cut to a commercial."

Gail's stylist raced to care for her. "Oh my god, what happened!"

She couldn't say a word.

Gail, her head woozy, tears in her eyes, tried to brace herself. Light-headed, Gail fell face-first onto the desk.

"No, no, Gail, don't . . . not there!" Thump. . . "Yuck!"

It took several minutes to get Gail to her feet and escort her back to her dressing room. She could barely speak. Her speech, more of a low, nauseated release, "Emmitt, you fucking asshole."

That was all she could say, supported on each arm and escorted into her dressing room.

Gail had changed her dress and rehydrated herself. She was too weak to go and punch Emmitt in the face. The first phone call she took was from her good friend Vera.

"Gail, are you okay?"

"No, not really, I'm sure that video will go viral."

"What are you going to do about it?"

"I'm going to pick myself up, hold my head high, and go back on the air tomorrow night, apologize, and explain what an asshole Emmitt is."

"Maybe you were really sick," Vera said.

"I was thinking that," Gail responded. My stomach hasn't been right for some reason. I've felt a bit off for several days now. Sometimes I cry for no apparent reason."

There was a pause on the phone.

"Vera, Vera . . . are you there?"

"Yes, Gail." But Vera stayed silent.

"You're quiet, Vera. Come on. Tell me what's on your mind."

"Gail, you know when you told me the story about what happened on the cruise ship and that Marie set you up with the casino dealer."

"Yes!"

Gail turned white. She read Vera's mind.

"Gail, do you think for a teensy moment you might have morning sickness?"

"You mean, I might be pregnant?"

"You didn't have your period?"

"I'm three weeks late. Passed it off as stress. It's happened many times."

"Gail, come to my house. I have a pregnancy test kit."

Chapter 23

I'm pregnant!" Gail said, holding the pee stick, rotating to show the positive result to Vera. "I don't know what to think."

"You are with child. It's a good thing no matter what," Vera said. "According to my wise mother, she often lamented there is never a good time to have a baby. When I think about her words of wisdom, she was right. Just accept the result, Gail." Vera wanted her to look on the brighter side.

"I don't know who the father is. I've no clue."

"Marie Battar might know," Vera suggested. "You are a good investigator with plenty of resources at your disposal, why don't you hunt her down and ask?"

Gail went into Vera's kitchen and tossed the stick into the wastebasket. "Guess I need to start somewhere."

"Call Emerald Cruise Line. Ask for Human Resources," Vera suggested. "I'm sure they kept track of Marie."

Gail returned home. She wasn't sure if she should feel elated or troubled. "Am I ready to have a child?" A feeling deep inside said, "Yes." It's what she'd wanted, but not this way, not knowing anything about the genetics of the father. *What if my child has olive skin, or curly hair? I must know who the father is. If not for my own sanity, then for my child.*

That afternoon, Gail dialed Emerald's phone number. She was placed on hold for nearly a half hour until finally, someone answered. "Emerald Cruise Line, how may I direct your call?"

"Human Resources," Gail requested.

"One moment, please."

"Hello, HR," an Indian voice said.

"Ah . . . yeah . . . hi, I'm Gail Stroud from WKMC TV in Tampa. I'm trying to locate one of your cruise ship employees."

"Is this a family emergency?"

"Well, yes, kind of."

"What's the individual's name?"

"Marie, Marie Battar."

"One moment please."

There was music for several minutes.

"Did you say Marie Battar?"

"Yes, her husband was a doctor on the *Sapphire Orchid*."

"Madam, they no longer work for the cruise line."

"Can you tell me where they went?"

"We are not permitted to provide that information, even if we knew, madam. I'm very sorry that we can't help you."

"Thank you," Gail said, disappointed.

"Thank you for calling Emerald Cruise Line." The person hung up.

Gail was at a loss. Marie and Lou could be anywhere in the world. If she called other cruise lines, it was unlikely they would not tell her anyway.

What to do? she thought. *Find a doctor. I'm having a baby.*

It was fortunate for Gail that she had started on the evening news, since she had severe morning sickness. The late-day broadcast afforded the capacity to get her tumbling stomach under control. Each day before work, Gail searched for Lou and Marie, but was careful not to contact Emerald again. They were in possession of the video of her naked in the dining room trying to screw any man that was close enough.

Several weeks passed, the child growing inside beginning to show. Her TV anchor contract required her to notify the station of a pregnancy, which she did. And the station loved it, because it drove up ratings—the social networks' conversations amongst female viewers about her on-camera appearance and maternity outfits as the child inside her lived. Plus, boutique baby retailers, pediatric practices, and pharmaceutical firms paid a premium for commercials, a fee that escalated as Gail's baby bump grew larger.

At ten weeks, Vera went with Gail for a fetal Doppler to hear the baby's heartbeat.

"I guess it's me and you, Vera. You are the surrogate father," Gail said, lying on the obstetrician's table, feet in stirrups.

Vera, supportive, loved the fact Gail included her in the pregnancy. Still married to Ian, Vera had not conceived yet.

The medical assistant smeared lubricant on her bulging stomach. "Are you sure you're only ten weeks along?" the sonogram tech asked.

"Yes, absolutely sure," Gail said with a puzzled look.

"For a woman of such a small stature you are bigger than the most."

"I'm having twins," Gail joked. "The mambo said so."

"Mambo?"

Vera interrupted. "Yes, Gail has a voodoo curse placed on her, she going to have twins, one boy and one girl."

All three women laughed.

Voodoo Cruise

The medical assistant smeared more jelly and slid the sonogram about. There was a swishing sound. "Hear that?" she said. "It's the heartbeat."

Everyone listened as they looked at Gail's tummy, then at each other.

A surprised look came to the technician conducting the test. "Oh, oh . . . mambo, who?"

Vera and Gail exchanged a confused look. "I was just kidding about twins," Gail said, her tummy protruding, the position awkward for a conversation.

"Your mambo friend is pretty powerful . . . Listen." There was silence in the room as she adjusted the volume. The squishing grew louder. "Hear that?"

"Hear what?" Gail asked, not understanding what she meant.

"A second heartbeat."

Again, silence and the discernible second echo.

"There are two? Are you sure?"

"Absolutely."

Gail was shocked. The mambo's blessing came true.

Vera grabbed a towel and wiped down Gail's tummy, then helped her from the stirrups to her feet.

Gail's legs were rubber. "Vera, I have to sit."

The pair sat there quietly, digesting, as the technician packed and left them alone. Vera waited patiently as Gail weighed the gravity of her news.

"Why am I not excited about this?" she asked. "There's an emptiness."

Vera, knowing how Gail worked out her problems, understood enough to let her think this through. *She'll come around,* Vera thought.

"I don't know who the father of these children is. I'm unable to share the experience with him. That's what troubling me," she told her good friend.

Sitting next to Gail, Vera hugged her. "We'll locate the father, wherever he is. He must know for the sake of your children and your peace of mind."

With tears rolling from her eyes, Gail released a smile.

Supportive, Vera dabbed them away.

Chapter 24

It was the RJA Foundation seal Milan peeled off a school book while sleeping in the Lekinioch schoolhouse that led to a clue as to who might know the source of the Utopia diamond. There were other items on Lekinioch as well, with the same foundation's seal—a top of the line, quiet-running generator that powered the one-room elementary school. However, the generator was rarely used, due to the self-sufficiency of the island inhabitants and the fuel cost to operate. Several boats that families fished with on the open ocean and traveled to the neighboring atoll of Ta had the same foundation's label. It was clear from the poor economic conditions on other islands that Lekinioch had a western benefactor.

When Milan escaped from the tuna trawler and remained stranded on the Lekinioch, a Chuukese family took him in, trading labor for housing. Milan was careful to keep to himself, working whatever odd job was required. He was certain the RJA foundation stood for the Ruth & Jason Applegate and that they were judicious with funding, not wanting to upset the subsistence lifestyle by westernizing the inhabitants too much.

Milan had learned the likely benefactor had lived in the Mau's hut. That it was Jason, found floating alone on a catamaran, his parents missing, taken in by Mau. And as custom in the Polynesian culture, Grandfather Mau passed along knowledge of Pacific navigation in the form of a story, leaving for those that could interpret an idea where certain islands were located, and how to get there. The location of the sunken island was likely embedded in such a story within Jason, Milan surmised.

After spending nearly three months on Lekinioch, Milan had earned enough in barter, collecting a vast quantity of coconuts to trade for passage on a miserable, unreliable, rust-bucket vessel that supplied the many small islands of Micronesia. During his stay, he visited Grandfather Mau often. And to garner his respect, he learned Chuukese, thanks to the teaching of French-speaking Mariel. Also, so not to tip off Mariel, he asked Mau directly the more penetrating questions in his native language.

Once off the island, Milan immediately set out to find Jason. Which wasn't difficult, as the RJA Foundation was based in Washington, DC. IRS Form 990, easily accessible online, provided the street address, Ruth's residence. The foundation generated $3.2 million last year in charitable contributions. A sub-schedule listed Jason as the primary funding source. Milan had to ask, who was this young man, raised as a child by the elder Mau, who had come across such great wealth? The logic was easy. Jason knew the source of the Utopia diamonds, mined them, and released them rather judiciously to meet the funding needs of the foundation—to help orphans like him. If there was bitterness to Milan's endeavor, he wanted to know what Jason's role was in sending him to prison in New Guinea.

Milan staked out Ruth's Washington, DC home for several months, again working at a nearby five-star hotel, this time as a bellhop. From the second-floor mezzanine, he could see across the avenue and a third of a block down the street to Ruth's brownstone's front door. Though he never saw Ruth enter, Jason came and went several times. Milan dug through his garbage, but did not gather a shred of information, except for an empty envelope with Emerald Cruise Line as the return address. It took tailing Jason to the Haitian Embassy on two occasions, and a flight to Fort Lauderdale, home to Emerald's corporate office, to put together Jason had some sort of project with Emerald in Haiti. And in IRS Form 990, there was a social benefit narrative of the orphanage, the good, and that it placed many of these well-educated boys and girls, once they came of age, in jobs on cruise ships, primarily Emerald's.

When Milan confronted Gail on the Tortola ferry and heard her falsely use Jason's last name, Applegate, he was excited. Here was a connection of sorts. After tailing Jason for months, he had run out of money and not made much progress. It seemed Jason was onto him. And when he arrived in Tortola, after assuring Jason had gotten onto the *Sapphire Orchid* in Fort Lauderdale, he spent his last dime getting to the *Orchid*'s second port of call, Road Town. With the sudden rain event and the retail shops empty, Milan found an easy target, breaking into a jewelry store, which likely had a safe with a cash drawer. For him, an expert, safecracking was easy. But what was the chance the heist would be interrupted by a desperate, drenched woman, seeking shelter as he robbed the jewelry store? The chance that she bore a direct relationship to Jason? He'd doubled down on his luck.

Hiding in the jewelry store as the lights of Jason's pickup shined into the window, Milan suddenly had many more questions. Who was the woman seated next to Jason? What role could she play in forcing Jason to reveal the source of his diamonds?

The next day, in Tortola, he staked out the orphanage and followed the pair, then snuck onto the ferry without Gail noticing, hiding in the bathroom until they were underway. Not knowing a thing about Gail, Milan felt it best to approach, to learn who she was. For him, women were more vulnerable. Men such as Jason, shrewd, traveled, and worldly, quickly caught on, distrusting from the beginning. If he'd any chance to finding the location of the Utopia diamonds, it must be through the woman Jason had an attachment to.

As Milan waited for his flight to Fort Lauderdale, the sinking of the *Sapphire Orchid* was everywhere. But Milan didn't care. He needed to tail this woman who had gotten a head start the day before.

Landing in Fort Lauderdale, Milan called the number Gail had written on the business card. And as suspected, it was the wrong number. Gail was onto him. But she'd left a clue, the area code. She used the Tampa 813 area code . . . That's where he headed next.

Arriving in Tampa, Milan did what he was accustomed to doing. He applied for a job, this time at the Hard Rock Casino as a valet. It wasn't long before he caught Gail's newscast and found the barfing episode on YouTube. But what was of significant value was that she was pregnant.

Patience, stalking his prey, was Milan's strongest trait. It was unlikely Gail was going anywhere. He wanted to get close; inside the news station, befriend staff. Milan had set up a war room in his tiny 22nd Avenue apartment. He gathered photos of each WKMC employee from their website. Memorized faces and tried to determine who was most vulnerable . . . It wasn't long. While Milan was working at the casino, Emmitt Stooch passed at the north entrance. Milan immediately recognized Emmitt, tailing him to the Let It Ride card table.

For the next two weeks Milan studied Emmitt, his routine of arriving at the Hard Rock after the morning news. How long until his money ran out. What kind of drink he preferred, an Arnold Palmer. Soon, Milan found himself sitting next to Emmitt drinking Arnold Palmers as they gambled.

Milan made sure he lost more than Emmitt to gather sympathy, funds stolen locally. When they drank enough free liquor at the gaming table and Emmitt had lost all his money, Milan invited Emmitt to the bar for more drinks. That's where the conversation and friendship began.

Voodoo Cruise

"So, what brings you to the casino so early in the morning?" Milan asked. "I take it you work a nightshift."

"Where do you work?" Emmitt asked, in the habit of following an inquiry with a question before answering. A redirect.

"I'm the valet, here at the casino," Milan replied. "Spending my tip money before I head home. Not going to get rich any other way."

They both laughed and drank more.

"I work across town," Emmitt said, answering Milan's initial question.

Milan nodded and allowed him to continue.

"With a bunch of good-looking women, unfortunately."

"Unfortunately!" Milan said, pretending to be shocked. "How can that be bad?"

Emmitt thought for a moment. It was two in the afternoon and he'd tied a good one on.

"I guess you are right in a way, shouldn't blame them, it's this damn TV industry. Women on camera get much better ratings. Good journalism is dead. It's not how good you are as a reporter anymore, but how good-looking you are to capture and hold the attention span of the viewers."

Emmitt was on roll. Milan kept quiet, already knowing Emmitt's place of employment. All he needed to do was guide the conversation to Gail somehow.

"I saw that barfing episode of the pregnant reporter," Milan said.

"Yes," Emmitt, said. "I feel bad about that. But my job feeds my recreational gambling habit. If I don't get high ratings, my employment is toast. There are few jobs these days for older male reporters. It's about tight outfits, how to stand at an angle to the camera to look skinny. How much skin to show without offending. A long leg shot and designer high heels. There is a definite economic advantage to the presentation of a female reporter's body. Men are bland. Kinda sucks for us."

Milan shook his head in agreement.

"I heard the barfing newscaster had twins."

"Yes, and we don't know who the father is. She went on that damn fertility cruise ship that sank just after she abandoned ship. Got knocked up by one of the crew members. Then the lucky shit gets a job as an evening news anchor because of it."

"Crew member?" Milan asked. "What was she doing there alone?"

"She dumped her husband 'cause he couldn't knock her up." Emmitt knew that wasn't the entire truth but the alcohol was talking and it sounded good.

"Gail's a great gal even though I messed with her too much. Guilt, explains why I'm here in this chair smashed and broke. I'm in a dead-end job," Emmitt said, sadly.

Milan debated. How could he get this guy to tell him something relevant?

"Do you think it was really a crew member that knocked her up?"

Emmitt smiled. "You mean like the immaculate conception?" He laughed then ordered another drink.

Milan paused . . . then chuckled as he turned to look at a soccer game on the TV above the bar.

"You know what?" Emmitt offered. "If Gail got knocked up on the cruise ship, you'd think the dad would be around. There ain't been the hint of a father. Unlikely that she'd not let the father know who he is. She's too good for that. The thought always bugged me."

"Did you ever ask her who the father is?"

"Yes, made a big deal of it. In fact, I'm such an asshole, I did it on air. Gail don't like me too much. I've compromised her reputation to keep ratings high, so I can gamble here at least every payday. I honestly think if she knew who the father was, we'd all know by now. Us in the newsroom, are a close bunch. But you know what else is odd?" Emmitt said, downing his drink.

Voodoo Cruise

"What?"

"She was flat broke and in the poor house. Her husband had left her in a big financial mess. She didn't even have a car. Had to Uber to work when she got back from the cruise. But suddenly, Gail was happy. Started buying new outfits, expensive purses, and brand name shoes. Like her financial worries had disappeared. Everyone in the station noticed."

Bingo. Milan was onto something. Emmitt was reduced to a drunk and blabbering reporter. That's what made Milan successful.

"When she worked the morning news, Gail had two makeup stylists to keep her looking pretty. The stylists said she cried often because she was so broke. They had to work heavy-duty to make her look normal on-air. Said she was so broke and might have to live in a shelter. The IRS was about to take her home. But that changed after the sinking. She didn't lose her home. Bought a brand-new car. Someone bailed her out, financially."

"Maybe it was the father of her twins. Maybe one of the husbands of a rich couple on the boat had knocked up Gail and didn't want to be blackmailed so he gave her some money," Milan surmised.

"You know," Emmitt said, slurring. "I'd never thought about that. Never guessed Gail would be that kind of a slut. It's not her."

That's all Milan needed to know. Jason had dropped her off at the Tortola ferry, and likely paid her passage back home, given that she was flat broke and likely a lot more. The woman would eventually lead her to Jason, if he stayed close.

Milan helped Emmitt in a cab and that was the last he saw of him.

Chapter 25

Delivering two beautiful babies, concerned she'd lose favor with the station after the birth of her twins—her body less beautiful, stylists working overtime, Gail returned to WKMC after six weeks of maternity leave. Vera had dumped Ian and moved in with Gail to care for the twins. A hefty pay raise from her nighttime anchor position, a healthy savings, thanks to Saul, Gail paid Vera to be the nanny.

It was late January, one of Florida's busiest snowbird months. Gail routinely visited the Channelside District on weekends with the twins in the stroller, hoping she could catch Marie or Lou by some dumb luck while the cruise ships were in port. But she felt it unlikely; they could be working anywhere in the world.

But luck changed one week before the Tampa Super Bowl, when a passenger ship called the *One World* arrived. The cruise ship was famous for the fact passengers were permanent ship residents. Once a year, oddly during Super Bowl week, it anchored in Tampa for repairs and a good cleaning. The onboard tenants took to hard land for ten days.

For WKMC, Super Bowl week was hectic. A good story to always run was about this unusual cruise ship, where passengers had no country except for the ship. And as was the routine, Gail sent a newbie reporter to gather footage and capture a few interviews for a change of pace. That afternoon, as Gail prepared for the evening news, reviewing the final footage for a segment on the *One World*, she saw Marie pass in the background.

Immediately, she called in the cameraman and asked questions, pausing the video. "This woman, did you or the reporter talk to her?"

"Yes," the cameraman said. "Regina thought it would be interesting to inquire about how healthy passengers were, given they didn't have a real home and never cooked for themselves. Regina had interviewed the ship's doctor . . . Ah, I believe his name was Dr. Battar, and asked Marie a few questions also. But we edited out Marie. She never made it into the segment."

"Do you have footage?"

"Yes."

Gail watched the scrapped interview. It was Marie Battar. "Where is the crew staying?" Gail asked.

Regina said she heard they stayed at the Hyatt, over in Rocky Point.

As soon as Gail finished her newscast, she raced to the Hyatt and pleaded with the front desk clerk to let Marie know she was here. Gail was nervous. This was the opportunity to find out the father of her twins; perhaps he's at the hotel as part of Marie's team.

The front desk clerk called the room. The person on the other end picked up the room phone.

"I have a Ms. Gail Stroud down here and would like to speak with you."

The clerk nodded and said, "She'll be right down."

Five minutes later, as Gail anxiously waited to learn the father of her children, the elevator doors opened. It was Marie—her hair thick, wearing freshly applied ruby red lipstick and a big smile.

"Gail." Marie hugged her. She stood back and looked at her. "Baby fat. You had a child."

"Twins," Gail said. "Just as the mambo said."

"Come, let's sit, Gail, and catch up." The pair crossed the lobby and found a comfortable place to sit and chat.

"What a tragedy with the *Sapphire Orchid*," Gail said. "I'm so glad everyone ended up safe."

"The captain didn't take the mambo seriously. Now the *Orchid* is at the bottom of the sea."

"I tried to find you after the *Orchid* sank, but the cruise line would not tell me where you went."

"You know Lou and I, this is our life. Where are your children?" Marie asked. "I want to see how beautiful they are."

"That's why I'm here, Marie. I need to let the father know."

Marie's face turned pale. "You mean Jason didn't tell you?"

"Jason, how would he know who the father might be?"

There was a long pause. Marie smiled and let Gail figure it out.

Gail eyes widened. "Jay . . . Jason is the father? But he said he was in his cabin working that night."

"No," Marie said, smiling. "Given the state you were in, it was unlikely any of the crew would have obliged you. You overdosed. Jason was the only choice. He knew about the effect of the honey, and the only way to stop it from harming you was to make love to you."

Marie smiled. "I'm glad for Jason. You two make a good couple. Besides, it wasn't only the mambo trying to help you out. Lou and I wanted to help Jason. Seems like the mambo worked a miracle on both ends."

Gail was shocked. Why didn't Jason tell her they made love that night? It all made sense; the shoe left in her cabin, it was his. And why he was suddenly so kind and gave her the diamonds.

"Does Jason know?" Marie asked.

"No, I had no idea it was him and Jason never let onto it."

"You must go tell him!"

Voodoo Cruise

"Have you been in contact with Jason?" Gail asked.

"Lou has," Marie said. "He's in Lekinioch. Jason considers the island people his family. Says leaving western civilization from time to time centers him."

"Is there a way to get hold of him?"

"No, not likely; there's no phone. It's a pretty remote place. Only way is to go there yourself."

Gail thought about that. She had Vera to rely upon, and needed to tell Jason he was a father. *What if something happens to me?*

"Go visit Jason," Marie said. "He deserves to know. Make it the most important thing you do."

The couple talked until almost midnight, mostly about Atabeira and that the *Sapphire Orchid* could not be refloated.

"It's getting late, Marie. I'm going to head home."

"We sail in two days," Marie said. "Good luck finding Jason."

"The earth is not that large that I can't find him," Gail said, standing. They hugged and parted ways.

As Gail headed out of the Hyatt lobby, the man sitting in the high-back chair with its back facing them raced to the restroom. It was Milan Petrovich. Overhearing the conversation, having drunk entirely too much coffee, he couldn't risk being seen by Gail leaving his seat. And he didn't want to miss the entire conversation. Gail's twins were Jason's.

Milan had to get ahead of this. Jason was in Lekinioch, likely gathering more diamonds. Gail was heading there. A compulsive woman, she wouldn't rest until she met the father of her twins. Capturing Gail, the mother of Jason's children, trading her for the location of the Utopia diamonds, was his plan.

Needing some cash to make the trip and anticipating the unexpected, Milan had to pawn one of his diamonds. His trip wasn't going to be cheap. Fortunately, he'd been in Tampa long enough to scope out jewelers, as was often his habit. Milan never knew where the next opportunity may come from. On his days off from the Hard Rock, he'd drink coffee and eat pastry outside the Hyde Park cafes, walking past the boutique jewelers that handled the higher quality jewelry, scoping out the wealthy women married to Tampa plastic surgeons, high-level Mac Dill defense contractors, shyster lawyers, and financial advisors. He learned the highest quality stones came from Ybor City and an old man by the name of Saul and considered the best in GIA ratings. Saul lived on a side street in rather meager quarters. He bought and sold only good quality product. If the stones were any good, Saul would pay a fair price.

Having no car, Milan took the downtown trolley into Ybor City. He went during the Super Bowl broadcast, when virtually everyone was glued to their televisions.

Climbing the stairs to Saul's residence, Milan knocked. There was no answer. He knocked several times, but still no answer. With nowhere to go, Milan figured he'd sit on the steps and wait for the jeweler to arrive. Not long after, the door opened.

"Can I help you, young man?"

Milan turned. "Yes, a Mrs. Maddon on Azalea Drive said you pay the fairest price for quality stones."

"What's your full name?" he asked.

Milan didn't like using his name when pawning. "It's Alfred Pisarro. I'm here with friends for to the Super Bowl."

"And why aren't you at the game?"

Milan thought fast. He showed some embarrassment. "I have a bit of a gambling problem and pawned my tickets."

"And you want to sell me something?" Saul asked, hunched, eyes angling up just a bit.

"I gambled too much at the Hard Rock and based upon the score of the game, I'm in trouble if I can't pay off my bet if I'm on the wrong side of the end result."

"Sounds like a plausible reason. Come in."

Milan could see this jeweler was no dummy. There were cameras recording every move. Milan wasn't in a mood to get caught ripping this guy off. He had too much at stake to spend more time in prison. It was a Jewish man named Yaakov who had caught him the first time, kidnapped and sent him off to New Guinea.

"Come over to the workbench and show me what you have." And just as he did, a large man came from the other side of the room from a dark corner into the dull light.

The man's presence did not intimidate Milan. It was common in such situations to have a bodyguard. Particularly if the product was hot.

"I hope you don't mind that my friend here makes sure everything works out well for both of us."

"No, I just need the funds to settle my debt," Milan said, pretending to be nervous as he laid the soft cloth onto the bench and unfolded the corners.

As the fluorescent light struck the diamond a rainbow cast throughout the room.

Milan wasn't sure if this old guy, given how he squinted, could grade the stone. But the old man's eyes widened as if he recognized the gem right away. He picked up the stone and held it to the light, then went through his traditional grading motions, putting the stone beneath his microscope, holding it up to the light, producing another stone and comparing it. But he added one last thing. From a drawer in his workbench he pulled out a clarity chart. At the far end, where the clarity was greatest, was an exact copy of the diamond he held in his hands.

"Yes, indeed, this is perhaps the greatest quality stone I've ever set my eyes on."

"How much do you want?"

"Three hundred thousand," Milan said.

The old man studied the diamond some more. "I think we both know it's worth more, but it's not for me to ask where you got it. I'll give you half."

"I'm out two hundred fifty grand in gambling money. I need that much, plus another five thousand to get back to New York."

"Two hundred thousand," the old man said.

Milan nodded.

Saul signaled to his security guard to come and stand over them both while the old man disappeared into what looked to be his bedroom. Minutes later he returned with the stacks of cash and set it on the table beneath the light.

Saul picked up the stone and put it in his pocket.

Gathering the cash, Milan lifted his shirt and unzipped a money belt around his waist. Carefully, he filled the pouch, then pulled down his shirt, leaving it loose so no one could see the bulge.

Saul signaled for the security guard to open the door. "Show Mr. Petrovich out," the old man said, an admission he knew he was a diamond thief all along.

Hearing his real name came as a shock to Milan. This old man knew who he was dealing with all along. What to think of it? He wasn't sure. How much would it affect him? He didn't like it much. Kill the old man, highly unlikely; he was too shrewd.

Within an hour, he'd be out of Tampa and on his way to Lekinioch.

Chapter 26

Gail felt compelled to leave for Lekinioch right away to find Jason. But how? It would take many days to plan. She asked a big favor of Vera—care for the twins while she traveled halfway around the globe. She requested a Family Medical Emergency leave from her employer. The station was reasonable and granted her request.

It took a week to settle her affairs in case she didn't return safely and to plan how to get to Lekinioch. The first leg seemed relatively easy. A flight to Hawaii and a United Airlines Island Hopper to Weno, Chuuk, on a 757. The Peace Corps office in Washington, DC, was kind enough to tell her how to get to the Mortlock Islands, three atolls in proximity to each other. Lekinioch was the southernmost island. Caroline Airways, a small family-operated carrier, shuttled Peace Corps volunteers and sick islanders to and from the outer islands of Micronesia. The airline routinely relied upon a Japanese WWII runway to land. They recommended she fly to the Satowan Atoll, then hire a boat to get to Lekinioch. They warned her it would be expensive, given the remoteness of this Pacific region.

Gail's journey to Hawaii was as expected and on time. The next day, she caught the Honolulu to Guam Island Hopper. It was a grueling flight, the Hopper landing on island atolls famous for atom bomb testing and WWII battles. Weno was the fourth stop. Arriving, Gail found hotel accommodations primitive. No air conditioning. The electricity unreliable. Though living in Florida provided an instant acclimation to the humidity, Gail was thankful for the clothing she wore, nylon shorts and a breathable top to keep comfortable.

The next morning, Gail skipped breakfast, fearful of getting sick. She must get to the Mortlock Islands and figured the post office was a good place to start. The one person working there directed her to the Peace Corps Office, where Gail hoped to find Jason, or at least find where he might be living.

There was no one there except for a native hired as a staff member. Able to speak marginal English, the attendant said she knew of the man, but a picture would help her memory.

"Do you know of an island called Lekinioch?" Gail asked.

"Yes," the attendant said, pointing south. "In that direction, toward the equator."

"Is there a way to contact someone there?"

"Yes, by satellite telephone. But you must wait until tomorrow morning when the volunteers are contacted on each of the atolls to make sure they are safe and report their progress."

Gail spent the remainder of the day familiarizing herself with Weno. There was a marina capable of handling large ship repairs. She learned the Japanese tuna fleet operated out of the port. She eventually found a decent place to eat. But no word about Jason. She'd thought people might know him, but got the odd feeling that unless you were a native, the community protected their own by not being forthcoming.

The next day Gail arrived at the Peace Corps office extra early. "Lekinioch will expect us to call in at eight thirty," the senior volunteer informed her, the accent clearly Australian.

Voodoo Cruise

When 8:30 came and the office contacted the Lekinioch schoolhouse for what served as the government center; a desk with a radio, the volunteer on the island answered and confirmed that Jason lived there. She indicated he left on his catamaran for several days as he did when he was home.

"I've got to get to there," Gail said to the Weno volunteer. "How can I do that?"

"Caroline Airlines leaves in an hour to the Ta part of the Satowan atoll. From there you must hire a boat."

Gail left immediately, taking a taxi to the airport and a small steel building near the end of the runway.

Directly in front, a twin-engine plane waited, pieces of luggage piled next to it. With nowhere to sit, several Chuukese passengers stood a short distance away.

"I was told this flight is going to Ta," Gail asked of what appeared to be the person responsible for managing the flight.

"Yes, the Chuukese," man said, smiling. "I have one seat left."

Using the credit card that got her here, she paid for the flight.

The plane quickly rising in altitude, the cool air that entered the cramped cabin was a welcome relief for Gail. "Do you have any idea how I can get to Lekinioch?" Gail asked, once the plane leveled off and the strain of the twin engines relaxed a bit.

Passengers looked at her with blank faces. Micronesians were polite people; it wasn't that no one knew, they didn't want to talk over the person who might speak first.

The pilot finally spoke but in Chuukese, above the engine noise.

A squished woman who nearly occupied two seats interpreted. "You must hire a boat. Could take days."

Gail thanked the woman and asked her to thank the pilot.

It was a two-hundred-mile journey across the vast Pacific. All around were rain clouds and several rainbows. Gail was a bit nervous; she couldn't see land.

Finally, a white stretch of sand appeared. Then three atolls came into view. "The Mortlock Islands," the pilot said in Chuukese. The women who spoke English interpreted again. She pointed. "The atoll to the left is Lekinioch. We will land on Ta. It is thirty miles between them."

The plane descended, banked hard over the ocean, and landed on a concrete WWII runway. There were trees all around. *How did they build this thing here?* she wondered.

The twin engine plane taxied to what was nothing but a small shack. The cabin went from cool to hot as they crawled from the crapped aircraft. Gale snatched her backpack from a lump of luggage piled next to the plane and went to the shed.

"Can I hire a boat to get to Lekinioch?"

The person that seemed to be in charge just looked at her. Then there was another voice, in English. "She doesn't understand your English."

Gail looked across where there was another door. "Hi, I'm Rita," the English-speaking girl said. "I'm the Peace Corps volunteer and heading out on this return flight to Weno for my quarterly physical. You want to get to Lekinioch?" she asked.

"Yes," Gail said. "It's important."

The volunteer spoke in Chuukese to the woman at the window. The woman pointed out the back of the shed, to the lagoon inside the atoll. There was a catamaran anchored about twenty yards out.

"You are lucky," Rita said. "A catamaran showed up here a few days ago with word it is for hire. You must pay cash."

Chapter 27

Milan had landed on the island of Pohnpei almost two weeks prior to Gail's journey to Micronesia. His plan was to kidnap Gail when she arrived, hold her hostage, and trade for the location of the diamonds. Pohnpei was much more westernized than the Chuuk, living conditions significantly more palatable, electricity reliable, and five hundred kilometers from the Mortlock Islands, a cluster of atolls, where Lekinioch was second largest. An experienced sailor, having learned to sail in the Mediterranean for the quick getaway purpose of his profession as a thief, Milan had a better chance of chartering in Pohnpei without Jason catching on.

Leasing a blue-gray catamaran, Milan was pleased; the color blended well with the ocean horizon, making him nearly indistinguishable when not under sail. He had to register his destination, which worried him. Someone might know Jason, given the reach of the RJA Foundation. He penciled in the Satowan Atoll, fifty kilometers west of Lekinioch.

Fighting a stiff headwind, Milan arrived in Satowan after a three-and-a-half-day sail across the open Pacific. Once again, as was his approach, he hung out with locals, playing with the children, whom he found to be a great resource of information on the RJA foundation.

Milan quickly relocated his boat when he learned Jason came on his own catamaran regularly. Short teachers, fluent in Chuukese, said Jason taught in the Mortlock High School in Satowan. This posed a dilemma for Milan—how to keep out of sight? Further south and about five kilometers along the atoll was the tiny village of Ta. At low tide Milan learned he could sneak into Satowan by foot from Ta. Also, if Gail were to arrive in search of Jason, Milan determined she'd need to land on the Ta airstrip and then hire a boat to get to Lekinioch.

Milan had loaded his catamaran with plenty provisions and waited. And when Jason sailed through the eastern break in the Satowan Atoll, Milan, hidden, uncovered his scuba gear concealed within a coconut grove. He slipped beneath the surface from the water's edge and made his way to Jason's catamaran a half kilometer away and secured a tracking device to the hull so he could discreetly follow Jason.

In Ta, the twin-ending plane taxied to the runway as Gail unslung her backpack and walked over to the corrugated shed. Poorly painted graphics to the right of the opening said something in a language she couldn't remotely understand. Inside were several Chuukese women, oblivious to the fact the plane landed. They were digging in each other's hair, picking. *Are they looking for lice?* Gail wondered. Directly behind the shed was a parcel of hardpacked sand that tapered to the clear water of the atoll and the swaying green seagrass beneath the surface.

"Where the hell am I?" Gail asked, her stomach still tumbling from the freakish landing, where the slightest miscalculation dumped you into the Pacific.

As plane engine revved for takeoff, the prop-blast struck Gail and sent her to her knees. As she stood back up, her blue nylon shorts tightened against her thighs. She felt out of place. This was an entirely different experience than Atabeira. There was no greeting or notice of the new arrivals.

Voodoo Cruise

Anchored not far from the shed, near a crumbled pier, was a blue-gray catamaran. A dark-skinned Chuukese man chewing beetle-nut spotted Gail and her now-what-do-I-do expression.

"Excuse me, do you speak English?" Gail asked, passing the preoccupied lice pickers, coming beneath tightly spaced palms into limited shade. The man reclined in a lawn chair that had seen better days, pitched forward, and spit a cud from his mouth.

"Yes," he said, teeth missing.

"Is that boat for hire?" Gail pointed offshore.

"To where?"

"Lekinioch."

"Depends," he said.

"Upon what?" Gail asked, thinking he was going to work her over on price.

"Weather."

"Oh, is the weather bad?"

He looked at her, confused. Divergent cultures; neither understood the other.

The dark-skinned man left his chair and waded into the seagrass to a submerged seawall, where it broke the surface. He stood there staring to the west, the direction a stiff wind, the plane banking, cutting across the sun.

Looking at the sky for several minutes, he then nodded. "We go now, the older sister is in charge."

"Huh? Please explain," questioned Gail.

"There are two sisters that make the weather. When the younger sister is moody and angry at the older sister, the ocean is unhappy. We do not sail when the youngest is in a Terrible."

Gail recalled during her trip preparation, reading the secrets of Polynesian navigation passed from generation to generation through story. Much like the Ybor City cigar rollers in Tampa, up on the second floor of the factories was a reader, someone who told stories of the Cuban homeland.

Gail felt she'd lucked out. She wasn't sure where she'd stay if she remained here on this narrow strip of sand; perhaps sleep underneath the palms, lice crawling into her hair.

"Let's go," the Chuukese man said, leaping from the pile of crumbled stone, wading in chest-high water, climbing the ladder into the catamaran.

Gail looked at him, perplexed. "You mean I must do the same?"

He said nothing. She had no choice but to lift her backpack overhead and wade to the bow. The short, shirtless man took the pack and tossed it on the net that spanned the gap between the pontoons of the catamaran. Then he helped Gail from the top of the ladder.

"You must pay for gas and your fare, three hundred US dollars."

"What!" Gail said. "That's robbery."

"How much do you think it costs to get the gas we need for this boat to our island?"

He was right. Fuel was unlikely to keep well, and the livelihood of getting around depended upon fuel and a reliable watercraft.

Gail pulled out fifteen twenty-dollar bills from her soaked fanny pack and handed it to the stout man.

He lifted the anchor, and they set sail. The catamaran traveled at a snail's pace, along the inside arc of the atoll. At intervals the tall coconut groves disappeared, leaving a barren strip of washed over coral. On the south side, waves raced onto what remained. Where the atoll thickened, and the elevation a tad higher was the village of Satowan. Gail studied the shoreline as the village came into view. An inflatable left from the shoreline and headed their way.

"It's the captain," the man said. "He will sail you to Lekinioch. I was hired to clean and fuel the boat."

Voodoo Cruise

"Uh . . . okay," Gail said, sitting on a plastic chair on the starboard bow, watching the small boat speed their way. The tiny craft swung to the port side stern. Wearing a broad-brim hat, the captain's face was concealed. She watched as he lashed his craft to the stern cleat. Shirtless, the captain's skin was lighter than the Chuukese, but still deeply tanned. Gail wasn't paying attention to the exchange of captains. The inflatable sped off and headed for the village. But when Gail saw him take to the helm, removing his hat, she turned ghost white.

"It's you, the . . . the jewelry store."

She was in shock.

He had a pistol stuck in his belt.

The catamaran speed picked up. She was too far offshore to leap and swim away. Frightened, Gail didn't move from her spot.

"My name is Milan Petrovich and I want nothing to do with you, except use you to find Jason. But I will kill you and Jason and orphan your children, if need be."

Gail was speechless. Halfway around the world—how could this be? She had to think

"Jason isn't the father of my children." Gail tried to deny that fact, speaking nervously.

Milan stared at her as they headed for the open Pacific. "Tampa, Hyatt. I was sitting in a chair not facing you, as you learned from the Lebanese lady, Jason was the father of your twins."

"It's the diamonds you want!" Gale said.

"Yes, I want to know their source."

"Are you going to kill me?"

"I generally don't. I'm a thief, not a murderer. But I wonder if your Jason is. Seems he likes to keep track of the precious stones he releases in the world. I was kidnapped and left for dead in a jungle prison."

And as they entered heavy swells of the deep Pacific, Milan told Gail of the tuna trawler, using slave labor from New Guinea prisons.

"I don't need you to tell me where Jason is. However, I'm sure you will come in handy. Keep your distance, and I won't dump you over the side to be eaten by sharks."

At the rise of each swell Gail saw land. She was in a hopeless situation. The island to the south disappeared. Gail guessed it was Lekinioch, her destination. And based upon the angle of the sun, they headed east.

"If you prefer to get out of the sun, you can go down into that pontoon. There's food and facilities for you."

Scared, looking again at the gun in his belt, Gail went below. But it was only seconds later when the overhead hatch flipped and slammed shut. Then a click.

"Insurance," Milan called out to her. "You'll remain below until we find Jason."

"You bastard," Gail yelled, pounding on the hatch.

She was trapped.

Many hours passed. The sun had set. Hungry, rummaging, Gail found a can of Spam. There was no escape as they sailed the entire night. But at one point the boat had stopped. She guessed Milan needed to sleep. And when daylight came and she called for Milan, he said nothing.

The morning wind stiffened as Milan's catamaran headed into the rising sun. He sailed east for the entire day, finally picking up Jason's catamaran on the faint signal of the hidden tracking beacon. He was careful, closing the distance, keeping at least twenty kilometers between him and Jason. When Jason anchored for the night, so did Milan. But as several other large blips came to the screen, Milan became concerned. Large merchant vessels tracked north, slicing between him and Jason.

"Damn tuna fleet," Milan complained, not caring to be reminded of his hard labor, the most painful experience in his life.

Voodoo Cruise

Milan opened the distance and diverted south, staying out of the fleet's way. They were onto a school of tuna, circling. The memory of toiling for hours on the unstable sunbaked deck, covered in fish guts, returned. Milan cursed.

Below, Gail complained. "I'm burning up in here."

"Open a porthole." Again, he threatened to toss her overboard if she annoyed him too much.

At sunset, it was clear Jason's vessel had stopped and anchored. Milan smiled. *He's over the diamonds.*

Quickly, he accessed a map of the seafloor on his laptop's navigation chart. There was no evidence of an underwater formation; this remote area of Pacific was not terribly accurate. He marked the spot, but wanted to see for himself, confirming this was the location of the Utopia diamonds.

To Milan, Jason seemed exceptionally elusive. Milan was distrustful of Jason's intellect. He was a smart one. And as the sun set once again, he told Gail, "Soon you will see the father of your children. Be quiet or they will be orphaned."

Milan turned off all power on the catamaran. In the pitch-black, he raised the mast and sailed toward Jason's anchor. It took five hours in a near dead breeze to close the distance. By daybreak, relying upon the blue-gray color of his vessel, Milan felt he was close, perhaps two kilometers. Looking through his binoculars, he spotted Jason's white hull. He saw Jason fumbling with scuba gear.

Milan waited and watched as Jason slipped over the side.

He's going below to collect diamonds.

Once Jason disappeared, Milan raised the mast to let the gathering morning wind fill the sail. Off to the north, Milan could see the tuna fleet working another school.

"Get me out of here," Gail cried, banging on the locked hatch from beneath.

"Be quiet!" demanded Milan. "No more banging."

Traveling at six knots, the firm wind full to the sail, Milan closed the distance and came alongside Jason's craft, leaving a space of about fifteen meters between.

It wasn't long before air bubbles gurgled between the nearly identical catamarans. As Jason's head broke the surface, Milan, at the helm, started the engine to hold his vessel stationary. Griping the wheel, he removed his pistol from its holster and pointed it at Jason.

"Go ahead and climb aboard your vessel, Mr. Applegate," Milan said.

Jason removed his diving mask, the regulator dropping from his mouth. Jason gave Milan a hard and bold stare as he swam to the ladder. A thin line attached to his shoulder ran into the water. It hung tight.

"I have a present for you." Milan released the wheel, went to the starboard pontoon, and kicked open the deck-latch.

Gail's head popped out. "Jason, he's got a gun," Gail warned, her elbows hanging over the rim.

Jason still didn't say a word.

"Jason, it's me, Gail! Don't you recognize me?"

He did not respond.

Milan came behind Gail as she climbed from below and stood at the edge.

He shoved his foot into her butt and pushed her overboard.

Splash!

Gail landed in the ocean.

But again, as Jason hung from the ladder, he didn't say a word.

"What's beneath you, on the line?" Milan asked.

Jason removed a serrated knife attached to his weight belt.

"I'll shoot you and her if you cut that line," Milan threatened. "I take it you've got what I'm looking for at the end of that string."

Jason pulled up the line.

Voodoo Cruise

A half-full mesh bag had glittering diamonds inside.

"Hand over the diamonds or the mother of your children dies."

Jason looked down at Gail bobbing in the water.

"Yes, Jason, it's true," she said, attempting to swim toward him.

Milan called out to Gail. "Don't swim any further!"

He fired one shot directly in front of her.

Gail stopped and treaded water.

"Here!" With one hand, Milan undid a bungee strap that held an inflatable raft in a half-barrel. Pulling a string that activated a CO2 cartridge, he kicked the raft overboard as it inflated.

Gail swam to the raft and clung to the side. "I can't climb in."

"You care to help the lady before I wound her so the sharks can eat?" Milan said, pointing the pistol.

Jason still didn't say a word. He continued his hard stare as he made his way to the top of the ladder.

"Mrs. Applegate, you are going to help me," Milan demanded, intentionally calling her by a different name than her own.

"Push the raft over to the father of your children and tell him to drop the diamonds into the raft and swim it back to me. And I'll let you be with Mr. Applegate, now that I know we are over the diamonds."

Swimming, Gail, shoved the yellow life raft ahead of her, spitting saltwater. The raft nudged the side of Jason's catamaran and bounced back. Jason leaned overboard and snagged the rope.

"Don't make any sudden moves, or your woman dies."

Locking his leg in the top rung of the ladder, Jason lifted the diamonds up high. Then he poured the glittering gems from about six feet up.

"No!" yelled Milan. "Lower the bag." He shot into the side of Jason's catamaran, missing Gail.

The sun, reflecting off the tumbling stones, refracted and intensified, like laser beams shot in a thousand random directions. Milan became blinded. And as the bag emptied, Jason tugged on the rope of the life raft. The diamonds rolled in the bottom, sending another array of brilliant, blinding lights, beams seemingly shooting everywhere.

Milan blinked, shot again, and missed. Closing one eye, trying to keep sight of Jason and Gail, finger on trigger and a third miss. But as Milan remained paralyzed by the glitter, Jason dove from the ladder, landing on Gail, grabbing her by the waist, dragging her underwater, beneath the raft and under the catamaran. A fourth shot, this time into the water.

Jason and Gail had disappeared.

Milan pointed the gun, waiting for an opportunity. But none came.

Gail and Jason had surfaced on the other side of the pontoon, beneath Jason's boat.

Milan needed to maneuver to get sight of them. Quickly, he pushed the throttle and spun the wheel to where he could see between the pontoons of the split hull.

Gail's head disappeared underwater. Again, he shot. And again circled, each time, Gail diving as she saw Milan's bow appear.

Finally, out of breath from the repeated dives, Gail had grown tired. Jason had disappeared, having not surfaced for the past two dives. Milan pointed the pistol with Gail dead in the crosshairs. Her big brown eyes grew wide and frightened. She was frozen. Milan took a few extra seconds to assure his aim would not miss. But suddenly, Milan felt a jolt between his shoulder blades, and the gun misfired. Milan flew overboard, landing in the ocean.

"Gail, Gail, climb aboard my boat," Jason said, speaking for the first time, standing where Milan once stood.

Gail quickly swam to the ladder off the stern and climbed aboard Jason's boat.

"Lift the ladder," Jason said. "And stay put."

Voodoo Cruise

"There's no way for you to get on my or your boat, Milan," Jason called to Milan, as he surfaced. Jason lifted the ladder on Milan's catamaran.

"Go ahead, climb in the life raft with your precious diamonds. They have no value to you now."

Jason drove Milan's boat to the starboard side of his own vessel and jumped aboard with Gail. Quickly, he lashed the two catamarans, started the engine, and put a considerable distance between him, Milan, and the raft. And when they were at a good distance, Milan bobbing far away, Gail embraced Jason.

"Thank God you are alive," Jason said.

"You are the father to my twins. I was coming to tell you and was kidnapped by Milan."

Jason smiled. "Mambo and her damn voodoo."

"What should we do with Milan?" Gail asked. "We can't kill him."

"I've had a plan all along," Jason said. He opened a small storage hatch and lifted the beacon Milan had attached to the hull. "But I didn't anticipate finding you with him."

Jason went to his radio and flipped to a marine channel. He keyed the microphone. "Man overboard. Man overboard." Then he reached for an orange waterproof box in the same storage hole and opened it. He pulled out a flare gun and shot two flares into the air.

Off to the north, Jason could see the white smoke from the trawlers. He waited, then fired another flare. Minutes later he saw two flares rise into the sky.

"Jason, what are you doing?"

"Seeing our thief here gets rescued."

"But what about the diamonds?"

"That will be taken care of shortly."

Jason maneuvered the attached catamarans closer to Milan.

Milan, helpless, had climbed into the raft, surrounded by diamonds.

Jason reloaded the flare gun and shot it at the raft. It ignited the rubber and deflated the tiny lifeboat. Milan slipped over the side to get clear of the flames. The rafts, with its valuables, sank.

"Look!" Gail said. "He's shoved some diamonds into his shorts!"

"Got that covered," Jason said, as he brought the boat around one more time. "Hand me a lifejacket."

Milan bobbed in the water.

"I'll trade you a lifejacket for your shorts. I'll give you sixty seconds."

At about thirty seconds Milan tossed away his shorts.

Milan bobbed, naked in the ocean chop, as Jason tossed him the lifejacket.

"Aren't you going to leave me my boat?" Milan asked.

Jason pointed in the distance. "There's your ride."

He called into the radio. "Man overboard." And gave coordinates, firing a final flare.

"Farewell, Milan," Jason said.

With his arm around Gail, and Milan's catamaran in tow, Jason pressed the throttle forward and headed south.

Bobbing in the Pacific for a good hour with the rise and fall of the seas, Milan heard the familiar grind of the tuna trawler, but could not see it. The sound grew louder. Finally, as the towering hull appeared, a net swung over his head and lowered. Milan reached and clung to the same net that he'd used to lower himself in the dark night many months ago. It lifted, brought him onboard, and dumped him to the deck like a caught tuna. The familiar rattling of shackles—prisoners working the tuna fleet, gathered around him.

And as a tall bearded man approached, the legs of his wool pants dragging on the deck, the shackled prisoners stepped aside. The man looked down at Milan and said, "We finally meet, Mr. Petrovich."

Voodoo Cruise

Milan, frightened, nervously asked, "Who are you?"

"Yaakov Kirshenbaum," he said. "Welcome aboard."

Chapter 28

As a healthy afternoon easterly trade wind filled Jason's sail, the compass held a steady southeast for several hours. The glare over the royal blue Pacific grew pale, a sign the seafloor was rising beneath them, until finally, Jason released the sail and dropped anchor.

"It was all a setup!" Gail said, watching the anchor chain rattle, then go slack. "We weren't over the sunken atoll, were we?"

"Yes, a setup. I was onto Milan for a very long time, before Fort Lauderdale," Jason said.

"How did you know?" she asked.

"The green cap. It was an odd color green. He wore it at the cruise ship terminal and while snooping through my trash in Washington." Jason then explained his relationship with Yaakov and the need to protect the diamonds' source. "Discovery of this location and the exceptionally large quantity of diamonds below where we anchored would disrupt and destroy the market for virtually any lower grade stone. That's what Yaakov's interest is, protecting the entire diamond marketplace."

"Did you have anything to do with his imprisonment?" Gail asked, concerned as to the civility of Jason's character.

"No, I'm not a fan of such torture, and only learned of it now. It's cause for concern and forces me to rethink the matter. But the thief did shoot at you, with the intent to kill, and likely deserves the end result. My focus must be the good I can do."

"The sunken atoll, its location," Gail replied, using an educated guess to connect the dots—the puzzle fully assembled except for one item. "The book without an author, left for the children of your orphanage to read?"

"Exactly," Jason said. "Just as I had learned from Mau. After all you've been through, you remain a passionate journalist," Jason added, the sun to his back.

"Just as you are passionate about the generosity of your wealth and life journey. Me pursuing your truth has allowed me to return to my core belief."

"So, I'm a father?" Jason said, putting his arm around Gail and hugging her.

"I learned from Marie what happened the night I took the honey. Why didn't you say anything?"

Jason, sitting close, their shoulders touching, struggled to find the words.

"I guess you are just as fallible, aren't you?" Gail looked deep into his eyes.

"I'd not been with someone in quite some time. The trajectory of my life is entirely different for you to enter my world. But I must add, the mambo works in strange ways. You are here with me right now. It's likely how the mambo wanted it to pan out." Jason took Gail's hand and held it.

She smiled, her big brown eyes considering his; a lonely, deserving young man. She could see his affection, but it might take some time for him to allow her into his life. *The cautious Chuukese in him,* she thought. *He's not completely westernized.*

On the horizon, they could see the trawler. "They are done for the day," Jason said. "Likely heading back to Weno."

"You are not getting off that easily," Gail said, smiling, feeling a mutual respect, a bonding, knowing it was likely he appreciated her efforts to find him. With twins, they were connected forever.

"You read the entire story, didn't you?" Jason said. "It's the Amelia Earhart mystery, isn't it?"

Gail nodded. "I read your entire book." The one she read to the children in Tortola. Able to speed read, after the children went to bed, she finished it. That was why she never woke for breakfast that morning. "Polynesians pass along secrets of their navigation skills through story."

Jason nodded. "You did your research."

"I had plenty of time to learn about your side of the world as I looked for you. You wrote the story so the secret you hold can be passed along for generations if needed."

"Yes," Jason said. "It must not get lost. It was Mau who passed me the story of *The Missing Night*, the location, and sinking of the atoll. I did not know who Amelia Earhart was until Ruth adopted me. Even then, it was many years until she pieced together what I was taught in Chuukese. She was known as the Great Lady, not Amelia. To have the truth to be never known for all eternity would be a sin. Passing it along in this way allows it come alive on its own."

"Don't you think that time is now?"

"Can't, not in my lifetime."

"Why?"

"Her plane is directly below us, surrounded by the diamonds."

Gail finished what he was about to say. "Locating the plane would not be a good idea."

Jason nodded.

Gail smiled. "So, what was her story? The one I must keep secret until you die?"

Voodoo Cruise

"It was the night of the coming of the bright light. Amelia, low on fuel, flew off course toward the light and crash landed inside the atoll. Her plane sank to the bottom. And as you read in the children's version, she met Mau as a curious child. And together, they discovered the atoll was about to collapse into the ocean. Tonight, I will show you. In just a few hours, as darkness arrives, the bright light will come. You can no longer see it unless you are right over it." Jason showed Gail on his underwater radar that they had anchored over the remains of a sunken atoll.

"Your story did explain why the atoll sank, but not what created such an abundance of diamonds."

"Meteor," Jason said. "A direct hit into the center of a volcano caldera. A fluke. The impact, the sudden intense heat, so great it created such crystals millions of years ago. When the oceans rose to fill the caldera . . ." Jason paused. "Tell you what, I think it's best you see what I mean. Come let's sit off the bow. The sun is about to set." Jason took Gail's hand and led her to the edge of the bow. "Have a seat and look in the water."

As the sun went below the horizon, Jason held her close. The water beneath turned gray-green as if a cloud had formed beneath the catamaran. There were flecks of silver. "Anchovies," Jason said. "They arrive en masse as the sun sets. Look." Jason pointed into the eastern horizon.

"It's a full moon," Gail said. "Just as you described, the coming of the bright light in your story. Is it true?"

"Wait and see for yourself." And as darkness came, the anchovies filled the sea, so thick the water seemed a paste. As the moon brightened, the ocean broke into a boil. "The flickers are here."

"As in your story, the flickers had undermined the atoll, chewing at the rock to ingest the diamonds to help digest the anchovies. It was the Great Lady, the mysterious woman on the island, who helped Mau convince the elders to leave before everyone was swallowed by the Pacific."

Jason smiled. "The story will live long after us."

The surface of the ocean boiled for nearly an hour. The flickers darted beneath the boat. Their eyes glowed and as the moonlight struck, a kaleidoscope of color lit the water. And as she watched, as the moon neared its peak, the ocean lit up like a gigantic underwater batholith.

"Come." Jason led Gail into the small cabin where his underwater radar was. On the screen was an image. All around were the diamonds. The seafloor glowed. But there was one spot where it didn't. A shadow in the shape of a plane.

"The Great Lady likely lived out her life there. One of the most remote places on earth at the time."

Gail came close to Jason and set her head on his shoulder. She looked at the screen, then out the window, where the entire surface of the sea glowed, as the flickers leapt like mullet, feeding, flicking at an angle, no doubt diamonds mashing the swallowed anchovies in their gizzards to digest their meal. But like spawning salmon, it would be their last meal, for they would drop their fertilized eggs to lie upon a nest made of diamonds, then die.

Gail, listening, found herself wrapped tightly in Jason's arms. She looked deep into his eyes, and they kissed.

The End!